Deadly Deals on the Sound

On the Sound Book Two

Gemma Christina

Jpenname Publishing LLC

Contents

Chapter One

Ms. MJ Brooks moved between groups of desks. Her eighth-grade language arts students were in teams of four preparing for an upcoming debate.

The teams each had a different side of a topic, all likely to get students passionate in opposition or agreement: requiring school uniforms, banning video games...things unlikely to happen, but issues of interest to thirteen- and fourteen-year-olds.

Their task today was to find text evidence to support their claims and smash the opposing views with excellent rebuttals. So far, they had impressed MJ with their progress.

She stopped to observe a team near a bank of windows in the back. Sunlight poured in as summer lingered outside. MJ let her eyes rest on the blue sky for a moment. This was her last period of the day. Then she'd finish up a few things and head home to take her dog Edgar out on the kayak. No one enjoyed being inside this time of year.

"This is a good one," said Kaylee Boeser, sitting up and pointing to an article so her teammates could see. MJ listened in as she explained.

"It says that school lunches don't really—"

Thwack!

MJ's head shot up.

Jada Lausch was standing, glaring down at Cade McCann, one of her three group members.

"Shut up, you idiot!" Jada's normally placid face flared an angry red.

"Ms. Brooks," complained Cade with a fake whine. "Jada threw her pen at me."

Drew Taylor, their other group member, snickered.

Jada stared at him with eyes of fire, another marker in her hand, ready to launch it. "You're lucky that's all I threw."

"Alright, you two. In the hall," MJ ordered.

Jada threw the marker down on the table so hard it bounced. Then she marched to the door.

Cade just sat there. He wore a grin, but it looked forced, as if looking casual took an effort. Whatever happened, thought MJ, Cade did not expect Jada to explode in that way.

"You too, my friend. Let's go." MJ pointed toward the door.

With a groan and dramatic eye roll, he got up and followed Jada.

The rest of the class stared in silence as Cade walked out. MJ wasn't the only one shocked by this behavior.

Jada and Cade were best friends. They'd even told MJ about their families vacationing together in Mexico. It was still early in the year, but she'd never heard a bad word between them.

"Listen up, everybody," MJ said to the class. "Keep gathering your evidence. Remember, each person needs at least two pieces of evidence and a rebuttal. Make sure you know who is doing your opening and closing statements."

The students would most likely spend the time talking about what just happened, but that couldn't be helped.

MJ stepped into the hall. Jada stood by the door with her back against the wall and her arms folded tightly across the chest. She stared down the hall, away from MJ. Cade stood awkwardly on the other side of the door, swaying back and forth nervously on his long, spindly legs. He wore the typical Washington boys' middle school uniform of jeans, hoodie, and a baseball cap.

As soon as the door closed, he started pleading his case.

"I swear, I didn't mean anything, Ms. Brooks. Jada just freaked out for no reason." He cast a nervous glance at the girl. "I mean, we joke about stuff all the time."

Jada continued to stare down the hall without saying a word.

"Tell me what was said."

Cade swallowed. "We have school uniforms for our topic, so I was just joking around, and I said if we had school uniforms, Jada's dad would save millions not having to buy Jada's clothes." He glanced at the girl again. "I mean, she does have a ton of clothes. I've seen her closet."

"Shut up!" shouted Jada, turning to face him.

"Whoa, Jada," said MJ, moving between the two.

Jada locked her arms over her chest again and turned away.

This is not about Cade, thought MJ. While it was an unnecessary and insensitive comment, Jada would normally laugh it off, or even feel a little flattered. MJ sensed a bigger issue caused Jada to lose it.

"Cade, I think you should apologize. I'm sure you can see that, whether you meant to, you upset Jada."

"But she threw a marker at me. She missed, like a typical southpaw, but still, she threw it."

"I will deal with that too, but one thing at a time."

He stared down at his feet. "I'm sorry Jada. I didn't mean to make you feel bad."

The girl's arms relaxed slightly, and MJ caught a wave of emotion on her features before she turned even farther away from them.

"Okay, Cade, head back inside."

He opened the door but stopped and looked at Jada one more time. "Is she going to be okay?"

"Let's give her a minute. Go ahead inside."

When he opened the door, MJ peeked inside to make sure all was well and no one was climbing on cabinets. So far, so good.

Cade went inside and the door closed again.

MJ took a deep breath. Sometimes these kinds of conversations led to unexpected disclosures.

A few years ago, she had a student named Kaitlin Waters. She'd been showing some uncharacteristic behavior in class. When MJ asked her if something was bothering her, the girl revealed that her mom's boyfriend had just been released from prison. That same boyfriend, who had a history of violence, was at Kaitlin's house babysitting her little sister. Kaitlin's stress about her sister had turned into yelling at classmates and being disrespectful to adults.

She didn't know what to expect from Jada. The outburst with Cade was so out of character for the girl; something had to be bothering her. She was a part of MJ's homeroom class, a group that stayed with the same teacher throughout middle school. MJ had learned over the past two years that Jada was concerned with grades, nice to her classmates, and confident with her friends.

A few situations had stirred MJ's curiosity about the girl's home life. The family seemed well off, but there were days when Jada didn't want to go home. Like when the ASB sponsored a volunteer clean-up day after school. Long after everyone else had bailed, Jada kept asking for things to do, insisting no one would be at her house. They had chatted for another hour while weeding the rhododendron bushes at the school's main entrance until Jada's dad showed up to take her home. He seemed like a caring dad, but he also was busy.

That day, MJ sensed Jada's need for adult interaction and approval, and she'd worked to continue building a positive relationship with the girl over the past two years, especially after learning about her parents' pending divorce.

It had always been Jada's dad who came to parent-teacher conferences. MJ never met Mrs. Lausch, but she could tell things were strained between the parents. Mr. Lausch never mentioned his wife and didn't offer any excuses for her absence. It didn't surprise MJ when she heard they had separated.

Still, MJ's history with Jada wasn't helping much at the moment. They were only two weeks into the school year. With puberty wreaking havoc, middle schoolers could change dramatically over the summer. Those changes could be even more significant if they experienced a shake-up in their family life.

"Jada," she said softly. "Is everything okay?"

Jada still didn't look at her. Shaking her head, she reached up and wiped away a tear.

"Can I help?"

"No," she said quickly, wiping more tears. "There's nothing anyone can do."

That sounds ominous, MJ thought. Teen drama or something worse?

"Do you want to go to the office and talk to Ms. Davis, the counselor? It might be good to talk to someone."

She shook her head with vehemence. "No, I'm fine." She wiped her face. "Are you going to write me up?"

MJ shook her head. "This is our first issue, so just a warning, but you need to apologize for throwing the marker."

Jada nodded. "Can I go to the bathroom?"

"Sure."

Jada pushed herself away from the wall and strode down the hall to the girls' restroom, her long, expertly balayaged copper and chocolate hair looking salon perfect. MJ watched, wondering what could be bothering her. Clearly, everything was not fine.

***

When the last bell rang, MJ followed her students out of the class-room. She cautiously entered the chaotic stream of students heading for the exit. It was like getting caught up in the rapid current of an adolescent dam break. There was the usual jostling, holding hands, grabbing each other's backpacks, and words the kids wouldn't say if they knew a teacher was behind them.

"Antonio," MJ cautioned.

A tall Hispanic boy turned around, throwing his head back to shift his long black bangs from his eyes.

"Oh sorry, Ms. Brooks. I didn't know you were there."

"Obviously," she said with fake sternness. "And to think, you've learned so many exceptional words this week."

He shrugged, a smile playing on his face. "Habit."

His attention drifted back to his friends, and he was soon swept away.

MJ shook her head. It was like shoveling in a snowstorm. Veering away from the crowd, she ducked through the staff entrance to the office.

She hoped to catch Shannon in an extremely unlikely moment of freedom. The month of September meant the counselor hardly had time to breathe between adjusting student schedules, registering new students, and running meetings with teachers and parents.

Getting to Shannon's office meant passing what used to be the office of the principal and MJ's mentor, Troy Danielson. It was now Carrie Chadwick's office. Following the tragic bombing of city hall in downtown West Sound last year, the school district hired Carrie, the former assistant principal, to assume the position left vacant by Troy's passing.

With fresh paint, new furniture, and Carrie's myriad of Washington State University kitsch, the room had a completely new look. The changes helped some, but not quite enough.

Troy's death devastated MJ and the community. It didn't matter who was in that office. She would always feel a deep pang of sorrow every time she passed it. She missed him.

Next to the principal's office was an empty room that housed workbooks, paper, and a new copy machine. It used to be the office of Jay Butler, dean of students. After Troy's death, Jay packed up his family and moved to Yakima to take an assistant principal position. MJ was glad to see him go. They did not get along, and Jay had the moral compass of a toad, except that was insulting to toads. He'd burned his bridges in West Sound. The district chose not to fill the dean position, and the staff gained a new storage room.

They did, however, hire a new assistant principal. His name was Adam Schwartz. MJ did not know him well, but she'd only heard good things from the rest of the staff.

Neither Adam nor Carrie were in their offices. That was not unusual. They were likely in the halls or outside by the buses during dismissal.

MJ approached Shannon's door, which was open. To her amazement, the counselor was there by herself, typing on her laptop. She looked up as MJ's figure darkened the door.

"Oh hey, I was just going to call you."

"What about?" asked MJ.

She sighed. "New student. I think she'll be in your fourth period. Her name is . . ." She hunted through a stack of files on her desk. "Tatiana Eubanks."

"When does she start?"

"Monday."

"Great. That gives me a few days to get ready." MJ stepped inside the office and closed the door.

Shannon arched a brow. "What's this about?"

MJ sat in a chair next to the circular table Shannon used for meeting with students.

"I was wondering if you have heard about any issues between Jada Lausch and Cade McCann. They had a blow up today."

Shannon glanced to the side as she thought about it. She looked back at MJ, shaking her head. "I haven't heard anything, but that's odd. Aren't they good friends?"

"Yeah, but I've got a feeling something is up with Jada that may have nothing to do with Cade. I just wanted to check with you to make sure there isn't something I should know."

"Nope. Do you want me to check in with her?"

"Maybe. Let me see how things are tomorrow." MJ didn't want to overreact, but she couldn't shake the feeling that something was going on with Jada.

"We're still on for tomorrow night, right?"

MJ gave her a blank look. "Tomorrow night?"

"Oh, come on, MJ. You promised!"

Shannon had to attend a cousin's wedding. She'd begged MJ to go with her to avoid the awkwardness of going alone.

A wicked smile crept up MJ's face. "Relax. Of course I remember."

Shannon glared at her. "Good. I can't face my Aunt Susan alone. She's going to set me up with every single weirdo in attendance."

MJ laughed. "Don't discount it. Maybe your Mr. Right will be at our table."

"Not a chance. I know my cousin's family. They don't attract my type."

MJ stood up. "I am looking forward to meeting them. Sounds . . . interesting."

"Even if it's not, I appreciate you coming with me."

The relief in her voice filled MJ with a bit of regret for teasing her. When MJ woke in the hospital after the explosion at city hall last year, Shannon was there at her side. MJ was supposed to be in the city council meeting to receive an award. She narrowly escaped dying in the explosion because she was late. Her only injury was a concussion and some bruised ribs. The explosion had thrown her to the sidewalk just as she reached the entrance to the building. Shannon stayed in the hospital all night to ensure MJ wouldn't be alone when she woke up and discovered their principal had died.

"It's not every day I get an invitation to the Fairview Valley Clubhouse. I've heard that it's quite elegant."

Shannon rubbed the back of her neck as her eyes narrowed. "I know. Don't ask me how they're paying for it. My uncle is a manager at a tiny bank."

MJ's eyes widened. "Maybe we're in the wrong profession."

Shannon sighed. "I think that a lot, but it has nothing to do with the money."

Over the past decade, mental health issues and antisocial behavior had grown alarmingly common. Funding from the state and the federal government in no way supported the needs of their school. Shannon, as the only school counselor, had a shocking caseload.

MJ rested a hand on Shannon's shoulder. "I'm glad you're here, and don't worry, no matter who is or isn't at the wedding, we are going to have a blast on Friday," she said firmly, her eyes twinkling with mischief.

Leaning back in her chair with her palms up, Shannon said, "Whoa, now you're making me nervous."

MJ laughed lightly as she headed to the door. "Alright, I'm leaving. See you tomorrow."

"Yes, get out of here. I have work to do." Shannon shooed her away with a grin.

Chapter Two

Curtis wove his way around the sand trap. He loved early fall. Six in the morning and the sunrise was already well underway. The sound of the mower, muffled by his giant green sound-blocking headphones, didn't interfere with his thoughts, all of which revolved around a certain girl. A smile floated to his lips as he mentally replayed the moment he first took her hand during the movie last night.

"I was wondering what you were waiting for," she'd teased, her eyes twinkling in the low light of the latest cartoon offering from Disney. He would do anything for Izzy. The night had been magical. If it wasn't for Roger standing by the eighth fairway pond waving his arms like a madman, he might have continued mowing in a romantic trance for the rest of the morning.

He waved back at Roger and turned his mower toward the pond. The man wanted something. Maybe his mower had conked out on him.

Once Roger knew he had Curtis's attention, he turned to look at the pond with his hands on his hips. This reminded Curtis of the body position his dad would take when he couldn't quite figure something out. Roger always reminded him a bit of his dad.

Curtis pulled up beside the older man's mower, shut off his engine, and jumped down, his curiosity growing. Izzy had temporarily lost her starring role in his thoughts. As he approached, Roger turned to him with an ashen face. His wrinkles seemed deeper and his eyes hollow beneath his well-worn Mariner's cap.

Roger turned back to the pond, motioning toward it with his head. Following his gaze, Curtis at first saw nothing unusual about the tangle of grass, cattails, and other vegetation that regularly choked the side of the pond. Then he saw it. A hand, a man's hand, he thought, floated in between the green cattail stalks. He inhaled and drew back, shooting a horrified look at the other man.

Roger glanced back at him, but he appeared stunned, as if he couldn't fathom what he had discovered.

Knowing he'd regret it, Curtis turned back to inspect the pond again. He realized the hand was just the easiest part to see. The entire body was there but effectively camouflaged in the leaves, stalks, and other muck of the pond.

"What the ...?" Curtis choked out. "Is he dead?" It came out in a whisper.

"Yeah, I'd say so," Roger said, taking his hat off and pushing his hand slowly through his hair. "I just don't..." He put his cap back on and his hands back on his hips.

"I guess we need to call the cops," Curtis said, feeling nauseous. The longer he stared, the more details came to the surface. At least he was face down, Curtis thought. A face staring up at him was something he couldn't have handled. The man appeared to be wearing a white t-shirt, but the pond had discolored it.

He turned away. Mood ruined.

Chapter Three

West Sound Detective Jefferson Hughes set a perfect pick. So perfect that his teammate, Detective Mendez, got open for a layup that would have given their team a four-point advantage. Unfortunately, Detective Rory Jackson made an athletic leap, stretching his five-foot-ten frame to knock the ball away from the basket and into the hands of his teammate, Officer Fogarty.

Jefferson raced down the court after him, getting between him and the basket. Fogarty took a shot that barely tapped the rim, and Jefferson snatched the rebound out of the air. He sprinted back toward the other basket with Detective Greg Larson and Rory on his heels. With two more long-legged steps and a leap, he slammed the basketball through the hoop.

"Woo-hoo!" shouted Mendez, clapping his hands. He reached out for a high five from Jefferson and their third teammate, a rookie officer named Evie Hanson, Fogarty's new partner.

"Now that's what I'm talking about!" Mendez gave a good-natured elbow to the ribs of his partner, Detective Larson.

"Whatever. It's too early in the morning for this crap." Larson ran a hand over his bald head. "I should learn to stay out of the gym when you youngins play. That was a nice block, though, Jackson."

Rory stuck his chest out a little farther. "Yes, yes, it was if I do say so myself."

"You always say so yourself," said Jefferson as he chucked the ball at him with a wry smile.

Rory caught it just before it hit his chest. "Awe Jeffey, you noticed."

Jefferson and Rory were partners and worked with the rest of the basketball crew at the West Sound Police Department. They had been enjoying a lighter caseload that allowed them time to get in a basketball game or two per week at the West Sound YMCA, provided they early birded it. Recent events, however, suggested their recreational time may be ending.

Just then, a sharp ringing from one of their phones echoed through the gym.

They all turned toward the wall where they'd thrown their hoodies and phones.

"I bet that's yours, Larson," said Mendez. "The senior officer's phone always rings first. Isn't that how it goes?"

"Yep," said Larson. He pulled up his T-shirt hem, wiping sweat from his face with a sigh. Then he headed over to answer the call.

"We're done anyway," said Rory. "I only booked the gym until seven a.m."

"And we're on shift in an hour," Fogarty said, motioning toward Evie.

"And you better shower first. I have to sit in a car with you all day." She held her nose above her full-lipped smile.

"What? I always smell good, like the ocean mist." He wafted the air in front of his face.

Jefferson chuckled at this comment, but his attention shifted to Larson on the phone. The senior detective had one hand on his hip and a grave look on his face.

"This doesn't look good." Rory was also watching Larson.

"No, it doesn't," agreed Jefferson.

The group started moving to gather up their things. Larson ended the call, slowly shaking his head as the others gathered around.

"Let me guess. The Underhill was right," said Mendez.

Larson nodded. "Two more overnight. They were found this morning in separate areas of the city."

"That's four dead in four days." Fogarty's hazel eyes were wide in astonishment. He looked a bit like a giant baby with his round face and smooth complexion, which held a workout-induced pinkness.

Larson glanced at him. "Thank you for doing the math."

The pink of Fogarty's face deepened.

Jefferson felt for the guy. He was young and eager, and so honest that he said whatever he was thinking.

"This really changes things," Jefferson said solemnly, sensing their basketball days were ending.

Three days ago, staff at the Room at the Inn homeless shelter discovered two dead men in their overnight shelter. Assuming drug overdoses, Aspen Klein, the owner of the shelter, called 911, and medics took the two deceased men to the hospital morgue. Dr. Stacey Underhill, the Rainier County Medical Examiner and someone Jefferson had briefly dated, suspected the men had taken fentanyl or crack cocaine laced with something. Exactly what she couldn't say yet.

They'd all been on pins and needles, hoping these deaths were isolated cases. But if Underhill was right, someone was selling a dangerous batch of drugs, and the WSPD could expect more casualties. The chief had ordered officers to post and hand out fliers warning people of the dangers.

Two more dead meant Underhill was spot on.

Jefferson picked up his keys and phone from the ground. "What's next?"

"Chief has called a special briefing at eight a.m. Patrol officers are securing the scenes and forensics is on the way since these cases are looking like more than the typical overdose." He reached down and picked up his sweatshirt. "So get your showers, grab something to eat, and I'll see you at the station in an hour."

***

Chief Carlson sent instructions for all officers on duty and the four West Sound PD detectives to be at the morning briefing. When Jefferson arrived at the station, the packed briefing room reminded him of the grim meeting after the explosion that rocked city hall last year, killing three people and injuring many more. However, the room today, while full, was missing the FBI and other federal agencies who'd been on hand that morning.

The room boasted functional gray carpet and white walls with one dark walnut conference table spanning the length of it. The city added technology upgrades two years ago. Hidden in the ceiling was a screen for displaying videos, slides, or other documents, with a projector ready to connect to laptops or phones. A case board hung on one wall for investigations involving multiple groups within the department.

Jefferson straightened his navy, gold, and brown Drake silk tie. Spotting Rory standing against the far wall, chatting with Mendez, Jefferson moved to take a spot next to him.

"You spiffy up so nice, Jeffy," Rory said with a smirk hidden in his ginger beard.

"Just trying to keep up with you, Jackson." Jefferson gave his partner a closer inspection. "Is that a new suit?"

"Ah, now I see why you are a detective," Rory said, smoothing his lapels. "My beautiful wife picked this little gem up for my birthday. Top of the line." He eyed Jefferson. "I knew you'd be jealous."

Jefferson nodded. "It is a beautiful suit."

"I meant that I have a wife to pick it out for me."

Mendez snickered.

Maintaining his relaxed crooked smile, Jefferson shook his head at Rory. "Yes, you do, and you got the better end of that deal. She's a saint for taking on the likes of you."

Of the four detectives, Jefferson was the only one not married or attached to a significant other. He didn't mind it that way for now. The job kept him busy.

"Alright, everybody." Chief Keith Carlson's voice boomed through the crowd. "Let's get this started. We won't be long—we need to get out to join the forensics teams at the two overdose scenes."

Everyone found a seat or a spot against the wall.

The chief, his silver hair combed back and trimmed with precision, stood at the head of the table, rigid in his uniform. "As you probably know by now, we have seen a sharp increase in overdose deaths recently, especially among the homeless population. Larsen and Mendez have been handling the investigative work to this point, but this situation is likely to require many more hands on deck." He glanced at Larsen. "Give your update, detective."

The chief sat as Larsen cleared his throat and stood.

"Thank you, sir. The first two reported deaths occurred Tuesday night at the Room at the Inn. According to Dr. Underhill, we should treat these as overdose deaths, though confirmation from toxicology is pending. Both of the deceased were male, ages twenty-three and thirty."

"Aspen Klein—most of us know Aspen as the woman who runs the shelter—reported that the two men did not seem to know each other or hang out together. That doesn't mean they didn't hang out in the same area of the street or get their drugs from the same supplier. We are still working on that connection." He took a deep breath and glanced down at his notes.

"Unfortunately, overdose deaths aren't unusual among the homeless population; we've seen our share. But two more deaths today means we could be dealing with a dangerous drug cocktail. And it's making the rounds through the community."

Larson picked up a stack of papers from the table and motioned for them to be passed around.

"You may remember," Larson continued, "the bulletin from Seattle that highlighted the combo of fentanyl with xylazine, an animal tranquilizer. Some dealers use the xylazine as an adulterant. The combo goes by street names of tranq or tranq dope. It restricts blood flow and slows the respiratory system more than fentanyl alone, but it can also give addicts a longer high."

"Our ME, Stacey Underhill, believes we could be dealing with something similar, as well as other combinations. Whoever is making this stuff is likely just throwing together combinations of pure drugs and garbage ingredients to increase their supply and, as a result, their bottom line."

A general murmur went around the room as people reacted to this information.

Jefferson lowered his head. An all-too familiar pressure was building in his chest. He worked to control his breath, trying to slow the anger that was always on a carefully contained simmer with this topic. He clenched his jaw and stared at his shoes.

As if the regular street drugs weren't bad enough, he thought. Now dealers were using any means necessary to increase profit. They didn't care about killing off their customers. There'd always be another addict in the queue.

The drug trade and the victims in its wake were personal to Jefferson. His little brother, Alex, met the wrong people, made a series of poor decisions, and before long, was willing to hurt the people who loved him to feed his addiction. Jefferson hadn't seen Alex since he caught him trying to steal their father's watch just one day after they'd buried the man. The memory still punched him in the gut.

There was a time when he spent every waking minute trying to help Alex. He searched for him on the streets of California, followed him to Oregon and Washington, trying to convince him to accept treatment. When their father died, Jefferson knew he had to let it go. He needed to focus on protecting his mother, and himself, from Alex's desperate plundering of their resources and emotions.

He shifted his position against the wall, trying to get himself mentally back into the meeting.

Rory glanced at him. "Great news, eh?"

Jefferson squeezed his eyes shut and ran his hand over his face. "They just keep finding more and more disgustingly creative ways to kill people."

Larson picked up a stack of papers from the table. "Everyone take one of these."

As the papers made their way around, Larson continued. "Toxicology tests don't routinely include xylazine, so it's difficult to know just how widespread it is. One sign of its use is nasty sores that spread really fast. Underhill observed sores on one of the deceased, one reason she believes xylazine is at least one drug we're dealing with.

"She'll add it to the toxicology tests for the two recent cases, but we all know how long those take."

He held up his copy of the paper they all now possessed. "This is an information sheet from the Drug Enforcement Administration. Our friends at the DEA have a deeper understanding of this stuff than we do. Take a minute to read it over, and then I'll try to answer questions, but once you read this, you'll know about as much as I do."

The room went quiet as they scanned over the information.

"This isn't good," Jefferson said to Rory as he finished reading the handout. "I knew xylazine caused people to stand in weird positions or lie around like zombies, but I didn't realize it could make naloxone ineffective."

"And we just barely got everyone trained on using the naloxone nose spray," added Rory. "That stuff only takes seconds to reverse an opioid OD. Kind of amazing. But now this." Rory shrugged his shoulders. "Throw in a little of this and a little of that, and now the nose spray may not work."

Jefferson shook his head. Fentanyl was already cheap. Why would dealers cut it with the other junk unless their goal was to kill people?

Despite his best efforts, his thoughts drifted to his younger brother again.

Living the life of an addict pushed people like Alex to pathways of destruction. Taking the drugs could kill. People who sold those drugs were often dangerous and unpredictable. Drug addicts hung around with other drug addicts, erratic people who could snap at any minute. And now criminals were purposefully adding ingredients that made those street drugs even more deadly.

For addicts, there were too many ways to end up dead.

Larson looked over the crowd, now mostly in conversation. "So...any questions?"

Fogarty raised his hand. Jefferson cringed. He hoped for Fogarty's sake that he had a relevant question.

Larson nodded in the young man's direction. "Fogarty."

"Thank you, sir. I was just wondering if the deaths are still considered overdoses if the people didn't mean to overdose. I mean, it's more like they were poisoned, right?" He looked around the room for any sign of agreement.

Larson folded his arms and squinted toward the ceiling as he formed an explanation. "Legally, it is the same. There are some instances of unintentional overdose, but those usually deal with prescribed medication or drugs given in a medical setting."

He scanned the room. "Regardless, we need to do all we can to communicate the danger posed by these drug combinations." He shrugged. "We can't say with certainty that the victims were unaware of what they were taking. Maybe they knew; maybe they didn't." He glanced at the chief. "That's why we're spending the time and resources to get in front of this 'poisoning,' if you want to call it that. In time, we should have more answers."

The chief nodded his agreement. "I know overdose deaths can be tricky to investigate as there's not usually a culprit to prosecute, but with several deaths in a short amount of time, we have a good chance of finding not just low-level sellers, but those up the food chain. Most importantly, we can get this garbage off the streets."

Larson scanned the group again. "Any other questions?"

The room was silent. What they wanted to know was their next steps, and that was up to Chief Carlson.

"That's all I got," Larson said.

"Thank you, detective." The chief stood just as Kathy, the department's administrative secretary, walked in carrying a box. He quietly thanked her as she set it on the table.

"We have more fliers here for distribution. We need all patrol officers to take a stack and hand them out in your area. Concentrate on the homeless population, but don't stop there. One death we are investigating today is in a wealthy neighborhood, so just get them into people's hands. We will hold a press conference as well. Families should be aware of the issue and the available resources, especially if they are caring for someone who is addicted."

"Hughes and Jackson, you two head over to Fairview. The groundskeepers found the victim in a pond on the eighth hole."

Jefferson raised a brow. "So what makes this case part of the drug investigation?"

"I am not one hundred percent certain it is, but Meyers and Souter, the responding officers, reported a syringe floating near the body. This isn't an area where we normally find drug paraphernalia, so, on the surface, it appears relevant."

He lowered his chin as his steely eyes bored into the two detectives. "Be prepared for pressure from the folks in that neighborhood to get this closed up fast."

Rory smirked. "It's not good for property values to have bodies floating in your ponds."

The chief pressed his lips together with a stiff nod. "Something like that."

"Larson and Mendez will head to the scene at the homeless encampment just north of the Shopside Docks."

Mendez moaned quietly, his copper eyes glaring at Jefferson and Rory. "Maybe I should buy a new suit," he muttered in his soft Mexican accent.

Jefferson lowered his head to hide a chuckle. He was sure there was an element of truth to Mendez's complaint, and he couldn't deny his gratification at pulling the Fairview scene. A body found in a rich community like Fairview heightened his suspicion.

The police were rarely called to that neighborhood for anything. It was far enough off the beaten path that opportunistic thieves had little to no access. Even with a car, a stranger would have to get past the security gates.

There had to be more to this case than met the eye.

Chapter Four

Mendez sat on his haunches holding a small flashlight, using his gloved hands to pick through the contents of a tattered gray backpack near the body.

Larson stood next to him, hands on his hips, envying Mendez's youthful knees. That position would kill him these days.

The poor dead soul was a young man, probably younger than thirty. He lay on his back in the center of a urine-soaked blanket, wearing just soiled black sweatpants and socks. His skinny bare chest bore several small sores, as did the scalp of his shaved head. His bruise-colored lips would smile no more.

A forensics officer kneeled next to Mendez, ready to bag anything the detectives thought worthy of closer inspection. Another member of the forensics team was finishing up photos of the scene.

Larson brought his forearm up to his nose as if that one act could blot out the smells surrounding him. Even without a dead body, this block of the city always held the scent of trash and human decay.

"Ah-ha!" Mendez held a driver's license in the air. He unfolded his body and stood while reading the card. "Assuming this license belongs to the victim here, his name is Christian Greene." He held it out to Larson. "Expired four years ago."

Larson took it. Though scuffed and faded, the picture on the front showed a curly-haired youth with the muscled neck of an athlete. He wore just the essence of a smile, a pretend man getting his first license.

"Date of birth 1998, so twenty-six. From Tacoma." He squinted at the picture and then moved around to get a better look at the face of the dead young man.

He scowled. This could be the same kid, but if it was, drugs had thoroughly destroyed him. "It's probably him, but we'll need to contact the family and get forensics confirmation." He took a picture of the license with his phone before passing it to the forensics officer for bagging.

"Detective Larson?"

Officer Hanson stood just inside the yellow tape of the crime scene with a short, bulky man next to her, his hands stuffed in his pockets. "This man says he might have some information for you."

As Larson scrutinized him, the man rocked back on his heels and raised his white-bearded chin.

During the police operation, most of the homeless individuals who occupied the tents and other makeshift shelters along the sidewalks near the Shopside Docks had dispersed. The Room at the Inn shelter, just a block away, never had enough capacity for the city's growing homeless population. As a result, an overflow of people camped on the sidewalks near the shelter to take advantage of the free meals at breakfast and lunch.

Larson knew this guy. He was a self-appointed spokesperson for the homeless, and he often found reasons to be critical of the city and the police.

Larson turned back to Mendez, who continued his hunt in the backpack.

"What do you want, Joey?" Larson said, without looking at him. "We're busy here."

He felt a slight annoyance towards Hanson for allowing this guy to bother them, but considering she was new, he couldn't blame her.

"Come on, detective," Joey shouted in his rough voice, his enunciation hampered by missing teeth. "I'm the one that called you all."

Larson groaned.

Mendez looked up and smirked. "Have fun."

"I should make you do it."

"I already have a job here." He motioned to the backpack. "You're the one standing around watching me work." He grinned. "Besides, maybe he knows something."

"I'm sure he thinks he does." Larson took his gloves off and threw them in the discard bag as he walked.

"This better be good, Joey."

Larson guessed Joey to be in his sixties, but homelessness was an age accelerator. Hard living took its toll.

The old man pulled one shaking hand out of his pocket and pointed toward the body. "I can tell you this kid, poor sucker, ain't one of us." The motion upset his balance, causing him to shift his feet. He shoved his hand back in his pocket as if it were cold. In reality, the morning already felt too hot for a day at the tail-end of summer.

Larson sighed. "Please elaborate."

His watery eyes shifted to Larson's and then quickly away again. "You seen me talking to folks. I know everybody 'round here, right? Heck," he chuckled, "all the people like talking to me, no matter how rough. You seen me, right? I look out for 'em, you know. Help 'em when you all are harassing 'em. Or when they need food or get sick—"

"I do not have time for this." Larson turned away.

"Don't you want to know 'bout the fella that was with him?"

The detective looked up at the sky. "How about you lead with that next time, Joey? Alright, out with it."

Joey tilted his head toward Evie Hanson while flicking his eyes between her and Larson.

The detective sighed as he pulled his notebook out. Joey was one of those guys who, despite his obvious low condition, still thought himself superior to women, especially a Black woman like Evie.

He turned his steely eyes on Joey. "Officer Hanson stays, so whatever you have to say, spill it."

Joey shrugged. "Suit yourself." He gave Evie a side-eye without speaking.

The young officer arched her brow. "Maybe I should just take him down to the station. He might find that more comfortable."

"Oh no, no." Joey waved his hands in front of him. "I'm fine here."

"Then start talking," Larson demanded.

"Okay. Don't get so antsy." He took a breath and expelled it with a loud sigh. "So, that guy there, uh ... the dead one. He showed up 'bout a week ago. He had another fella with him. Neither was too friendly. But the dead guy, yesterday he was out of it, like he was messed up." He pulled at the end of his beard and flicked his eyes up at Larson. "I ain't no snitch, so I'm only telling you all this cuz I know them others died too. Something's going on, man." He shook his head solemnly.

"I get that, Joey. So tell me about the other man. The not dead one."

Joey ran a hand across his nose. "He didn't stick around much, just like in the mornin', like he was checking on the other guy. Then he's off again." He motioned with his head for Larson to lean closer before saying in a whisper, "Pretty sure he was dealing."

The detective nodded understanding. "When did you last see him?"

"Just before it was dark, probably like eight last night. He must've buggered off sometime later when he seen his friend was..." He drew a finger across his throat.

"Description?"

"Medium-sized guy. Usually wearing them baggy jeans and a black t-shirt...sometimes a gray hoodie. He's all tatted up the arms. Never could make out much of it, but I seen a letter N on his neck when I was passing him on the street. Just an N; I couldn't tell nothing else. I don't do no staring with them mean fellas."

"Where on his neck? Left side, right side?"

"Um, like right here," he said, pointing to the area just below his left ear.

"Hair?"

"Shaved like the dead guy."

"Did you hear him speak? English? Spanish?"

Joey shook his head. "Nah, like I said, the dead guy," he said, reaching a trembling hand toward the body. "He was jus' out...like he was dead before he was dead. That other guy...he sort of took care of him. But nope. I didn't hear nothing. I gave 'em their space."

"Anybody else see anything? Hear anything?"

Joey chuckled hoarsely, rolling his eyes up at Larson. "You all can try, but..." He shrugged. "They ain't gonna talk."

"Come on, Joey. You know everybody. You never got the guy's name?"

He moved his head slowly back and forth. "Nope. Like I said, I ain't getting too close to those hard-looking fellas."

"Anything else?"

"He had him a phone." He stroked his beard. "Never saw him talking on it, just staring at it most times."

Larson snapped his notebook closed and stuffed it back in his pocket. "If you see him again, call me directly." He handed him a card. "Or if you find someone else who knows something. We may need you to come in at some point, so stay close."

Joey snorted. "You mean no trip to the Bahamas?"

Larson glanced back toward Mendez, who was now standing next to the body talking with the forensics officer. "Nope, Joey. No Bahamas."

Chapter Five

The blazing sun lit the way as Jefferson and Rory wove through the interior of West Sound. Fiery red and gold leaves of the maple and other deciduous trees were making their last brilliant gasp of life against the deep shadow of the evergreens. The day wasn't just clear; it was stunningly clear, like the sky had been polished to its purest blue.

Jefferson rarely made it out to this part of the city. The Fairview community overlooked Tillison Bay on the east side of West Sound. The police station and all other city services were in the downtown area, on the Stanton Inlet side.

Criminals found more opportunity to break the law within a few miles of downtown, where there were more people, petty thefts, burglaries, and drugs. The miles between downtown and Fairview were rural—fewer people, less crime.

As Jefferson turned off the highway, a fortress of gates supported by two stone guardhouses greeted the detectives. A muscular man in black slacks and a gray polo stepped outside as their car approached.

The guard read their identification badges with dramatic scrutiny before signaling for another guard to open the gate.

"You'll want to turn left at the third intersection," he told them through the open car window. "From there, you'll see the other police vehicles parked on the side of the road."

They thanked him and drove through the gate into the manicured world beyond.

For a half mile down the lane, they passed nothing but trees on either side of the road. Not a leaf was out of place, even with the colorful evidence of fall still clinging to the maples lining the sidewalks. Soon, the road opened up to reveal the first of the mini mansions piercing the blue sky.

Rory whistled. "Man, you could fit a dozen of my houses into one of these."

He was right, Jefferson thought as he took in the enormous structures. Fairview was the only neighborhood in West Sound made up only of sizeable luxury homes. Despite being built in the 1990s, most of the houses had a classic style and were well maintained, preserving their high value.

"These homes might make yours seem small," Jefferson said, "but you've got more land than almost this entire subdivision."

Rory's wife Marissa grew up with horses, so she insisted their kids do the same. They owned a twenty-four-acre ranch just outside of town.

"True," Rory agreed with a grin. "He with the most land wins."

Jefferson grunted. "I don't mind being the ultimate loser in this contest. Smaller mortgage than these people and less work than you."

They turned the corner and, just as the guard had promised, a line of emergency vehicles came into view, including that of Stacey Underhill, the Rainier County Medical Examiner.

Jefferson tightened his grip on the steering wheel. He still couldn't see Stacey without feeling awkward, even though they'd only gone on a few dates a year ago. She made him feel like a twelve-year-old in front of the cutest girl at school.

"Looks like the Underhill is here." Rory cast a sideways glance at Jefferson.

"Just don't," Jefferson warned as he turned off the car.

Rory shrugged with wide eyes. "I wasn't going to say anything."

"Let's keep it that way."

They walked from the road toward the fairway on a path meant for golf carts. As the view opened to the wide expanse of velvet green turf, the detectives spotted the crime scene cordoned off by yellow tape next to a long pond bordering the fairway.

Jefferson tipped his head to the officer guarding the perimeter. "Meyers."

"Good morning, detectives," the young officer replied.

"You were on night duty?"

Jefferson's question elicited a yawn. "Yep," Meyers said with a sigh. "County Sheriff was the first here, but Souter and I weren't far behind. Now I'm just trying to keep my eyes open while waiting for my replacement."

Rory reached down and grabbed a pair of gloves from a box at the officer's feet. "There's a crew on the way. We left about the same time, but Jeffy was in a hurry to get here and see what Dr. Underhill has to say."

"Do you ever stop?" Jefferson pulled his gloves on with a snap.

"Stop what?"

Jefferson shook his head and turned his attention back to Meyers. "So where's Souter?"

"Oh, they needed help removing the body from the water, so Souter volunteered to go in. He got soaked." He wrinkled his nose. "It was nasty." He raised his shoulders in a shiver. "I told him to go home. His girlfriend came and got him."

The sound of car doors shutting echoed from the street.

"Sounds like you are about to be released. Have a good one."

He thanked them and the two detectives made their way to the scene.

Stacey Underhill kneeled near the edge of the pond, the lifeless body lying face up on a plastic sheet in front of her. She pointed to something on his arm and directed the forensic photographer to document it.

She glanced up as they approached. "Good morning, gentlemen. Glad you could make it to our little waterside shindig."

"Fancy venue," said Rory.

"You're telling me." She picked up her clipboard and stood, mud covering the legs of her white protective suit. "This is not where I expected to examine the latest potential overdose victim."

"So it was an overdose?" Jefferson looked down at the man. He had dark hair and wore nothing but a stained white t-shirt and gray boxers. His eyes were closed, but he looked far from peaceful with his hair full of dirt and plant debris and his face marred by cuts and bruising.

The corner of her mouth lifted in a smile. "I know you love to move on quickly, but if you listened closely, you'd remember that I said *potential*."

Jefferson hurried his gaze back to the body to avoid her smiling eyes. She made every comment a cryptic swipe at him for not continuing to ask her out.

"So you're not sure?" he asked without looking at her.

She sighed before continuing. "It could be, but it also might not be." She reached down, grabbed a clear evidence bag, and handed it to Jefferson. "Found this in the pond."

It was the syringe mentioned in the briefing.

"We've swabbed the inside, but until we get it back to the lab, I can't tell you what was in it. And even then..." She shrugged. "It's likely too waterlogged to be useful."

Jefferson turned the bag over once before handing it to Rory.

Stacey bent over the man's left arm. Turning it gently, she pointed to a bruise on the upper arm. "I'm guessing this is a puncture mark." She looked up at them. "There may be some evidence of an injection here, so if toxicology says drugs, then I'd put money on that being the source." She pointed to the bag still in Rory's hand.

"So why do you sound skeptical?" asked Rory.

She showed her full, brilliant white smile, her brown eyes crinkling as she looked up at Rory. "You're very observant, my friend."

He bowed slightly at the compliment.

"Although...it's not that I'm skeptical as much as curious." She reached for the victim's other arm and lifted it from the plastic. "I've done a cursory examination for needle marks, and other than the potential puncture on his left arm, there is no other evidence of drug use, at least with needles.

"I mean, we all know that habitual drug users leave the traces of their addiction all over their bodies. If he injected himself, it may have been the first time. But I'm just guessing here. I need to inspect the tissue."

Jefferson raised a brow. "Any other theories?"

She shook her head. "Not yet. I can tell you he hasn't been in the water longer than overnight, and that's just my little piece of detective work. This is a busy course. Someone would have seen him before the mowers."

Jefferson agreed. "What about the damage to his face?" he asked, examining the man's features again. Tiny, jagged cuts ran across his cheeks and forehead.

"The water here is pretty shallow," Stacey moved closer to the man's face. "With the softening of the tissue, even with a short time in the water, the rocks, sticks, and shrubs here would easily damage the skin."

She pointed to scratches on the man's forehead. "You don't even need a current for that, just the slightest movement."

She glanced up at the two detectives. "Other than being banged up from spending the night soaking in pond muck, this guy appears to have been healthy; I'd even say he was uncommonly fit."

"What's the brand of his shirt?" Jefferson bent closer to the body.

"Interesting." She said, considering him with amused interest. "I have not checked that yet." She pulled the T-shirt collar out to read the tag. "Looks like—"

"Luca Faloni," Jefferson finished, his eyes widened with surprise.

Stacy raised a brow at him.

He shrugged. "I like Italian brands."

Rory snuffed. "Expensive Italian brands. So, we can conclude that this isn't the T-shirt of a poor lost soul who wandered into drowning in a gated community full of rich people."

As he stood and gazed around the fairway, Jefferson observed that all the homes lining the fairway had patios and yards that opened directly onto the golf course. A man drugged out of his mind could easily trip into the pond.

"He could definitely be a lost soul, but he looks more like a local who wandered out of his backyard," Jefferson said. "Any footprints?"

Stacey sat back on her heels, her long legs bending like a resting heron. "No. The mowers had already gone over the entire area before the maintenance guys noticed the body."

"I don't suppose we're lucky enough for him to carry a license or credit card in his boxers?" Rory asked.

Stacey cocked her head to the side, "Do you expect me to find all the relevant clues? Come on, you all need something to do."

"But you're the Wonderhill," Rory teased.

As he swept his gaze around the area, Jefferson noticed a golf cart coming down the fairway in their direction. The single occupant was a man whose white head bobbed as he rode over the grassy terrain, scattering a flock of Canada geese from his path.

Jefferson tapped Rory's arm. "We have a visitor."

The man stopped his cart in front of the three newly arrived officers just outside the crime scene perimeter. Jefferson couldn't hear their conversation, but the man kept pointing toward the detectives.

One officer eventually turned and strode over to Rory and Jefferson.

"Excuse me, detectives, but this man would like a word with you. I tried to take down his information, but he insisted on talking to one of you."

Jefferson assured him it was fine. "I'll go talk to him. He seems eager to tell us something."

Rory slapped him on the shoulder. "You go get 'em, cowboy. I'm going to take a couple of these officers and start going door-to-door to see what the neighbors might know."

"Sounds like a plan."

Stacey stood up and gazed at the man waiting by his golf cart. "Maybe he knows this guy."

There was truth in what she said. If this surprise guest knew the victim, it would save them the time of hunting for someone to identify the body. Jefferson glanced down at the dead man again. It was a lot to ask. Most people had never seen a dead body, except for the surreal stillness of those resting in a casket. He had to take the chance. With another potential overdose victim on their hands, wasting time could mean adding to the list of victims. The pressure was on to identify the seller of the lethal drugs before they ended up in the hands of more users.

Jefferson took out his phone and snapped a picture of the dead man's face. Making an ID wouldn't require seeing the whole corpse, and they didn't need another pair of feet walking around the crime scene.

"We'll see," Jefferson said as he slid his phone away.

The man was now standing outside his golf cart. In a few long strides, Jefferson approached him wearing a hard, all-business expression meant to communicate the seriousness of the situation. The last thing he wanted was to get roped into a lengthy conversation by a curious neighbor or a reporter... Until Jefferson could determine the visitor's intentions, he wouldn't give the man any invitation to waste their time.

"Ah," said the man. "Thank you for coming over."

"Of course. I'm Detective Hughes. What can I help you with, Mr. ...?"

The man watched as Jefferson pulled out his notebook.

"Oh, well, that's why I came over. I'm Brent Miller and I'm the president of the Fairview Neighborhood Association. I'm also the president of the Fairview Golf Club." He offered a gentle smile that was not as pompous as his titles.

Jefferson wrote his name down. "Did you see or hear anything out of the ordinary last night, Mr. Miller?"

He shook his head slowly. "No, unfortunately. Slept like a baby."

Jefferson narrowed his eyes. "So, do you have any information for us?"

"Oh, sorry," he said with a nervous chuckle. "As I'm sure you can imagine, the neighborhood is in a state of shock, and several of our older residents are just plain scared out of their wits; my phone is ringing off the hook. Of course, the golf course is closed, and the poor maintenance fellas are just in shock. And we have families with children..."

He stopped, suddenly noticing the impatience that had crept into the detective's eyes.

"Did any of the neighbors you've spoken with see or hear anything?" Jefferson asked, working to keep his tone civil.

"Not that I know of, but our social media site is going crazy with people speculating about what's happened."

"You have a neighborhood site?"

The man nodded. "Yes, but it's private."

Jefferson made a note without responding. Nothing on the internet is private, especially if it ended up in a murder investigation.

"So, Detective Hughes, I just want you to know that if you need, you know, sort of spokesperson for the neighborhood, to share information, or let you know what I hear, then I am willing to do that. I know pretty much everyone here."

Jefferson studied him for a moment. Not everyone could handle seeing a dead body, and in this case, the dead could easily be a friend or neighbor.

"Thank you, Mr. Miller. We will keep that in mind." He pulled out his phone. "I have one way that you could be really helpful, but I warn you, it won't be easy."

The man's eyes widened. "Anything, detective. Whatever I can do to help."

Weighing his phone gently in his hand, Jefferson considered the man. Brent Miller looked to be in his fifties or a youthful sixty-something. If he carried a lot of responsibility in the neighborhood, he likely had a steady disposition and could handle stress. A man of his age had probably experienced the death of family or friends, and while not the same, Jefferson decided Miller seemed able to handle the potential shock of recognition.

The detective squinted at the brightness of the sun illuminating the grass to a brilliant green. "I have a photo of the deceased here. If you are willing, I can show it to you, and you can let me know if the victim is familiar to you. What do you think?"

Brent Miller rubbed his chin, regarding the blank phone screen. "Is it very bad?"

"There's no blood or open wounds. There are some scratches and some bruising, but his face is otherwise untouched."

Miller looked up and nodded. "Okay, I can do it."

Jefferson tapped his phone and pulled up the picture. Then he held it out so Brent could see the image.

At first, the man's eyes narrowed with concentration, and Jefferson thought they'd hit a dead end. Then Brent's hand flew to his mouth as he backed away and bent over at the waist, taking several deep breaths.

"Oh my. Oh...my." He clutched at his forehead as he stood back up. Tears filled his eyes. The man looked wretched. "That's Dan," he whispered. "That's Dan Lausch."

Chapter Six

MJ watched as a straggling group of eighth-grade girls exited the hall toward the lunchroom. They were the last to go, almost every day, giggling and walking in a clump of long hair and jeans.

"Whoo," said Sandy Wright with a sigh. "They were wired up last period." She shook her gray head. Mrs. Wright, across the hall, taught U.S. History and two periods of language arts.

"The sun," MJ said, pointing to the glare coming from Sandy's classroom windows.

"Yep," the other woman agreed. "And I can't wait to get in my garden later today. Only three periods to go." She smiled with forced enthusiasm.

MJ chuckled. Sandy planned to retire at the end of the year, and she was counting the days.

"But for now," Sandy continued, "grade and grub."

"Grade and grub," repeated Garrett Long, a math teacher who had just opened his door. "According to our contract, you are entitled to a work-free lunch."

Sandy smirked. "Of course I am, but then I'd just have more grading to take home. So I choose to grade and grub."

MJ was only partially listening to this exchange. Her attention moved down the hall as she watched Cade McCann making his way toward them, his backpack slung over one shoulder.

As he came closer, his eyes darted between the three teachers from beneath a furrowed brow. She'd never seen him looking so serious.

"Ms. Brooks," he said, clearing his throat. "Can I talk to you for a minute?"

She told him of course, wished the other teachers an excellent lunch, and opened the door to her classroom.

Once inside, the boy stuffed his hands in his pockets and looked down at his feet.

"What is it, Cade?"

As he looked up, MJ's eyes narrowed with concern as she saw the worry etched into the young man's face.

He hadn't missed her reaction, quickly lowering his head as he folded his arms across his chest. "I'm not sure what's going on. But, um..." He looked toward the windows and then back at MJ. "I think something is going on at Jada's house. Like something bad."

"Something bad? What makes you think that?"

He set his backpack on the floor as if to shed the extra weight before continuing.

"There were police in our neighborhood this morning. I only saw them because we were late leaving for school, but there were a lot of them. My mom brushed it off as someone's alarm going off accidentally or something. But they wouldn't send that many police cars for something like that."

MJ was about to speak, but he kept going. "I know that doesn't mean it was Jada's house, but I've been calling her all morning, texting, checking all her posts, and nothing."

"Could she still be upset with you?"

"No," he blurted. "We talked about what happened yesterday after school. That's what freaks me out. She said it wasn't me making her sad, it was stuff at home with her dad, but she wouldn't say what."

He shook his head. "I know something's wrong. She's not here today, and she never misses school. And no one else has heard from her either. I checked with everyone. I even called her dad's office, and they said he hadn't come to work yet. But no one is answering their house phone either."

"What about her mom?"

"She hasn't talked to her mom in months because they don't get along. And she lives in California anyway, so it's not like Jada would be with her."

"Has there been anyone new at the house, like a relative, or does her dad have a girlfriend?"

He shook his head. "It's just Jada and her dad."

MJ nodded as she considered this information. Given what she knew about Jada, this apparent silence seemed strange. But there could be a lot of explanations besides something that involved the police. There was likely no relation between the two situations. That didn't mean Cade's worries were without merit.

She folded her arms and leaned against a desk. "You're right. It's unusual for her to be gone. I can see why you are concerned." She smiled gently. "I also think there's a perfectly reasonable explanation."

His face fell. "But what if there's not? I mean, if something happened to her, then we would need to find her fast, right? You worked with the police before, when Mr. Danielson died last year, so I figured you could find out if they're looking for her." He ran a hand through his sandy hair. "I just need to know she's okay, and I don't know who else to ask."

MJ picked up Cade's backpack and held it out to him. "Right now, you need to go eat some lunch, and I need to get ready for my next class. As soon as school is out, I will check into Jada's absence today. I can't give you any personal information, even if you two are friends, but I can at least let you know that there is nothing to worry about. Okay?"

He slung his backpack over his shoulder. "Thanks, Ms. Brooks."

As soon as he was out the door, MJ picked up her classroom phone and dialed the front office.

"Hi, MJ. What can I do for you?" asked the always helpful Dolores Birkman, attendance secretary.

"Hi Dolores. Has anyone called in to excuse an absence for Jada Lausch? I don't have her until seventh period, but I've heard that she is absent."

"Um, let me check."

As she waited, MJ pulled up Jada's profile on her computer.

"Hmm, nothing yet," Dolores said. "But, you know, she could still show up if it's a dentist appointment or something."

"That's true."

"Is something the matter?"

"I don't think so. Just one of her friends raised some concerns, but they had a bit of a falling out yesterday. I'm sure everything is fine. Thanks for checking."

"No problem. I'll let you know if I hear something. And if she's not here by the end of lunch, I'll call the house."

MJ thanked her and glanced up at the clock. Just a few minutes left of lunch.

She dialed the phone number for Jada's dad. Tapping her fingers on the desk, she willed someone to pick up. Cade's worried face popped into her mind. She blinked it away, hating the dread growing in her own gut.

No answer.

Chapter Seven

"Here."

Shannon's simple text sent MJ into a flurry of last-minute tasks before leaving for the night.

She'd waited until the last minute to slip on her black sandals. They were slim and studded with black rhinestones—super cute. She had about a two-hour window before her feet would be howling.

Edgar followed her to the door, and she kissed his furry head in a last goodbye. "Be good, buddy."

The black and white Border Collie-Australian Shepherd mix watched as she slid her arms into a sheer lace bolero, picked up her small purse, and walked out the door.

"Whoa, you are stunning," Shannon said as MJ climbed into the passenger seat. "Seriously, MJ. You should wear dresses more often. That shows off your awesome figure, and that blue is beautiful. You even put your hair up."

Shannon knew how much work it was for MJ to tame her long, dark curls into a neat updo. Some curls were likely to escape about the same time her feet were done with the heels, and the car turned into a pumpkin.

"You don't look so bad yourself." Looking gorgeous was nothing new for her friend. With her expertly blended makeup, blonde hair, chocolate brown eyes, Shannon had to work at looking grungy, something MJ did rather well.

"Wow, but that view outside. Just one reason I love coming to your place."

MJ looked out the windshield as they backed out of the driveway. The Puget Sound was also wearing its finest today, sparkling like liquid sapphire under the bluest of skies. Mt. Rainier reigned over the scene in her crown of snow.

MJ never took that view for granted. Even on the worst of the rainy days, Stanton Inlet, her little piece of the Puget Sound, calmed her tendency to restlessness.

She rented the back apartment from her friend and landlady, Claire O'Neil. Claire led an active life as a retired park ranger. Her place was empty for the week as she was off visiting her sister in Arizona, probably trail running or some other crazy athletic endeavor. Every once in a while, Claire could convince MJ to join her on a hike or kayaking up the Puget Sound.

Shannon had her favorite country band on blast as they made their way down the highway. MJ had the visor down, using the mirror to apply a layer of lip gloss. She wanted to have fun tonight, to relax and enjoy Shannon's company with some good food and amusing people-watching, but the situation with Jada still weighed on her mind.

She hadn't been able to put Cade at ease during seventh period. Dolores tried calling the house multiple times. MJ even tried calling Jada's mom, who was listed as a secondary contact. No answer there either.

She shut the visor and turned down the music.

Shannon shot her a look. "I like that song."

"Sorry. Can I ask you a favor?"

"You can ask, of course." Shannon smiled, but it slowly faded as she saw the look on MJ's face. "What is it, MJ?"

"Probably nothing, but could we make a stop before we go to the reception? It would help me relax if I could check in at Jada's house...since it's in the same neighborhood as the clubhouse."

Shannon sighed in relief. "I thought for sure you were going to ditch me. Of course we can stop. I wouldn't mind getting this mystery solved myself. It's so strange not being able to contact anyone in the family. I mean, it's not all that unusual, but I could name the diffi-cult-to-contact families, and Jada's is not one of them." She turned to MJ with a reassuring smile. "Still, most of the time, I find it's not anything serious. So we'll stop by the house because I need you to relax."

MJ sat back against the seat with a sigh. "Thanks."

She rolled her head around, trying to get her neck and shoulders to release some of the tension, not wanting to ruin their fun evening by obsessing over this. Everything was probably fine, she told herself. It wasn't completely unusual for a parent to take their kids on a surprise vacation somewhere, or to have a relative get sick and make an emer-gency visit out-of-town without thinking to call the school. And with the parents' separation, they would have to deal with a lot of issues, emotionally and legally. Whatever was going on likely had something to do with that. At least, that's what MJ tried to convince herself.

Shannon turned the music back up, singing along with gusto. MJ laughed and joined in, thankful for the rare fall sun just beginning to sink in the sky. And her beautiful, exuberant friend.

***

When they arrived at Fairview, Shannon showed her wedding invitation at the gate.

The guard's dark eyes surveyed the inside of their car with a seriousness that seemed excessive for a golf club community. Then he walked around the car, shining a flashlight into the back window of the SUV.

MJ glanced at Shannon with a raised brow, her smile threatening to turn to laughter.

"Stop it," Shannon mouthed silently, holding back a snicker.

The guard returned to the driver-side window, bending down with a changed expression. Now, he was all smiles and friendliness.

"Alright, you ladies be sure to turn right at the first intersection. That road will take you directly to the clubhouse. There's another...um...event in the neighborhood just now, and I wouldn't want you going to the wrong place." He grinned with an air of importance, as if he had just offered them life-saving guidance.

"Oh, thank you. We'll do that," Shannon lied.

"You ladies have a good time," he said with a wink. Then he tapped on the car door and waved his muscular arm at the guard shack to let them through.

"What do you think he meant by 'event'?" asked MJ, as she opened her phone for directions to Jada's house.

Shannon shrugged. "Golf tournament or something?"

They were silent for a few minutes as they took in the view outside the car.

"Okay, you're going to turn left up here, where you see that gorgeous French Château-looking house," MJ directed.

"Can you believe this place?"

Fairview wore its name well. Every inch seemed lush with meticulous beauty. The wealth in this neighborhood had to be astounding.

What did all these people do to afford these homes? They weren't teachers; MJ knew that for sure.

The place seemed eerily quiet. Given the stunning weather, she had expected to see golfers around. Maybe it was too late in the day. Long shadows grew as the sun slid behind tall fir trees. MJ didn't golf, but she assumed daylight was important.

In no time, they made the last turn. MJ sucked in a breath at the scene coming into view as they approached Jada's house.

Police cars crowded the cul-de-sac. Men and women in uniform were milling around outside. People in white paper suits came out of the house while others went in.

"Oh no," breathed Shannon, stopping before a neighbor's house. Concern filled her wide eyes as she turned to MJ.

MJ turned to stare at the house, her heart suddenly racing with fear and adrenaline. Her gut had been right. Cade had been right. This was something bad. Very bad.

***

MJ unbuckled her seatbelt, ready to bolt from the car. Shannon grabbed her arm.

"Wait. Maybe you shouldn't go walking up there. We don't know what's going on."

"I know. That's what I want to find out." MJ opened her door. "It's okay if you want to stay."

Shannon groaned and unbuckled her seatbelt. "Of course, I'm coming. I'm not going to let you go alone."

The two women's heels tapped gently as they strode down the sidewalk. A group of four officers regarded them with raised brows. The dresses and heels were very out of place.

One officer eventually broke away and met them before they could make it to the driveway of Jada's house.

"I'm sorry. I have to stop you here." He put his arms out wide to show the area they would not be crossing. His youthful face had a serious expression, but it was relaxed and pleasant.

"Officer..." MJ glanced down at his tag. "Officer Payne, we both work at Mariner Middle School, and one of our students lives here. We'd just like some information. We've been worried about her."

"I see." He turned to look behind him. "You probably ought to talk to one of the detectives. Stay here and I'll check if anyone is free to speak with you."

MJ barely heard what he said. Behind him, two men in suits were descending the porch. The tallest one turned. His blue eyes met hers, and for a moment, the fear seemed to transform to the grief of a year ago, when she mourned her friend and mentor and met Detective Hughes for the first time. As they locked eyes, a flood of memories weighed down the moment.

He stood still, causing his partner to pause and follow his eyes.

Rory waved, and MJ became conscious that she had stopped breathing. Jefferson finally dropped his gaze.

"Isn't that your detective friend?" asked Shannon.

MJ nodded, swallowing hard at the sudden lump in her throat. Seeing him again shouldn't be so difficult, but it unleashed an unexpected wave of sadness, dredging up memories of the grief she had painstakingly buried.

"You know the detectives?" asked the officer as he watched the two men walk in their direction. "Saves me a trip. Looks like they're coming to answer your questions."

"Thank..." MJ's voice came out in a whisper. She cleared her throat. "Thank you, Officer Payne. I'm sure they will."

Well, maybe they will, she thought, doubt creeping in as she remembered Jefferson's resistance to letting her help with the case when Troy died. He firmly believed that she would only get in the way, make foolish mistakes, or end up injured. She'd proved him wrong, and he eventually trusted her. Sort of. But that was then.

Jefferson and Rory stopped to give instructions to the group of officers, sending two of them toward the house. One stayed to act as a sentry with Officer Payne.

Turning again toward MJ and Shannon, Rory wore a broad grin, his eyes sparkling with humor. Jefferson, on the other hand, checked his watch, looked behind him twice, and watched his feet, essentially looking everywhere but at her.

She fought the smile that felt very inappropriate in the moment. His demeanor reminded her that for all his confidence as a detective, Jefferson could be strangely awkward.

"MJ!" Rory said. "Fancy meeting you here, and looking so fancy, I might add."

"Detective Jackson," she said, shaking the hand he offered. She glanced briefly at Jefferson. "Detective Hughes." It came out more formal than she'd intended.

Jefferson smiled in his crooked way, looking at the two women. His eyes landed on her. "How are you, MJ?"

His voice was soft compared to Rory's boisterous one, and the question had a depth that went beyond the moment. The last time she saw him, he said something very similar, wishing her well from his hospital bed. That day was dark and light in so many ways.

Before answering, she exhaled a shaky breath.

"I am doing well. Thank you for asking." She hoped that her voice sounded more casual than this moment felt. In order to calm herself, she clenched her fists. She was doing well. It'd been a tough year, but she felt good. "And this is Shannon Davis. She's a friend of mine and our school counselor."

Jefferson reached out and shook Shannon's hand. "It's nice to meet you."

MJ watched in shock as Shannon grinned at Jefferson, a pretty blush on her cheeks. The detective smiled gently before letting the counselor's hand go.

Rory hadn't missed this exchange, looking at MJ with a raised brow.

MJ scowled, impatience replacing her momentary weakness at seeing the detectives again. They were not here for pleasantries or flirting. She needed to know where Jada was and why the entire police department seemed to be at the girl's house.

She stretched herself as tall as the heels would make her—all of five-foot-five—and reached down for her firmest teacher's voice. "While it's very good to see both of you, we need to know what has happened here. This is where one of our MMS students lives. Her name is Jada Lausch. She didn't come to school and we have had trouble contacting her family. We would appreciate any information you can share about Jada or her parents."

The two detectives looked at each other, their faces turning more serious.

Rory shook his head. "What we can tell you and what you want to know may not be the same thing."

Jefferson narrowed his eyes. "This is a long drive just to check on a student? Do you know something you should tell us, MJ?"

Just like Jefferson to ask questions rather than answer hers, thought MJ. Before she could say anything, Shannon spoke up.

"Oh, my cousin is having a wedding reception at the clubhouse tonight, so we were in the neighborhood," she said, her voice sounding bubblier and more melodic than ever. "Jada doesn't normally miss school, and MJ was already worried about her, so we stopped by. We never expected to see all this."

When she finished, Jefferson smiled warmly. "That explains the, uh..." He seemed to struggle with how to say it.

"Oh, the dresses," Shannon laughed. "Yes, we don't normally show up at our students' homes this way."

They grinned at each other again. MJ threw an exasperated look at Rory. A girl was missing, for all they knew, and no one seemed interested in that fact right now.

"Detective Hughes," she said, stepping closer to him. "Where is Jada?"

He clenched his jaw, but his eyes held something troubling in their blue depths.

"We don't know," he said, simply. "She's not in the house and none of the neighbors have seen her since yesterday."

"And her dad?"

Jefferson glanced at Rory, who shrugged. "It'll be out soon enough, partner."

"What will be out?" MJ asked, a sinking feeling in her gut.

"He's dead," Jefferson said softly, as if trying to keep the words from landing too harshly.

She could feel his eyes on her as she sucked in a breath, her mind reeling with what this could mean for Jada.

"MJ—" he started.

"How?" she choked out, too afraid of the answer. If someone killed him, what would they do to a defenseless thirteen-year-old girl?

"We can't say." He put his hand up as she interrupted. "Without a full report, we cannot say for certain what killed him, but..." He looked at Rory again before continuing. "I shouldn't even tell you this much, but it looks like a drug overdose."

"Drugs?" said Shannon, turning to MJ with wide eyes. "We know Mr. Lausch, and I can't imagine him doing drugs. Can you MJ?"

She thought about it. "He was a busy man, but if he was doing drugs, he hid it really well."

Rory folded his arms. "People get into drugs in all kinds of ways. Prescriptions can lead to dependence. I'm not saying that's this guy's case, but drug use is a problem all over."

Looking at the sky, MJ rested her hands on her hips as she tried to process what they were saying.

"So there wasn't any kind of break-in?"

Jefferson glared. "Stop trying to figure it out MJ. Just know we don't see any sign of your student being hurt or injured here, but we can't locate her right now. We have all our officers on the lookout, going door-to-door in the neighborhood, and if we don't find some sign of her soon, the search will expand, most likely to include the FBI. We are doing everything possible."

"Detective Hughes, you know we can help. We know her friends—"

"MJ." His voice lowered to a warning. "Go to the reception. We will let you know if we need your help."

Not one good-natured wrinkle disturbed the solid set of his jaw. This was his super serious face. But as usual, the hardness didn't extend to his eyes, which were the same gentle shade of blue, matching the fading color of the sky as the day gave way to dusk.

She didn't doubt that the police were doing everything possible, everything they knew how to do. But there was no time to waste with a young girl missing.

She met his gaze with a determination of her own, knowing that while she would do as he asked at this moment, her mind was already whirling with her next steps to help find Jada.

So MJ smiled, thanked them for the information, and headed with Shannon to the reception. Someone knew something, and she refused to sit around and wait for the awful news that someone or something had hurt Jada, or worse. MJ had to do something.

When would Jefferson learn she could be his greatest asset?

Chapter Eight

The unexpected meeting with MJ had Jefferson's mind in knots as he and Rory headed back to the station for the evening briefing. Thankfully, Rory had to take a phone call from his wife, sparing Jefferson the knowing looks and the humorous jabs his partner was sure to throw at him.

Jefferson enjoyed seeing MJ looking well after everything that had happened the previous year. He knew it'd been tough for her.

He rubbed his chin. She didn't just look well. She looked stunning. His jaw had almost hit the ground when he saw her standing there with her attractive friend.

A smile crept up one side of his mouth. The counselor was flirting with him for sure, and he found MJ's reaction interesting. She did not like it at all. He wondered if she objected to their flirting or just to him. Trying to read what MJ had going on in her head was not his best skill, yet she seemed to read him easily. He hated that.

As the memories of last year's investigation filled his mind, Jefferson bristled at the prospect of MJ getting involved in this case. While she'd played an important role in solving the city hall murders, her involvement caused him stress and worry that he didn't care to repeat. MJ is demanding, doesn't think before she acts, and runs headlong into danger, especially if someone she cares about is at risk.

He had to admit, however, that the daughter's disappearance was troubling. If they didn't hear something soon, the chances increased that something had happened to her, or that she knew what happened to her father and ran out of guilt or fear. One thing he knew for sure, with a student involved, it'd be a struggle to hold MJ back from pulling all kinds of stunts to find her.

Brent Miller provided them with a little more information, but seeing his friend's body took a toll on him, and they didn't want to push him too much. He hinted at some trouble in the dead man's marriage, which may have affected the victim's state of mind. They were perhaps looking at a purposeful overdose in this case.

When they arrived back at the station, Jefferson got a pleasant surprise when he saw Amber Wells sitting beside Chief Carlson as they walked into the briefing room.

She stood and greeted the two detectives with a warm handshake.

"It's good to see you, gentlemen. It's been a few." Her genuine smile softened her serious features. Amber Wells served as the Supervisory Special Agent for a small FBI office in West Sound. Her team covered a four-county region that extended to the Oregon border, so although they were in the same city, the agents often worked cases wherever their expertise was needed. They played a pivotal role in the city hall bombing case last year. Amber led the investigative team, which included her agents and the West Sound detectives.

"It's great to see you, too," Jefferson said before adding with a grin, "But this means we have something going on that the feds find interesting." Suspicion lined his brow, but his crooked smile negated its delivery.

Amber met his gaze with a steady grin. "We find recent events very interesting. There could be some definite overlap between one of our investigations and the deaths here in West Sound."

Jefferson's brow shot up. "Like?"

Amber laughed. "I'm guessing you're the kid who peeked at all your presents before Christmas."

"More like he interrogated his parents until they gave up the goods," chimed in Rory.

"Wait for the briefing, Hughes," the chief warned. "No need to make Amber go through the information more than once."

Amber sighed. "I appreciate Jeff's determination to get going. These drug cases take a heavy toll on the community."

Her hazel eyes were soft and full of meaning. Most of Jefferson's colleagues knew his background, how he'd forgone his law degree to become a cop, driven by an obsession with fixing his brother's drug addiction. After almost ten years of chasing that hopeless cause, he'd finally realized that no one could save Alex but Alex. That didn't mean he'd buried the anger, the hatred he felt towards those who created and used addicts like his little brother to line their pockets.

He folded his arms with a nod. "I can wait."

Rory gave him a quick arm bump. "Maybe we should have invited MJ."

"MJ?" asked Amber. "Where did that come from?"

Jefferson glared at Rory. "It came from a deep and disturbing desire to be annoying."

The ginger-haired detective grinned. "It's true. Marissa would agree one hundred percent."

"That doesn't answer my question. Why are we talking about MJ? Is everything okay?" Amber's eyes were wide with concern.

This reaction surprised Jefferson. He had sensed last year that Amber thought MJ provided valuable insight. She'd given the woman tons of leeway and trust last year, more than he'd expected, more than he wanted. MJ must have made more of an impression on the FBI boss than he'd realized.

"MJ is fine," he assured her. "She just showed up at the victim's house in Fairview. The guy's daughter is one of her students. When she didn't show up for school, MJ and the school counselor went to her home to check on her and her family."

The chief cleared his throat. "We'll have to discuss this further after the briefing. Larson and Mendez just walked in, so let's get going."

Amber touched Jefferson's arm before he could move to a seat. "Jeff."

Her eyes searched his from behind her slim glasses. Amber had twenty years on Jefferson, but tiny creases were only beginning to form around her eyes. She took her health and fitness seriously, and it showed. Right now, though, she looked at him with something like motherly concern.

"Some of what I share today is going to hit close to home."

His eyes narrowed. What did that mean?

Before he could ask, she turned and followed the chief to her seat.

***

The chief stood at the front while everyone else sat around the table.

"You all know Special Agent Wells, so I'll dispense with any niceties. Larson, you start, then Hughes, and last, Agent Wells will share any pertinent information from the federal agencies. Larson," he said with a curt nod before sitting down.

Opening his notebook, Larson placed it on the table.

"We tentatively identified the victim near the Shopside Docks as Christian Greene, twenty-six, of Tacoma. Mendez found his license in a backpack at the scene. We just returned from making a God-awful visit to his parents. They have yet to make formal identification, but..." He tapped his notebook with a pen. "We're pretty sure it's him."

He gazed down at the table and cleared his throat.

"Initial cause of death appears to be a drug overdose, very similar to the cases at The Room at the Inn. His body showed signs of long-term, habitual drug use. We did not find any remaining drugs with his belongings. His parents haven't heard from him in a year, but they passed on a few names of friends that we'll be tracking down to see if they know anything about his recent situation."

Sitting back, he ran a hand over his bald head. "You'll all be glad to know we had the help of our favorite homeless community organizer, Joey."

A few eye rolls and groans greeted this.

"I know. I know. We are not used to Joey being helpful, but it seems he was more concerned with outsiders in his territory than obstructing the police. According to Joey, the kid hadn't been in his area very long." He relayed in more detail the information from Joey concerning the unidentified man seen with the victim.

"An 'N' tattoo?" asked Rory. "Have we seen that before?"

Larson shrugged. "I haven't. And it could be meaningless, at least as far as we're concerned. Some Nancy, Nora, or...uh...Nathan might think otherwise." He gave a half-hearted grin as he closed his notebook.

"Or Nico."

Jefferson's head snapped in Amber's direction. She'd spoken so quietly that he wasn't sure he'd heard correctly.

"Did you say Nico?" Just saying the name shot ice through his veins.

She nodded as her eyes met his. Her face held her usual calm expression, but the tension in her brow showed her concern. Amber was the only person who knew his history with Nico, his brother's history with Nico.

Slowly, she moved her attention to the crowd at large. "I was going to wait until my time at the end, but this piece of evidence suggests a stronger link than we realized." She glanced at Jefferson again before continuing.

"Nicolas Lopez Guerrero, known on the street as Nico, has been an up-and-coming drug trafficker for over fifteen years. Originally from Nuevo Laredo, Mexico, he entered the country as a child with his parents, who took up residence first in Laredo, Texas, and then near San Francisco. This is where Nico began trafficking drugs as a teen. Small potatoes at first, but he is ruthless."

Jefferson attempted to swallow. His throat was as rough as sandpaper. He tugged at his collar, trying to calm his breathing.

Amber glanced downward, appearing to consult her notes. Jefferson noticed her deliberate avoidance of eye contact, fully aware of the impact this news would have on him.

Raising her eyes to the group again, Amber continued. "After a young girl's overdose death twelve years ago, there was too much heat on him, so Nico moved his operations to the Pacific Northwest, selling drugs from Salem to Tacoma. He mainly distributed for John Mejia, a California cousin of the Herrera family in Mexico. Nico gained control of a weak network in our area, and before long, he had the strongest network. He fled to Mexico when several of his people were arrested in Medford, Oregon, after an undercover operation by the FBI." She stopped and then added more quietly, "And others." She paused and then looked directly at Jefferson. "We believe Nico is back in the area, or at least his people are."

A wave of disgust fell over him with an oceanic level of hatred behind it. He stared back at her, trying to control the muscles of his face, his mouth, his throat, his hands. All wanted to shout, yell, pound the table.

Amber looked away, and Jefferson ran a hand over his face as if that could wipe away everything she had said.

Nico was back. There was no man alive that Jefferson hated more than Nico.

"This 'N' tattoo," Amber continued, "has been seen on Nico's closest associates, the guys charged with controlling each piece of territory. We find this whole tattoo thing surprising. Most of these guys operate with loose networks. Branding your people puts targets on their backs, either for law enforcement or drug-trafficking competitors. It suggests that Nico is as arrogant and ruthless as ever. It also suggests your unidentified man works for Nico. He may be a major distributor in West Sound."

Larson sat up and folded his arms on the table. "So where's this Nico guy now?"

"The FBI has been unsuccessful in locating Nico. The DEA may have more information, but their investigations are separate from ours." She adjusted her glasses. "We rarely know specifics about their operations until they have concluded."

"That's pretty stupid."

"Larson." The warning in the chief's voice silenced the detective.

Amber smiled patiently. "It's true. These dual investigations don't always make the most sense." A piece of blonde hair had strayed from her low ponytail. She tucked it behind her ear. "But the DEA has a source on the inside. I can't share those details, but we expect to know more about Nico soon."

Her gaze returned briefly to Jefferson, and then back to the chief.

Jefferson bent his head to stare at his hands interlaced on the table, hoping no one else could see the storm stirring inside of him. What did Nico's return mean for Alex? Was his brother back in the area? The last time he saw Alex, he didn't have a penny to his name. Jefferson doubted his brother was working for Nico then.

The chief's booming voice pulled him out of his thoughts.

"This makes finding the unidentified man one of our top priorities. If nothing else, he may know who supplied the drugs that killed Christian Greene and the others, if it wasn't the man himself. Larson, when will the Greenes ID the body?"

"In about an hour."

"Good. As soon as you have that confirmation, follow up with those friend leads. Also, check in with Aspen Klein. See if she's seen this 'N' tattoo."

"I can have Jared run the description through his security camera program," Amber offered. "It narrows the results quickly when we have identifying information that he can feed into the program. If he's tried to leave town, Jared will see him at bus stations, airports, train stations."

Jared was the local FBI office's young tech agent. Although he was not very talkative, he had valuable skills that saved them from wasting time on useless leads.

The chief nodded. "Of course. The more resources, the better." He turned to Jefferson. "Alright, Hughes, what do you have out of Fairview."

The detective realized he'd tensed every muscle in his body, including clenching his teeth so hard that his jaw ached. He took a deep breath through his nose. The case in Fairview had fled his mind.

"Hughes?" the chief repeated.

He paused, taking another breath to refocus himself. If he could just survive this meeting.

He clung to his notes like a life raft. "A neighbor identified the deceased as Dan Lausch, a member of the Fairview community. Mr. Lausch's home backs up to the pond in which the groundskeepers found his body. While we don't have a toxicology report, other evidence at the scene suggests he either overdosed on drugs or was high and accidentally drowned. Unlike Larson's victim, our guy does not appear to be a habitual drug user."

"Any word on his daughter?" asked the chief.

Jefferson swallowed and shook his head. "No. The officers on scene have almost finished going door-to-door in the neighborhood, and no one has reported knowing where she is or seeing her leave."

The chief let out a huge puff of air as he considered this. "I don't like this at all. Let's make her an official missing person. Do you have a picture we can get out to the media?"

"I have it," said Rory. "I took a picture from the house."

"Get it to Kathy and a copy to Amber."

"Yes, please," said Amber. "I can get the information out to all our offices. How old is she?"

"Thirteen, and her name's Jada," Rory said, as he began working on his phone.

Amber pressed her lips together. "Since she's over twelve years old, we can assist for now. If it turns out to be kidnapping or anything of that sort, the FBI will investigate more fully."

"Get a trace going on her phone," said the chief. "Making her a missing person means we don't need a warrant. If she's got it with her, that's our best tool at the moment. What else do we know about Dan Lausch?"

Jefferson looked at his notes as his mind threatened to go off track again. "There are indications from his neighbor, a man named Brent Miller, that Lausch was experiencing challenges, potentially depression. Miller suggested his friend may have been suicidal."

He paused as he read a little further. "He owned a company called Sound Home Title. The house was in order, with no obvious signs of a struggle. We also did not find any other drug paraphernalia in the house."

The chief folded his hands together on the table. "Until we know more about the cause of death, I'd like you and Jackson to focus on finding his daughter. If this case wraps up quickly, then you can join in the search for this unidentified man and the Nico character."

"Chief, I'd like to work specifically on the whereabouts of Nico. I think I can provide valuable assistance in that investigation." The words were out of his mouth before Jefferson could stop himself.

The chief cocked his head to the side, putting the full weight of his eyes on him. "I do not doubt your abilities, Hughes. This is my decision, and you can assist Larson and Mendez once we know Lausch's daughter is out of danger."

He wanted to object, but decided against it. Questioning the chief's decisions was a bad career move. Plus, he respected the man.

Find the girl. Then find Nico.

***

Twelve years ago, a young woman named Anna died in a run-down San Francisco hotel; one frail girl in a rising tide of lifeless young Americans washed up on the shores of the drug trade.

Anna was different. She was Alex's girlfriend, and her death, tragic in so many ways, made it clear to Jefferson that his little brother's addiction was carrying Alex toward an early grave.

He'd always known drugs were dangerous, but before Anna, Jefferson focused on trying to get Alex clean enough to have a normal life, maybe get married, or have kids. They could watch football together while grilling burgers in the backyard. Their mom might quit crying herself to sleep. He'd never faced the idea that his brother might die, and sooner rather than later.

Back then, Jefferson was a rookie cop in Redding, California. He spent his free time hunting for his brother, using police resources to get information he probably shouldn't have accessed.

It was an arrest report for Alex that led Jefferson to spend a few days off in San Francisco. He learned three things that weekend. Anna was dead, Alex was gone, and he'd left town with a man named Nico.

According to the San Francisco PD, Alex being mixed up with Nico meant bad news. And mixed up, he was.

Nico, an entry-level punk dealer, scaled his business in San Francisco, catching the attention of more influential figures in the narcotics distribution network. They had Nico's back when the police traced the fentanyl that killed Anna back to him, and investigators started monitoring him with increased attention. Those powerful traffickers facilitated Nico's move further north, helping him take over lines of distribution in Oregon and Washington.

Soon, Alex wasn't just using drugs; he was in deep with Nico, doing whatever role needed covering. Drug trafficking is a high-turnover enterprise, and there are always places to stick a rover.

About a year after Anna's death, a birthday card for Jefferson's mom came in the mail. It was from Alex. She'd cried tears borne equally of relief and sorrow. Jefferson knew this because he felt the same, though he didn't show those emotions outwardly.

Instead, he carefully folded the envelope away in his pocket.

Later, he took the envelope out and planned his upcoming week. He had four days off. He would drive to the postmarked city of Medford, Oregon; a trip of just two and a half hours.

The late spring drive through the southernmost part of the Cascade Mountain Range helped ground his emotions. The mountains, in their solid, silver indifference, reminded him he would need to be steady and clear-headed, no matter what he saw. He wanted to find his brother, but he had to be prepared for what that might mean.

Almost daily, Jefferson dealt with addicts, drug dealers, and the consequences of their actions. So many police investigations stemmed from someone involved in substance abuse. He saw the washed-out people, wasted families, and the persistent cycle of human misery that the drug traffickers used as food for their greed.

Perhaps it was a faulty perspective, but he never saw Alex in that light. His brother should have more hope and a desire to be better. These thoughts led Jefferson to believe that if he could just find the right combination of words or people, Alex would snap out of it and be the boy Jefferson remembered.

The part of him that knew the truth lay as dormant as the sleeping volcano inside Mt. Shasta.

Jefferson wouldn't lose hope until years later.

Once in Medford, it didn't take long for him to spot Alex. He only needed a few hours sitting in his car.

He watched a street corner that had all the markings of illicit activity: dark, no street cameras, people lurking about, others moving slowly but intentionally in for a quick greeting and out again.

The Medford drug trade, still in its infancy, had not yet invaded every unoccupied corner or green space of the city.

What Jefferson didn't know was that he wasn't the only one watching. One of the shaggy men on the corner watched him in return. That man called Jefferson's plates into his FBI counterparts.

Later, as Jefferson followed Alex away from the corner, a black sedan followed him. After he'd seen where his brother was staying, the same sedan followed Jefferson as he bought a takeout burger and booked a hotel room for the night.

Just as he settled down to eat, a knock on the door startled him into reaching for the weapon that wasn't on his hip.

He stepped quietly to the door and looked through the peephole. A slight blonde woman stood there looking directly back at him as if she knew what he would do before he did it. She held up a badge. He opened the door.

This was the first time he met Amber Wells.

***

"Jeff," Amber called over the office chatter as the group vacated the briefing room.

With his back to her, he stopped and worked his face into a calm expression. He wasn't angry at Amber for not telling him about Nico earlier, but the shock hadn't left him yet. He didn't want her to mistake that for anything more than it was.

Turning toward her, he forced the slightest upturn of his lips into a crooked smile. "Got more good news?"

She searched his eyes, which he quickly cast down. There would be no hiding the pain there.

"Jeff," she said in a whisper. "I'm sorry I didn't tell you before today. I hate that you got blindsided by this."

He gazed toward the door as people filed out. "Definitely blindsided. But I'm sure you had your reasons for waiting." He hoped she didn't take his forced control as sharpness.

She folded her arms, fixing him more intently with her hazel eyes. "I know this is throwing you for a loop, but until yesterday, we weren't sure Nico had a footprint up here. I didn't want to bring all of that history back into your life until we were sure." She let out a long sigh. "This time around, it's not an FBI case, so until today, I had little information. I've shared most of what I know because you and your colleagues need to know what is going on in your own area."

"Most?"

"We should talk later."

His stomach dropped into a splitting canyon of worry.

He nodded, no words available.

"I'll call you later." She touched his arm gently and walked away.

Chapter Nine

The aroma of delicious food filled the Fairview clubhouse foyer as MJ and Shannon stepped through the doors. A chandelier the size of the moon sparkled above them while marble urns overflowed with red roses and vines of star-like white flowers. A view of the sunset-bathed golf course poured through the floor-to-ceiling windows, offsetting the navy walls and dark wood of the room.

The reception dinner was in full swing, and they were late.

"Sorry," MJ whispered.

Shannon shrugged. "Don't worry about it. Stopping at Jada's was a good call, even if it just means we're more worried than ever."

She had that right. How could they have fun tonight knowing that Jada was gone, and no one seemed to know where or if she was safe? It gnawed at MJ's nerves. But she plastered a smile on her face for Shannon's sake.

A young woman with sleek black hair in a tight bun greeted them at the ballroom door. She smiled out of crimson lips, her black eyes mingling a welcome and a reprimand at their tardiness.

"Good evening, ladies," she said, picking up a gold clipboard. "Please tell me your names and I'll make sure you get to your seats right away. They've just served the main course."

"Thank you. I'm Shannon Davis, and this is my guest, MJ Brooks."

After finding their names on the list, the hostess led them through a maze of round tables to one near the front.

The wedding party sat at a long table on an elevated platform facing the other guests. A line of greenery and red roses ran the length of the table with white candles every few feet.

The bride spotted them and waved excitedly at Shannon before leaning over and whispering something to her new husband. Then she jumped up, gathered the flowing pieces of her dress in one hand, and negotiated her way down to greet them.

The bride pulled Shannon into a huge embrace. "I'm so glad you're here."

The family resemblance was stunning, especially for cousins. If she didn't know better, MJ would've thought they were sisters. She stood by awkwardly, smiling at the two couples seated at their table.

As the cousins pulled apart, Shannon made the introductions. "Aubrey, this is my friend, MJ. And MJ, meet my lovely, newly married cousin."

Aubrey surprised MJ by grabbing her in a silk, makeup, and perfume-saturated hug. "Welcome, thank you for coming."

"Of course," MJ said when the woman released her. "And congratulations on your marriage."

"Thank you so much."

"Everything looks beautiful." Shannon gazed around the room. The candlelight and roses mingled with the fading amber and forest hues coming through the expansive windows. It all combined for a spectacularly dreamy, romantic vibe.

Aubrey smiled as she too gazed around at the decor. "I know. I'm so in love with what Janice did. She's my wedding planner, and she is amazing." She glanced back at the family table. "The only downer is Daddy."

MJ followed her gaze to a balding man staring vacantly down at his plate of food.

Aubrey leaned closer to them. "One of his best friends was found dead this morning. They think it was suicide. Daddy's just heartbroken."

MJ and Shannon exchanged glances.

"You mean Mr. Lausch?" Shannon asked.

Aubrey raised her brows. "You know him, too?"

"Not really. But his daughter is one of our students. MJ has her in class."

Just then, a server asked if Shannon and MJ would like plates brought out to them. Aubrey answered for them, insisting that they both get the prime rib.

"I better get back to the table. They'll be starting all the speeches and stuff soon." She kissed Shannon's cheek. "We'll catch up later." Then she whisked away.

***

With the formality of the dinner finished, the atmosphere shifted from a rose-infused romantic getaway to a dark, strobe-lit dance club.

"Are you all ready to get funky!" yelled a DJ from the front of the dance floor.

The crowd cheered as the first bass-thumping song dropped.

Music pulsed through the air, and the DJ's throbbing lights were the only illumination, making it difficult to hear or see who was doing what. After a few minutes, many of the older guests said their last goodbyes and shuffled out the door.

Throughout dinner, MJ's gaze kept returning to the father of the bride, Shannon's uncle. The man was trying to look happy, and he gave a lovely speech about his daughter and new son-in-law, but when the spotlight was off, the pain returned to his face.

If he knows the Lausches well, she thought, there is a chance he knows something about Jada and where she might be.

Aubrey grabbed Shannon's wrist, dragging her to the dance floor. Shannon laughed. "Come on, MJ," she shouted over the beginning of Haddaway's "What is Love."

"I'm going to the restroom," she shouted back.

Shannon nodded her understanding before getting sucked onto the crowded dance floor.

About five minutes earlier, MJ had seen Shannon's uncle depart with another man, prompting her to head toward the foyer. The two men appeared to be in a serious conversation and wanted a quieter space to talk.

They weren't hard to find. The two men huddled near the foyer windows, now transformed into shadowy mirrors, with no daylight behind them. She positioned herself close to them, but not so close that they might suspect she was listening in, although that is exactly what she planned to do.

"I don't understand why he would do that," Shannon's uncle whispered while putting his hand to his forehead. "There has to be more. You have to tell me if there is more to it."

MJ couldn't hear the other man's answer. He faced away from her, keeping his words from floating easily to her ears. Whatever it was, it didn't console Shannon's uncle.

Shaking his head, he insisted, "I don't buy it. He wouldn't leave Jada alone like that. He loved that girl." The uncle wiped his eyes.

As the other man spoke, Shannon's uncle looked at him with wide eyes. "So you think he may have planned this whole thing? Sent her away before?"

The other man ran his eyes around the room and sighed. MJ caught his reply, "I think so."

The uncle stared in disbelief. Then his eyes narrowed. "You're sure? How can you—"

He stopped as the other man turned to inspect the guests milling around, including MJ.

She was making a great show of reapplying her lip gloss. He smiled warmly at her.

She smiled back before taking out her phone and pretending to dial a number.

That guy seemed to know a lot about Jada's dad. Talking to him could be the key.

Just then, a couple approached the two men. The husband reached out an enormous paw and clapped Shannon's uncle on the shoulder.

"Congratulations, Glen. It's been a great night," he boomed, his cheeks rosy with drink.

The thin woman next to him agreed. "Just lovely. Aubrey just beams. You must be so happy."

Glen found a smile for them. "Yes, yes, of course. I'm so glad you're having a good time."

The big man chuckled. "Too good. Margaret here says she's taking me home."

"Anyone who has seen his dancing will thank me," added Margaret. "Please give our love to Susan as well."

"I will. Thank you for coming. I know Aubrey appreciates it, too."

The woman grabbed her husband's hand and turned to walk away, but the big man didn't budge.

"Hey Brent," he said, "how are you liking that new Mercedes G-Wagon?"

Looking surprised by the question, Brent replied, "Oh, yeah, it's great. We are loving it."

"You know, so many people get the black one, but that white is just beautiful. We only had a couple in stock, and now we're down to one. It's got your name on it, Glen."

Margaret shook her head. "I'm sorry. This man thinks he has to talk shop twenty-four-seven. Let's go honey."

"Alright," the man finally agreed. "See you fellas on the course."

They all exchanged gentle hugs or handshakes before the couple headed for the exit.

"I should get back in there," said Glen.

The other man agreed. "Yes, tonight is about your family."

Glen nodded quietly and walked back into the ballroom.

Glen's friend now stood alone, his hands in the pockets of his expensive, well-tailored suit. A rather attractive older man, he had golden skin that suggested he either traveled a lot or spent the entire summer outside. That kind of tan was hard to achieve in West Sound, but it contrasted well with his white, expertly trimmed hair.

Sensing her inspection of him, he looked in her direction.

There's no time like the present, she decided.

A big smile plastered on her face, MJ walked toward him.

"Excuse me," she said in a light, overly friendly tone. "Do you live in this neighborhood?"

He gave her a reserved smile, as if he did not easily trust such questions. "Why do you ask?"

"Oh, it's just so beautiful here. This is my first time in the club-house, and I'm wondering how you get to be a member. I mean, do you have to live in the neighborhood? Because I could never afford one of those beautiful homes." She blinked innocently at him, hoping she wasn't overdoing it.

His face relaxed just the slightest bit. Apparently, she was giving off enough harmless vibes.

"So you golf?"

"Hmhm. Yep. All the time. I love golf," she lied. "But I just use the West Sound public course over by the high school. I'm afraid I'm not great, but I'm working on it, especially putting. You know 'drive for show, putt for dough,'" she chuckled. "That's what my dad always says."

She'd just said everything she knew about golf. The last bit was a phrase her ex-husband Justin was fond of using. He considered himself to be an excellent golfer.

She stuck out her hand. "I'm MJ, by the way."

He took it. "Brent Miller. And yes, I live here. I'm also the golf club president. If you're interested in a membership, I can set you up with a tour. Then you can see everything we have to offer."

Clearing his throat, he added, "It is quite expensive for a non-resident, but you know, that's up to you." He shrugged one shoulder and moved his eyes to his feet, apologetic in his stance. Then he pulled out his wallet. "Here's my card. Call me when you've got some time to see the course."

Skimming it, MJ stuffed it in her clutch purse. "So, you're a real estate agent?"

"Yes, I'm the owner and broker for Eagle Home and Land."

"That's good to know," said MJ. "I'm not buying a house just yet, but someday," she said with the breathy voice of a dreamer. "But I'd still love to do a tour. Some of my kids live here in the neighborhood. I'm sure they could tell me all about it, too."

He screwed up his face. "Kids?"

"Oh," she laughed. "I can see how that sounds odd. My students, I should say. I'm a teacher at the middle school."

"I see. That makes sense."

"Yeah, in fact, I just heard that the dad of one of those students died. I can't even imagine how she is going to handle it. Poor girl."

Solemnly shaking her head for effect, she couldn't hide the actual ache in her face. She'd known grief recently with Troy's death, but she couldn't even imagine being a young girl and losing her dad in such a horrifying way. The news would have devastated her.

But how Jada would cope was second on MJ's list of worries. Finding her was all she cared about right now.

Brent Miller's face tightened, and he lost a bit of color. "You mean Jada?"

MJ nodded. "I've been worried about her all day. She was absent from school today, so I've been calling her dad and her mom." Then she added in a whisper. "I guess we know why her dad didn't answer."

Brent allowed a gentle smile to come back to his face. He glanced toward the reception room where the music had suddenly softened to a slow song.

Turning back, he said, "I can tell that you care a lot about your students, MJ." He reached out and took her hand as if to console her, squeezing it with his a well-manicured hand. "But I don't think you should worry too much about Jada. I think Dan..." A catch in his throat stopped him and he dropped her hand.

Murmuring an apology, he continued. "The police seem to think he overdosed on drugs. Dan would have made plans for Jada before he would do drugs in front of her, I'm sure of it. It's shocking to think of him doing drugs at all, even if life wasn't always easy for him, especially with what he'd been through with his wife. No, Jada must be with a family friend. That's just how Dan was." A tear hung in the corner of one eye, and he looked away.

"I'm sorry. I can see you were friends."

He nodded without meeting her eye.

"Losing someone like that..." she trailed off, wondering if broaching the subject was wise. Mr. Lausch's death had deeply affected him. But for Jada's sake, she had to pry some information from him.

"I feel so bad for Jada," MJ continued. "She already doesn't see her mom, and now she's lost her dad. Is her mom someone Jada could live with once the police find her, or is that not a good situation?"

Turning wide eyes on her, shocked she would ask, he said, "I couldn't even say. That will be up to the authorities, I'm sure."

"Oh, of course. I'm sure they will do what is best for her." MJ wondered what Mr. Lausch had "been through" with his wife, but it was clear Brent Miller would say nothing more about it.

Earlier, the detectives hadn't mentioned a conclusive cause of death, and yet this man seemed sure it was suicide. After his reaction to her last question, asking about that might risk shutting him down, but she had to know why he felt so certain it wasn't an accidental overdose.

She took a deep breath and with gentleness in her voice asked, "Do you think he did this on purpose? I mean, that he took his own life."

Brent still didn't look at her. He put his hands in his pockets and contemplated his shoes for a few seconds longer before meeting her gaze.

"I wish I could say absolutely not."

Neither of them spoke for a minute.

"Do you have any idea where Jada might be? I mean, I think the police are about to put out a nationwide search for her through the FBI."

Brent's eyes widened again. "Me? No, I don't have any idea, but I'm sure the police will find out where she is soon." He leaned in a closer and whispered, "I understand why you are worried, and it makes me glad to know we have such caring teachers serving our kids. I'm sure she'll turn up. No FBI searches needed. That's just what my gut tells me."

Thanking him for sharing what he knew, MJ did not feel the least bit consoled by his confidence that Jada was fine. He seemed like the type of man who was unacquainted with drug addicts and how they can get so lost they forget to worry about the welfare of their kids. She'd seen too many students living in the reality where addiction is a merciless master that requires total fidelity, even at the expense of the most helpless.

Maybe Mr. Lausch didn't plan on dying. Maybe he didn't know what the drugs would do to him. And maybe his death had nothing to do with his state of mind at all.

Someone has to know what happened to Dan Lausch.

She had a terrible feeling that Jada was in more trouble than anyone wanted to believe.

Chapter Ten

"Callie B's. 8."

The text from Amber came as Jefferson and Rory finished checking a lead from the missing persons hotline. A female caller insisted she'd seen Jada Lausch in the dressing room section of a local Target store. When they arrived, the detectives quickly discovered that the attendant working the area was Jana, a twenty-one-year-old student at West Sound Community College. In fairness, she bore an older-sister resemblance to the missing teenager.

The chief told them to go home. The night crew would alert them if any leads came through. Officers were continuing to search the neighborhood, including the forest and nearby parks. The detectives would be the first to know if they found anything.

Amber loved to meet at Callie B's, a coffee and dessert bar that stayed open late on weekends. Jefferson didn't mind so much. The owner, Callie Brown, had a dessert daily special that always knocked his socks off, no matter what it was. She served a few sandwiches, but the menu consisted mostly of mouthwatering sweets and baked goods.

Amber had already taken her seat, with a steaming cup of coffee and a chocolate-filled croissant in front of her. He knew exactly what it was because Amber always ordered the same thing.

Taking a breath at Carrie B's meant taking in an atmospheric level of coffee aroma. Jefferson didn't drink coffee, but he didn't mind the smell. It conjured up comfortable memories of his grandparents, parents, aunts, and uncles, who drank coffee in the old way—black or with very little else in it. Nothing like today's artistic coffees that commanded a pretty penny.

As he sat down, a pleasant man in his fifties approached their table.

"Hello, Detective Hughes. Can I put in a drink order for you?"

"Good to see you, Nate. I'll just have sparkling water with lemon. Thank you, and what sandwiches do you have tonight?"

Nate's face lit up. He was Callie B's husband, a construction manager by day; night help at Callie B's on the weekends. There couldn't be a more proud husband in West Sound. He spoke about his wife's food like it was manna from heaven.

"Tonight, Callie's got an amazing French dip—homemade bread, piled high with roast beef, everything made here." He beamed.

"Sounds perfect."

"Dessert? She's got a few chocolate chip cookies left."

Jefferson chuckled. "Bag those up for me for later."

"You got it."

Amber took a sip of her coffee and then set it down slowly. "Any news on the girl?"

Jefferson smirked. "You would probably know before me."

She picked a piece from the croissant and put it in her mouth, nodding once to acknowledge his point.

"Anyway, no. We've followed up on every good lead, and called the mother half a dozen times. Still nothing. The chief said he would call down to LA and have someone do a welfare check at her home."

"Good move."

He settled his gaze on her, his heart already beating a million miles a minute. He didn't want to hear what she had to say, but he couldn't bear not hearing it either. "Tell me what you know and how it involves Alex."

She sighed, sitting back and dropping her hands in her lap. "It's not much, and I only know what I know because I called in a favor."

Tense and alert, Jefferson knew he must look like a cougar ready to pounce.

Before Amber could continue, Nate set his sparkling water on the table.

"Sandwich will be right out."

Jefferson thanked him, and the man had the good sense to notice the serious conversation between these two law-enforcement patrons, quickly leaving them to it.

She glanced down at her coffee mug. "There have been some communications in Nico's group referring to 'H.'"

Jefferson hung his head. "Hamilton."

"Yes."

Though he couldn't see her, he could feel her steady gaze.

"Drink some water, Jefferson."

Without argument, he did as she said.

That night, many years ago, when Amber showed up at his hotel room in Medford, she knew he was a cop, and she knew he was Alex's brother. She told him everything he didn't want to hear: his brother was one of Nico's most trusted couriers, meeting suppliers up and down the coast, carrying drugs and money across multiple state lines, and when needed, collecting money from the small-time street corner dealers. Nico called him H, short for Hamilton, Alex's middle name.

Amber had solicited Jefferson's help, asking him to meet up with Alex on the following day. Plant a bug in his phone. They could nail his suppliers, and they wouldn't touch Alex.

Amber took another sip of coffee, still watching him.

"So he is back with Nico," he said without looking at her.

"I'm sorry."

It seemed unreal. He wanted to slam the table in frustration, but he had to keep it together.

"How? After everything we did to get that scumbag to leave the country, how is it possible that Nico is back?"

Tipping her head to the side, her eyes were kind, but her expression said that this was a stupid question.

"Come on, Jefferson. You know the border's a sieve. And Nico has more resources and contacts than most. It was only a matter of time."

His sandwich arrived. Nate set it down with a quick nod.

Jefferson stared at it, suddenly feeling nauseous. He took another drink of water.

"I know this is hard to hear, and I hate that this is causing you pain, but my concern is with you, not your brother."

His eyes narrowed. "What does that mean?"

She sat forward, lowering her voice. Her eyes were stern. "Nico never knew where the leak in Medford came from. But Alex figured it out."

Jefferson sat back, shaking his head. "No, he wouldn't."

"Don't be so naïve. He's not the kid you remember. And if he told Nico, that could put a price on your head. And I don't like that at all."

The unusual earnestness of her tone shocked Jefferson. He'd rarely seen her so agitated.

"Then you need to get me on this case."

"I'm not sure that's a good idea right now. Besides, that's the chief's call."

"He would listen to you."

"Are *you* listening to me? I think you could be in danger. If Nico finds out you are on this case, he won't need Alex to put two and two together. Maybe he already has."

"I'm not afraid of Nico."

She looked toward the street and shook her head. "I know you're not afraid, Jeff. I'm just not sure your head will be in the right game." She turned her eyes on him again. "If it comes to sending your brother to prison, can you make that call?"

For a second, he met her eye, but then he looked away as he considered his answer.

"If you have to think about it, you're not ready to be on this case. Besides, you need to tell the chief about your involvement in Medford. He needs to know."

"Then he'll definitely keep me off the case."

She shrugged. "Maybe that's for the best, but you won't know until you tell him." She sat forward again, her eyes steely. "And don't put me in the position of having to tell him."

Amber was right. They both had an obligation to make sure Chief Carlson knew about Nico, his brother, and Jefferson's hand in sending some of Nico's network to prison.

"Besides," Amber added, "finding a missing kid is important. And if she's just hiding out somewhere, it should be easy. If you can get that squared away without losing your head in this Nico business, the chief is more likely to believe your mind is in the right place."

"I don't know. Finding her has not been easy so far." He hadn't touched his sandwich. He'd have Nate box it up along with the cookies.

Amber regarded him with softened eyes, a slight upturn at the corners of her mouth.

"You won't like this," she said, "but you should use MJ's help." She put her hands up as he protested. "I know, I know, but hear me out. She's motivated to help. You know she can make some crazy connections, and she's trusted by parents, kids, and community members. Her reputation is solid after what she did to help us solve the case last year." She ate another piece of her croissant. "If you really want to find this girl sooner rather than later, call MJ."

As if on cue, his phone buzzed in his pocket.

He checked the call. It was from the station. "Hughes here."

"Detective Hughes, it's Officer Meyers. We just had a call on the hotline from a woman claiming to be Jada Lausche's mother."

"She called the hotline?"

"Yes, sir. She said someone stole her phone, and she didn't get any of our calls, but then she saw her daughter's picture on the news."

"You're sure it's her?"

"As sure as we can be. I asked her the series of questions outlined in the missing persons protocol. She knew it all."

"Does she have Jada with her?"

"No. She's frantic, I'd say."

"So she doesn't know where she is?"

"No."

"Do you have a phone number?"

"She hasn't bought a new phone yet and doesn't have a landline. Anyway, she's about to board a plane to SeaTac, so you likely wouldn't reach her tonight. She's supposed to land around midnight."

He thanked the officer.

With a satisfied smile, he said to Amber, "It looks like I won't be needing MJ after all."

She raised her coffee cup to the knowing smile on her lips. "We'll see."

***

MJ brushed her teeth with the muscle memory of that repetitive task, her mind engaged in puzzling over the events of the day.

The same thoughts buzzed around her mind as she turned off the light and moved to her bed. Before she could reach it, her foot hit something solid and warm. Catching the edge of the bed with her hand, she saved herself from falling on top of what she realized was Edgar, his black body lost in the shadows.

The dog scurried away to safety.

"Sorry, buddy," she said as she found him in the darkness and ruffled his fur.

He took his place next to the bed again, and she climbed inside, pulling the covers to her chin. With her dog around, she never felt alone, but tonight was different; loneliness rolled over her like a thick fog creeping over the sound.

Thinking about Jada, worrying that she was alone and scared—or worse—stole MJ's ability to relax in the darkness when she turned out the light.

The wind kicked up outside, whistling around the house like it wanted inside, trying to convince her it had nothing but good intentions.

MJ pulled the covers up tighter and closed her eyes. It didn't help that her landlady, Claire, was out-of-town visiting a sister in Arizona.

Maybe Jada didn't have her phone, or maybe it was dead, and she didn't have a charger. She wasn't using it, that was clear.

MJ tossed to her other side, the moonlight flickering in and out of her bedroom window as clouds drifted across the lunar path.

Jada must know by now that people are looking for her. If she's not being held against her will, then she surely would have seen the missing person report on TV or heard it from someone. Why was she staying hidden? Or maybe she's not. Maybe the police have heard something but haven't shared it publicly. She thought about calling Jefferson Hughes and then pushed the thought away.

How else could she try to contact Jada?

Her eyes flew open with the realization that she hadn't tried everything.

Throwing the covers back, she ignored the rush of cold air on her skin and the chill beneath her bare feet as she felt her way through the dark to her small office. Once there, she unplugged her laptop and took it back to the bedroom.

She climbed back into bed, propped herself up on pillows, and opened the computer. With a few taps, she had her school email open.

"Jada, please contact me as soon as possible. Many people are looking for you and are worried about your safety. Please let me know if you are okay, where you are, and what I can do to help. Ms. Brooks."

MJ pushed "send" and then waited. After refreshing the page for fifteen minutes, to no avail, she closed her laptop and set it on the nightstand. She'd check in the morning. It was a long shot, but worth a try.

Chapter Eleven

S aturday morning, MJ woke to a mass of gray outside her window. She yawned and rubbed Edgar's head as he danced around her, ready to eat.

The weather wasn't too disappointing. Summer had blessed the Pacific Northwest with an extended stay, but it couldn't last. She'd already mentally prepared for the ensuing darker, shorter days, knowing the switch could flip any day.

She fed Edgar and drank a quick cup of her favorite tulsi mint tea as she checked her email.

There were some new notices of free webinars and offers from educational companies promising to sell her the next best thing for teaching language arts, but there was nothing from Jada.

It felt like such a good idea last night, but she had to admit to herself that Jada was not likely to be checking her school email.

She prepared to take Edgar down to the beach by slipping on her boots and raincoat. The sky hung low, but so far this morning, it was holding its watery load. With any luck, she'd be able to get in a long walk and some ball-throwing for the dog before any raindrops hit the ground.

Edgar flew around the beach, kicking up sand each time MJ released his dirty tennis ball through the air. She envied his pure enjoyment of this simple exercise. She, on the other hand, couldn't get all the events of yesterday out of her head.

Could Jada be hiding out at a friend's house? Wouldn't she at least contact her friends? Admittedly, MJ knew Jada's school life much better than her home life, but it seemed weird for any thirteen-year-old girl to not be on her phone, seeking support from her friends. Then again, if Mr. Lausch sent her off somewhere because he wanted to get high or to take his own life, Jada may not even know her father is dead.

MJ threw the ball again before reaching into her pocket for her phone. She scrolled to one of the local news websites. Sure enough, the top headline read, "West Sound man found dead in Fairview."

Slipping her phone away, MJ gazed across the rippling water. A heavy blanket of clouds scraped the tops of the evergreen-covered banks. In other places, thin mist floated down and hid the nearby homes overlooking the sound.

She shook her head. It didn't make any sense. MJ could not wrap her head around the idea that the girl was safe and warm somewhere and being cared for by some mysterious friends. Over the past year, she'd learned to trust her instinct, and it was screaming at her now that all was not well with Jada.

Edgar took a break from running to gnaw on his ball, rolling it between his paws. He was going to be a wet, sandy mess, as usual.

Suddenly, the dog's ears perked up and his eyes were bright and alert. He stood and locked his eyes somewhere behind MJ.

She turned to look just as Edgar took off in a sprint toward the steep and winding beach-access stairs.

Descending was her ex-husband, Justin.

As he laughed and ruffled the dog's head, MJ remembered she'd said Justin could have Edgar for the weekend.

Even though he didn't deploy as often as he used to, Justin still traveled a fair amount to train soldiers in other areas of the country and abroad. For that reason, he didn't want to get another dog, and he loved Edgar to pieces.

His feelings for her also played a role in his desire for dog sharing, a fact Justin never hid very well. She tried to be gentle with his emotions without giving him the wrong idea. Keeping Edgar away from him wasn't something she could do, even though Justin annoyed her with his constant need to protect her and tell her how to live her life.

There were still parts of Justin she cared about, like his absolute willingness to put himself at risk for others. She did not doubt that he would do anything for her. But that was part of the problem. He wanted to do everything for her, including decide for her. Maybe someday he would understand how suffocating it was to be in that kind of relationship, but he wasn't there yet.

"MJ," he called out, his brilliant smile covering his face. The outside of Justin still gave her goosebumps. She'd fallen in love with that smile, his crisp and open blue eyes. His face invited you to stare and get sucked in. No one could resist Justin's friendliness. Even her mother thought MJ was a fool for divorcing him.

Justin was also the fittest man she knew, with not an ounce of body fat anywhere. With his face, outgoing nature, and physique, she knew the only thing keeping Justin single was his hope that she could love him again.

She waved as he approached. "I almost forgot. Sorry, he's really dirty."

"Oh, that's no problem, is it, buddy?" He petted the dog with the furious scratching Edgar loved. Justin looked up at her. "How are you?"

She stuffed her hands in her coat pocket. "I'm fine."

His eyes narrowed as he glanced at her hands and then back at her face.

She willed her face to stay calm, but inside she cringed. The hands-in-the-pockets move was a dead giveaway.

"Are you clenching your fists, MJ?"

"No," she scowled. "It's cold." It was a lie, and he knew it. Even as a child, she'd tried to control her emotions by balling up her hands into fists so tight she sometimes had marks on her palms for days. It wasn't that bad today, but she didn't want him to see the worry on her face.

"Okay," he said, putting his hands up. "I'm not trying to pry or tell you what to do. I just want to help if I can." He picked up Edgar's ball and threw it. MJ watched as Edgar flew after it. Was it possible that the dog ran harder and faster to please Justin?

She sighed, feeling a twinge of remorse for getting so defensive. As much as she wanted Justin to remember she could handle her own life, she had to believe it, too. That meant being able to tell him the truth without worrying about his reaction.

"Seriously, Justin, I'm fine. It's just one of my students. Yesterday, her dad was found dead, and I have no information about her whereabouts or well-being. I'm worried about her, that's all."

He tilted his head and arched a brow. "Is that the guy they found at the golf course?"

"Yes. Shannon and I were out there yesterday for her cousin's wedding. We stopped by the house, and police were everywhere."

A tightness entered his jaw, and he pressed his lips together. "You went to the house?"

She ignored his change in demeanor. In the past, this is where she'd apologize for making a decision he didn't like.

"Yep, when we couldn't contact anyone, a home visit was the next step. Anyway, her neighbors seem to think she is staying with friends somewhere, but no one knows where, so it's a little weird."

He cast his eyes toward the sky. "A little weird? I know what you are thinking, MJ. You need to let the police handle it."

She snickered. "You sound just like Detective Hughes."

A flicker of something passed over Justin's face, but it was gone before she could consider what it meant.

"He's right," he said without looking at her. Then he whistled with a fierceness that rang in her ears. "Edgar! Let's go, buddy."

MJ grabbed the dog's leash from a nearby log of driftwood. "Take good care of him."

"Always."

He clipped the leash on Edgar's collar.

"You know, MJ, I think your student is probably fine. But until they know what happened to her dad, you should stay clear. You don't need to get yourself in trouble again. If you won't listen to me, then listen to the detective. He knows what he's doing."

Maybe, maybe not, she thought.

She smiled at Justin. "Have a great weekend. I'll see you Sunday."

***

Seven o'clock Saturday morning, Heather Lausch waited in an interview room for Jefferson and Rory. After landing at midnight, she stayed in a hotel near the airport before getting a rental car to be in West Sound as soon as the detectives were back on duty.

Jefferson had one Mountain Dew in him after a long night of tossing and turning, his conversation with Amber playing over and over in his mind.

It surprised and troubled Jefferson that they'd found no sign of Jada Lausch. None of the hotline leads had panned out, and searching the local area resulted in no new information. Amber was right. Despite his desire to find Nico, this girl deserved his full attention. The longer she remained missing, the more likely there'd been foul play—a thought that filled him with dread.

Jada's mom was not what Jefferson expected, given the family's wealth. Stringy brown hair framed her face like a neglected curtain, the remains of a light copper dye lingering on the bottom half. Sitting with her shoulders caved and her hands wedged between her knees, she made the on-the-edge, jumpy movements that Jefferson recognized immediately as withdrawal symptoms. This woman was an addict.

Her brown eyes tracked nervously between the two detectives as they sat across the metal table, notebooks in hand. In a plain olive hoodie, she folded her arms tightly across her chest as if the damp morning had followed her into the room. Every few seconds, she reached up and touched her lips with a quick twisting motion.

Rory thanked her for coming in so early.

"You need to find my girl," she said, a catch in her voice. Her fingers twisted at her lips again, as if reminding her to be quiet. "They say I can't smoke in here," she said gruffly.

"No, there's no smoking," Jefferson said.

"Well, let's get going then. I don't know how long I can last without a cigarette break."

"We can get you some water or a soda, maybe something to eat?" suggested Rory.

She pulled at her lips again. "A soda might help."

"Coke, Diet Coke, or Mountain Dew?" Rory asked, standing.

"Coke."

He glanced at Jefferson. "I'll be right back."

When he was gone, Jefferson smiled at the woman. "You've had a long night."

She nodded, tears forming in her eyes.

They'd overlooked tissues. He went to the door and told Rory to bring a box.

Jefferson returned to his seat. "I know this is difficult, Mrs. Lausch, but can you think of where your daughter might be?"

She shook her head, wiping a couple of tears from her cheeks.

"No, and I can't believe I didn't know she was missing. Somebody stole my stupid phone at work, and I can't afford a new one. Dan pays for my phone. I don't know what I'll do now."

Rory came back and set the Coke and box of tissues in front of her.

"But you and Mr. Lausch are divorced?" Jefferson asked.

She took a quick sip of the Coke, her hand shaking as she raised it to her lips. "Separated. He told me I had to leave, so I did. We just hadn't filed the papers yet." She ripped a tissue from the box and blew her nose. "I haven't seen Jada in a year."

A shiver racked her skinny frame, and she pulled the sleeves of her hoodie down to cover her hands.

"I know what you're thinking," she said. "You're thinking I must be a terrible person to not see my own daughter for that long."

"We are trying to find your daughter, Mrs. Lausch, not judge your parenting," Rory assured her. "Any information you provide about your daughter, or your husband, will only help us do that."

A deep furrow covered her brow. "I don't understand how Dan is dead. They said something on the news about a drug overdose."

Touching her fingers to her lips again, she shook her head. "There's no way that happened."

Jefferson raised a brow. "Why do you say that?"

"Dan never did drugs. He didn't even drink alcohol." She shook her head with energy, but her limp hair barely moved. "He kicked me out because I was smoking weed once in a while."

She glanced between them, her eyes reaching for wide and innocent. "It was just to take the edge off, you know. I'm not like a real addict. I liked to smoke a little once in a while, but Dan...he was Mr. Goody-Goody, always lecturing me. I'm clean now. And despite what Dan might have told other people, I never did it around Jada." She sat forward, leaning across the table, as if getting closer would make them believe this one thing about her. "Jada didn't even know."

Jefferson fought the smirk tugging at his mouth. He didn't believe for a second that Heather Lausch only had an occasional weed problem. The emaciation, the physical ticks... There was more to her addiction than she was letting on.

The woman's need to plead her case only further convinced him. Many addicts like to spin themselves as victims, failing to admit the impact of their actions on those around them. Even in her genuine distress about her daughter's disappearance, this broken mother wanted to first deny her addiction.

She lived in a fantasy world if she thought Jada was completely unaware of her mother's drug use, even if she only smoked cannabis. People who smoke it lose their ability to recognize the lingering smell in their house, in their clothes, on their breath.

Keeping his doubts to himself, Jefferson steered the conversation back to the search for Jada. "We'd like to talk more about Dan in a few minutes. First, can you think of any close friends or relatives Jada might stay with, either in this area or even in another city or state?"

With her elbows on the table, she let her face rest in her hands as if in deep concentration. "I just can't think of anyone you haven't talked to," she said. "The McCanns are the first people who come to mind. Jada and Cade are best friends. If he doesn't know where she is..." She moved her hands and grabbed another tissue as tears pooled in her eyes again. "I think it's bad."

At those last whispered words, the two detectives exchanged glances.

"What do you mean by bad?" Rory asked.

She blotted her eyes with the tissue. "She's in trouble—kidnapped or run away from somebody." Quiet tears dripped onto her cheeks, which she tried to contain with the now saturated tissue.

Kidnapping or Jada running "from somebody" struck Jefferson as alarming options too readily asserted by the girl's mother—unless she knew some reason that might be true.

"Mrs. Lausch," he said with as much firmness as he dared. "Do you know of someone who wants to hurt you or your family?"

She said nothing but continued crying quietly.

"Heather," he said more softly, hoping his words might not land as harsh as they were in reality. "Is there any way that your daughter's disappearance is connected to your drug use?"

Her head shot up, glaring. "This has nothing to do with me."

Interesting, Jefferson thought. Nothing to do with *her*?

"Who does it have something to do with?" Jefferson asked, his voice calm, unaffected by the intensity of her eyes on him.

Shifting in her seat, she looked at the door, touching her lips again. "I don't know. I don't know anything." She glanced at Rory, perhaps thinking him the more hospitable of the two. "I need a smoke."

He smiled. "Let's just clear up this one thing, then we'll take a break. Does that work for you?"

With longing, she eyed the door. She seemed in a battle with her identity as Jada's mother, and the need to ease her craving. If she was clean, she likely used the cigarettes as a substitute.

"I really don't know anything," she whispered.

"You said that," pushed Jefferson, "but I think there is something you're holding back, and if it can help find Jada, then you need to tell us now, for your daughter's sake."

Silence filled the room as they waited, the woman staring at her hands, which were folding in and out of each other.

They couldn't hold her. If she stood up, demanded to leave, and disappeared into the mist, they couldn't stop her. She came voluntarily, ostensibly to help find her missing daughter.

How could this even be a question for her? Though he wasn't a parent, Jefferson couldn't imagine not spilling everything he knew if he had a son or daughter missing.

Getting information from Heather felt more like interrogating a suspect. This woman believed her daughter to be in danger, even kidnapped, and yet, some piece of information supplanted finding Jada as the most important thing about this interview.

Rory made a slight head movement toward the door, suggesting they let her take that smoking break.

Jefferson sighed and nodded.

Before they could start this plan, the woman broke the silence.

"What's going to happen to the money?" It came out in a ragged whisper, as if she knew asking the question sounded bad, looked bad, a mental walk of shame that kept her head bent to watch her still working hands.

It was probably best that she didn't see the look exchanged between the detectives, expressions of their worst expectations fulfilled. Too often they found themselves seated across from people who held their own survival as the prize they must fight to take out of the room. It was just a shame that Heather Lausch had to be one of them.

Jefferson, feeling a rush of anger beginning to balloon on his tongue, motioned for Rory to ask the next obvious question.

His partner ran a hand over his ginger beard and closed his eyes. Then, in a voice now void of sympathy, almost bored, asked, "What money?"

She sniffled without looking up. "Dan has a lot of money." She glanced up. "I...I don't have a very good job, so I don't know what I'm going to do if his money gets all tied up."

"Why would it get tied up?" asked Jefferson, taming the acid with which he wanted to cover his words. "He probably has a will. Insurance might be an issue if his death is ruled a suicide."

"That's not what I mean." She put her elbows on the table, her hands on her forehead as if he'd said the stupidest thing in the world. Suddenly, she stood and started to the door, tears crowding in her eyes again. "I need a break."

Rory stood quickly to beat her to the door. "Let me show you the bathrooms, food, and the best way out if you need a cigarette. We meet back here in fifteen minutes?" He glanced at Jefferson for his agreement.

"Works for me."

"Fifteen minutes good for you, Heather?" Rory asked, his hand resting on the door handle.

She nodded; her eyes focused on the exit.

With Heather behind the station taking her smoking break, the two detectives waited next to Rory's desk in the large room, called "the hub," that was the heart of the West Sound Police Department. Only the detectives had their own desks in this massive space, all clustered in the corner closest to the wing of interview rooms. Officers used any open desk when on shift. The only office belonged to the chief.

"Well, this has been a bust," Rory said, sinking into his chair.

He was right. As far as getting information on Jada's whereabouts, they had learned nothing from Heather that would aid in the immediate search.

"I don't get it," Jefferson said. "She flies all night to get here, distraught over her missing kid, but then at the end clams up over an impending shut off of her cash tap."

Rory stroked his beard. "Well, I can't blame her there. I love cash taps even more than beer taps." He grinned and put his feet on the desk. "But, more seriously, are we sure she flew here last night?"

"What are you thinking?"

He shrugged. "Maybe she's been here the whole time. Maybe she knows how her husband died. Maybe," he said, narrowing his eyes, "she knows where Jada is."

Jefferson considered this thought, leaning on the edge of the desk, his eyes focused across the room. She's an addict. Her husband wasn't.

Suddenly, he stood up. "Jackson, don't let this go to your head, but you're a genius, and I see just the person we need to talk to."

They both watched as Amber Wells walked into the room.

With dramatic effort, Rory dropped his feet from the desk and pushed himself out of the chair. "You go have a chat with Wells. I'll go collect Mrs. Lausch from her smoking break."

Jefferson met Amber as she made her way to the detectives' corner of the room.

"Good morning, Hughes." She carried her computer bag like she expected to work at the station.

"Sort of." His crooked smile made a brief appearance. "It's been an early one and, seemingly not-so-productive."

"Seemingly?"

He recounted the interview with Mrs. Lausch along with Rory's latest thoughts.

"That's a dark theory," she said, the idea clouding her expression. "Do you think she gave him drugs, knowing the dose would kill him?"

When she said it like that, it didn't sound as workable, but he'd seen people do worse for drugs or money.

Before Jefferson could reply, Rory reappeared, trudging toward them, his hands in his pockets. A man perpetually in good spirits, his downcast eyes told the story before he opened his mouth.

Heather Lausch was gone.

***

"This day gets better and better." Rory returned to his desk chair.

Jefferson ran a hand through his hair, disappointed with himself. "We should have seen this coming."

Nodding, Rory agreed. "Yep."

"Well, gentlemen, I suggest you go find her," said Amber. She looked at her watch. "I'm due to meet with Larson and Mendez in a few minutes, but let me know if I can help."

"Any new info on Nico?" She wasn't likely to tell him, but Jefferson had to ask.

As expected, Amber responded with a patient smile. "Jeff, right now, you two should check out the station's exterior video to see what your interviewee was driving. She can't have gotten far."

Rory jumped up. "I'll go have Jonesy pull it up."

Officer Bianca Jones handled the security operations for the station. Her job involved monitoring access to recordings made inside or outside the station. A small office off the interview room wing was her domain.

"I'll meet you there." Jefferson had another idea he wanted to run by Amber before the other detectives arrived.

With Detective Jackson gone, she eyed him suspiciously, her two hands holding her computer bag in front of her. "Have you talked to the chief yet?"

He shook his head. "There hasn't been time." It was true. They started their interview with Heather Lausch before the chief was in the building. "And that's not what I want to talk to you about."

"Okay. What is it then?"

"I think there may be something to Rory's theory about Mrs. Lausch, but the only way to know for sure is to check her story."

Amber was already shaking her head. "She's not a suspect, Jeff. We don't even know for sure there's been a crime."

"I know, but she could have information regarding a missing child, her child. I mean, don't most kids go missing because of a parental abduction?"

Her blue eyes narrowed. He could see her thinking it over.

"You're right," she said. "You are absolutely right. And the fact that she took off is at least suspicious."

He hadn't expected her to agree so easily, but Amber had kids of her own, and she'd worked enough missing-person cases to know that time was the most important factor in finding people alive, especially children.

She turned as Jefferson's eyes flicked up at Larson's boisterous hello to someone else in the room.

Turning back to him, she said, "Get her information to me. I'll have Ron and Julia check it out."

"You're the best."

"Of course."

She eyed him closely before adding, "Nothing new with Nico. We're just going over background. So keep your head focused on finding that girl."

"I am on it. We'll find her."

"I hope so, for her sake."

Chapter Twelve

Though the gray sky only deepened its shade as the morning advanced, MJ decided it would be an excellent day to tour the Fairview Golf Club.

Or at least it was an excellent way of getting into the neighborhood and trying to squeeze more information out of Brent Miller. She also hoped to talk to some of Jada's neighbors and stop by Cade's house.

Cade was the first person to know something was wrong. He or his parents must be able to shed some light on Jada's disappearance.

She found the card Brent Miller gave her at the reception and dialed his number. He didn't answer right away, and she wondered if he might ignore the call, not recognizing the caller.

Just as she resigned herself to not getting an answer, his voice came on the line with a guarded, "Hello."

"Hi, Mr. Miller?" MJ said like the most excited golfer in the world.

"Yes?"

"It's MJ Brooks, the teacher from the wedding reception the other night."

"Oh, yes, I remember."

"Well, you suggested I come for a tour, you know, to decide if a membership is a good fit for me. I've got some time today and would love to spend it seeing your beautiful facility."

Was she piling it on too thick?

"Hmm, I tell you what. I've got a tee time in about an hour, so I'll be tied up after that, but I'll get Trevon, the club's assistant manager, to show you around. If you can be here in a half hour, I can introduce you before my game?"

It wasn't exactly what she had in mind, but it would have to do.

"Sure. That sounds great. I'll see you in thirty minutes."

Now, what to wear? She rushed to her closet to pull out a pair of khaki shorts. While looking, she found a white skort she'd forgotten about. She tried it on with a navy-blue polo shirt with her school's MMS ship-wheel logo on the pocket. Perfect!

To complete the look, she whisked her mass of dark curls into a ponytail with a white Las Vegas visor her mother gave her. She also grabbed a hooded windbreaker for the always lingering threat of rain.

The sporty look complete, MJ grabbed an apple for the trip, remembering she'd skipped breakfast.

After arriving at Fairview, she had no trouble getting through the gate. Brent Miller must have called and put her name on the guest list. The guards spent an extra minute admiring her rig, a restored 1987 Ford Bronco II, V6 red with a broad white stripe on the sides. Edgar and the Bronco were the only two things MJ requested in her divorce from Justin.

When he wasn't deployed somewhere with the Army Rangers, Justin spent his time restoring cars. MJ fell in love with the Bronco at first sight, and even more so when Justin finished it. Beautiful and tough, the Bronco was perfect for driving in the Northwest. People who knew and loved cars often showed their appreciation for such a fine vehicle.

Soon the clubhouse stood in front of her like a daunting mansion, its deep red brick and ivy-covered facade calling to mind a wealthy estate somewhere in the English countryside.

When she came here for the reception, the scene at Jada's house earlier that day kept the building from making much of an impression on her. Now, in the daylight, it felt more intimidating. She almost expected to meet a pompous butler acting as guardian at the entry. She'd be sent away for not having the proper attire.

In reality, no one met her at the entry. She walked into an empty lobby. From a hall to her left, lighthearted voices mingled with the clinking of silverware. She guessed that to be the direction of the club restaurant. Walking straight ahead toward the ballroom, she saw another hall opened up to the right of the large foyer. At the wedding reception, she'd followed that hall to the bathroom and remembered passing the pro shop. She headed that way, hoping the clerk could at least tell her where to find Brent Miller or the mysterious Trevon, her tour guide.

The door to the pro shop stood open with a mannequin just outside in the position of a frozen welcome. It modeled the latest in Fairview golf attire for women: a pleated, navy blue skort paired with a lavender polo that had just the faintest trace of a floral design. Just for fun, MJ turned over the tag dangling from the shirt.

Her eyes popped. One-hundred-and-fifty-dollars. Hiding her shock took a fierce mental effort. If that was the standard, MJ was woefully underdressed. But there was nothing to be done about that now.

She dropped the tag and walked into the shop.

Just as she stepped in the doorway, a man stormed out, knocking her roughly on the shoulder. MJ had to grasp the door frame to keep her balance.

The man stopped and offered a gruff, "Sorry."

To MJ's surprise, it was Shannon's Uncle Glen. He looked miserable. Dark circles hung beneath his eyes and angry pink patches stood out on his cheeks, a stark contrast with his otherwise ashen face.

"Oh," said MJ, overcoming her shock. "You're Shannon's uncle. I'm MJ. I was at Aubrey's reception. It was beautiful."

"Thank you," he said without looking at her.

It was then she noticed Brent Miller was in the shop. He leaned against a rack of shorts, watching their interaction with a peculiar mixture of sadness and impatience.

Shannon's uncle apologized again before shooting a glare at Brent Miller and rushing down the hall.

Miller sighed. "Sorry you had to see that."

She walked farther inside the shop. "What happened?"

"Nothing," he pushed away from the clothes rack. "He's just not coping well with Dan's death. Not that I blame him. The entire neighborhood is in shock, and Glen and Dan were close buddies. They also have some business deals together, so I'm sure that fact, and having just put on an expensive wedding, is weighing heavily on the guy."

"That doesn't seem like a good reason for him to be angry at you. I couldn't help but notice how he glared at you."

He pressed his lips together in a tight smile. "He just needed to blow off some steam. It's not a big deal, but that's enough about that. Trevon's just in the backroom with the new store clerk. I'll go grab him. Feel free to browse."

"Of course," she returned his smile, knowing there was nothing in this store she could afford.

***

Trevon Baldwin, a recent high school graduate, turned out to be the same Trevon that MJ had taught in eighth grade. Seeing him dressed in expensive golf attire and helping to run such a posh establishment took her by surprise. In middle school, he often wore the same clothes for days at a time, and the school provided him with school supplies and new shoes the year he was in her class.

He kept to himself in middle school and never seemed to have many friends. So it was even more shocking when Trevon greeted her with the warmth and confidence of a much-changed young man.

"Ms. Brooks, it's so wonderful to see you." Trevon held out his hand.

"And you too, Trevon," she said as she took it. "You've grown quite a bit since eighth grade."

He chuckled. "I cringe to remember the eighth-grade me."

"Don't we all," smiled Brent. He then excused himself to head to his golf game when he saw they were already well-acquainted.

Her young tour guide, marked by the subtle acne that sometimes lingers into young adulthood, still didn't look old enough to assistant manage anything. He'd changed significantly since middle school, but he still had a boyish smile. His competence became more clear when he began showing her the grounds and perks of the facility where his passion for golf and his maturity were on full display.

While she feigned joyous interest in the world of Fairview golf, she waited eagerly for an opportunity to ask him about some of the club members, particularly Mr. Lausch and Shannon's Uncle Glen. Trevon must have seen them interact and may have even heard things said between them, something that might give clues about Jada's dad and where Jada could be.

MJ seized the moment at the driving range. As Trevon explained how the reservation system worked, MJ spied Shannon's uncle hitting golf balls in one of the driving range tee boxes. His swing looked anything but relaxed.

MJ knew little about golf, but it looked like Glen was trying to kill the ball. The ferocity of his swing sent the ball flying in every direction except straight ahead. One ball skittered across the ground and came dangerously close to hitting another golfer in a tee box further down the line.

"Do you remember Ms. Davis, the counselor at the middle school? That's her uncle down there," MJ said to Trevon, motioning toward the spot where Glen continued his assault on the golf balls.

"Mr. Donovan? Wow, I didn't know that."

"Donovan, is it? I guess I didn't know his last name. Yeah, I hope he's okay. He seemed really upset earlier at the pro shop."

Trevon put his hands on his hips as he watched the man. "I'd say he's still upset. He normally has a really smooth swing."

"I think he got into an argument or something with Mr. Miller," she said, hoping Trevon might share anything he might have overheard.

The young man nodded. "I heard them talking loudly about something. I couldn't understand most of it, so I just kept showing the new clerk how to catalog merchandise."

He watched as Glen Donovan sent a ball ricocheting off a post. "People get mad at Mr. Miller all the time. He decides who gets in the golf club and whether people can get out of their contract." He shrugged. "Maybe it had something to do with that."

"Glen's a member, isn't he?"

"Yep."

"Why would he want out?"

"Oh, I'm not saying he does," he backtracked. "That's just one thing that gets people mad at Mr. Miller. They usually want out because they can't afford it anymore, they're moving, or they get sick or something."

She nodded thoughtfully, squinting her eyes at the unexpected blinding brightness of the cloudy sky. There was no denying the beauty of this place. Walls of towering Douglas Firs stood on both sides of the driving range, the depth of their shadowy green contrasting with the livelier green of the grass. The striking red and gold of maple and oak trees stood out like bold pocket squares in a man's suit. She could understand why people lived out here if they had the money.

MJ recalled Brent Miller saying that Glen Donovan and Jada's dad had some business deals together. She wondered if Lausch's death put a pinch on Donovan's finances.

"Did you know his friend, the one who died?"

"Mr. Lausch, yeah. It's hard to believe he's gone. It was just a few days ago he and Mr. Donovan were in the shop laughing as they checked in for their tee time."

"So, they were pretty good friends?"

"For sure. Their tee times were always together, Wednesdays and Saturdays at eight a.m., like clockwork. They'd be on the course right now if..." He didn't know how to end the sentence. "I just feel so bad for his daughter, and with her missing and everything. It's all just weird."

"Did you know her?"

"Not well. She's a lot younger than me. Mr. Lausch brought her out on the course sometimes. I think he was trying to teach her to play, but she didn't seem very interested. The few times I saw her, she was on her phone." He shrugged. "Pretty typical for a kid that age."

What he said was true, but she smiled at his use of the word "kid." It revealed a charming innocence in his perspective. But his description of Jada only made the girl's failure to contact anyone via her phone even more mysterious.

"He brought her into the shop about a month ago to try out some clubs," he continued. He seemed eager to talk about the Lausch's now, full of the pent-up anxiety people feel when tragedy strikes close to them, but talking about it feels too weird. "We only had one set she could use because she is a lefty like Mr. Lausch. To be honest, they were kind of ugly clubs, and I could tell she hated them. She took a few swings to make her dad happy, but they didn't buy them."

For a moment, she considered this young man. He was gazing out at the driving range but saw instead that day with the Lausches playing in his mind.

"It's hard to lose someone, even if you don't know them well," she said softly. "An empty space is an empty space, and you can't help but feel the loss. It's good to talk about it."

He turned to face her, his eyes a little misty. He wasn't in danger of crying, but she could see that Trevon Baldwin had a tender heart.

"Thanks, Ms. Brooks. He was a good guy. I met Mr. Miller and him when I worked at the Harrop grocery store in town. They said I had charisma." He snuffed at the memory, shaking his head slowly. "They gave me a chance to do something bigger than I'd ever imagined. Now I get to spend every day here. Mr. Lausch even lets me stay in his other house instead of renting it to someone else."

"A house in the neighborhood? That must be nice."

He agreed. "You have no idea. I grew up a poor kid. This kind of life was never in my plans."

She was glad for Trevon. He deserved to be happy, and it sounded like he'd found something he really loved. However, his story piqued her interest in just how many houses Dan Lausch owned. Could Jada be staying in one of those?

"Does Mr. Lausch own many houses in the neighborhood?"

"No, just mine and the one he lived in." He gazed out toward the driving range, calm but watching Glen Donovan with a slight furrow in his brow. "Yeah. The police came by the other night, asking if I'd seen Jada." He shook his head. "Man, I sure hope they find her. We don't need another tragedy around here."

MJ followed his eyes out to the frustrated Glen Donovan. The tragic death of his friend had abruptly altered his regular tee time, once a cherished tradition. That would explain the man's trouble on the driving range this morning. But she couldn't shake the feeling that it wasn't just their friendship Glen Donovan had lost. He seemed to grieve, yes, but he was also angry.

About what?

"Our last stop is the ladies' locker room," announced Trevon, the pep back in his voice. "I'll walk you over there, and then you can go inside and check it out yourself."

The locker room had all the plush comforts of home—not MJ's home, but the home of someone with money and expensive tastes. A chandelier of champagne-pink glass glittered in the center of the room. To one side, a lounge filled with soft, inviting sofas and armchairs beckoned to the weary visitor to relax and chat or have a drink from the nearby, elegant wine cooler, which held a variety of waters and sodas.

No one was in the locker room as MJ perused the area, but peeking at the lockers and showers, she had the uncomfortable sensation of invading someone's private space. She didn't stay long.

When they returned to the pro shop, Trevon gave her a cute tote full of brochures and other information about membership in the Fairview Golf Club. She told him she would study it all, lying like one of her students. Guilt nibbled at her as she thanked Trevon, who said he looked forward to seeing her on the course soon.

Chapter Thirteen

B ianca Jones's office was a jungle.

Potted greenery sat on every flat surface that did not already contain something electronic. The room smelled of dirt but not dirty, more like a freshly mowed lawn or tilled soil.

The sixty-something Jonesy, as they all called her, was on her fourth and, she said, last career. Before joining the police force, she and her husband Marvin owned their own security company, which they sold off to a national chain, taking in more than two million dollars, according to station lore. They spent most of the money to buy an opulent home on the water with enough property to build houses for their two adult children, a ruse for getting the grandkids close.

Owning the security company came after her job as a data analyst for the state. Before that, she served in the Washington National Guard where she met Marvin. The couple also had a small nursery on their property, and that was now Marvin's job, growing and selling local plants, trees, and shrubbery.

When Jefferson entered the office, Rory sat next to Jonesy, watching a monitor with keen interest. Neither of them turned but kept their heads close to the screen as if the most important moment of the movie was about to happen, Jonesy's right hand on a mouse. Rory's rust-colored hair contrasted with the woman's short black curls.

"There she is," said Rory, nodding toward the screen.

"Gotcha, honey," Jonesy cackled.

Jefferson moved closer to see the action.

Jonesy glanced at him and then back to the screen. "Hello, Detective Hughes. You're just in time."

"Sorry I'm late to the party. Looks like you found our fugitive."

Heather Lausch walked hurriedly across the screen to a white Toyota Corolla.

"Now we just need little miss here to drive away from the curb and pose at the stoplight for a pretty picture of her plate number," Jonesy said. "Then I'll send you two fellas off to do the rest."

Like she was following Jonesy's directions, Heather started the car and pulled straight up to the light. Jonesy froze the frame, took a screenshot, and quickly emailed it to the detectives.

Jefferson leaned in closer. "No sticker or plate-frame showing the car's a rental."

"Nope," agreed Rory. "Could be on the front."

"Let me play the rest of it so you can see which way little miss headed."

Jonesy started the video again. Heather was in the left-turn lane but decided not to wait for the light and lurched over to take a quick right.

"She's in a hurry," Jonesy chuckled. "But it looks like going right wasn't her first choice."

Straightening to his full height, Jefferson rubbed the back of his neck. They could run the plate easily enough, find out where she rented the car, if it was a rental, and check to see if any license plate cameras caught her, but that would all take time. While waiting for the technology to find her, they needed to be on the move, trying to head her off at the most likely places she would go.

He could only think of one.

"Jackson let's move. I think I know where she's going."

***

Cade McCann's house had a contemporary design that contrasted with the more traditional homes in Fairview. The home appeared newer, with its freshly painted exterior and modern architectural design. The landscaping reminded MJ of her home state of Nevada. There was no grass, only pea gravel, and she spotted dwarf palmettos and sand-colored boulders.

She rang the doorbell, not sure what she would say but relying on intuition. The massive oak doors had an intricate design of intersecting circles carved into them. She was deep into a study of it when the door suddenly opened.

"Ms. Brooks?"

It was Cade. He was in basketball shorts and a Washington State cougars sweatshirt. He stared at her with a puzzled expression as he took in her outfit. "Were you playing golf?"

"Hi, Cade. And, no. I wasn't playing golf, just checking out the course. But I was wondering if you've heard anything about Jada?"

Just then, a woman looking exactly like Cade but with shoulder-length hair walked up behind him, smiling curiously at MJ.

"Hi," she said. "Aren't you Cade's English teacher?"

"Yeah, mom," Cade said before MJ could respond. "She's just checking on Jada."

"Oh." The woman's face turned solemn.

"I'm sorry to bother you, but I am just so worried about her."

"We all are," said Cade's mom. "Why don't you come in?"

Once inside, as her son closed the door, the woman led MJ to the back of the house where an expansive living room overlooked the golf course. The ceiling stretched to the second floor and windows filled the outside wall. It created the illusion of being outside while inside. It was beautiful, but the design seemed risky on a golf course.

The woman motioned for MJ to sit on a long, black leather sofa encased in a metal frame. Cade sat on the opposite end and his mom was in an armchair of the same design.

"It's Ms. Brooks, isn't it? I'm Shelly McCann."

Shelly McCann wore a baby blue sweatshirt and sweats combo that shifted like silk every time she moved. Probably designer sweats, MJ thought.

"It's nice to meet you. Please call me MJ." She glanced at Cade. "But it's still Ms. Brooks for you."

He nodded. "Yeah, I know."

"I'm sorry that we don't have better news," said Shelly, glancing at Cade as if calculating his emotional state.

"You can talk about it in front of me, mom," the boy said. "I know she's missing, but I also know she's alive. We just have to find her."

Shelly's eyes shifted to MJ's. What passed there said the mom clearly did not have the same confidence as her son. While MJ's gut instinct also said Jada was alive, she knew it was dangerous to give false hope to Cade. She would tread lightly.

"You're right, Cade. Until we know something more, we need to focus on finding Jada," MJ agreed. "I'm just curious. What makes you so sure she's okay?"

Cade leaned toward her. "Remember the day Jada threw the marker?"

MJ nodded.

"Well, that was the first day I noticed her acting really weird, and then she told me that things weren't good at home...I mean, she didn't tell me exactly what, but she was really sad or something. So, I think she ran away." He sat back. "She usually tells me everything, but I think she knew everyone would come to me first to find out where she went because we're best friends."

MJ smiled as she sat in their living room, doing that very thing.

"You've thought this through. So...any idea where she'd go?"

"We've checked everywhere we could think of," Shelly chimed in. "We even had a friend check our house in Las Vegas. Jada's dad used to have a place in the same development, but they sold it last year," she paused, "after he and Heather separated."

"But Jada knows the code to get into our house," Cade said. "That's why we checked. But she's not there."

MJ mulled this over. Just how many homes did Mr. Lausch own? The idea of a vacation home hadn't crossed her mind, but it made perfect sense. People who had the money often bought a second home as a sunny escape from the drizzly, overcast Washington winters. If he sold the house in Las Vegas, maybe he bought one somewhere else. Could Jada be there?

"Did her dad own any other vacation properties?"

"Oh, I don't think so," said Shelly sitting forward and clasping her hands in front of her. "Dan liquidated everything after deciding to file for divorce, except the house here in Fairview. He may still have his rental here in the neighborhood. I only know about that house because it was a bit of a scandal."

"How so?"

Shelly waved a hand. "I mean, not really. I'm exaggerating, of course, but we don't have a lot of rentals in the neighborhood, so some residents were displeased with Dan. But then he used it as housing for the club's assistant manager. That seemed to settle everyone down."

Shelly narrowed her eyes as a thought seemed to cloud her mind. "I wonder what will happen to the rental and their home now that Dan is gone." She glanced cautiously at Cade.

He rolled his eyes. "Mom, stop. I'm not a baby."

She nodded. "I know. It's just sensitive stuff." She touched her fingers gracefully to her chin. "It concerns me that Heather may get any significant amount of money. Sadly, she is not in the right state of mind for that."

MJ knew Heather Lausch was Jada's mom. She'd already tried to call her several times. Now she wondered what could be so wrong with the woman that Shelly believed her incapable of handling money. It must be the same reason Jada was not on speaking terms with her. But if things were bad with her dad, it seemed natural that the girl might reach out to her mother.

"So," MJ said, her index finger lightly tapping her lips, "you're saying there's no chance Jada could be with her mom?"

Shelly stiffened. "That's highly unlikely."

"Jada's mom is a druggy," Cade hissed. "She left Jada because she'd rather get high than be with her daughter."

"Cade," Shelly said with a gentle shake of her head, "it's not always so simple."

He glared, not buying it.

Turning back to MJ, Shelly explained. "Heather, that's Jada's mom. She and I were good friends. I still miss her, the way she used to be." She took a breath to steady her voice.

"After a knee surgery a couple of years ago, she started taking pain medication. She was never the same after that. Dan tried to help her and send her to rehab, but when she came home, she relapsed and started buying illegal drugs from some shady characters. She wouldn't listen to me or any of our friends. Dan finally told her she had to stay clean, for Jada's sake, or she had to go." Shelly turned her palms up as if to say the rest is history.

Poor Jada, thought MJ. She lost her mother to the life of an addict and now her dad to a drug overdose. The story was too cruel. It also made little sense. Why would Mr. Lausch decide to divorce his wife for drug use and then turn around and do the same thing, leaving his daughter essentially abandoned by both her parents?

"I'm sorry," MJ didn't know what else to say. The more she learned about Jada's disappearance and her father's death, the more she saw the suffering extending out like infinite rings after dropping a pebble in a pond. Addiction is one monster the guards at the massive Fairview gates couldn't keep out.

"Thank you," said Shelly. "We appreciate your concern for Jada...for all the kids."

Across the room, a phone buzzed on a sideboard table. Shelly excused herself to answer it.

MJ turned to Cade at the other end of the couch. He watched her with a question troubling his eyes.

"What is it?" she asked.

He lifted his left shoulder in a half-shrug. "I was just wondering if the police have told you anything cause you're like friends with them. Maybe they know something they won't tell the rest of us."

This question belied the earlier confidence with which he declared Jada alive and well. He focused intently on his hands, pulling at the stretchy bands of his sweatshirt sleeves, a sign he worried about MJ's answer.

The idea that she was "friends" with the police seemed sweet and humorous at the same time. Sweet that Cade would see her work with the police last year as "friendship" and humorous because that very characterization would drive Jefferson Hughes mad.

"I have talked to the police," she said carefully, not wanting to upset the boy or give him false hope. "At this point, they are just as puzzled as we are, but they are using every resource possible to find Jada. They have a lot more ways to look than we do, so I'm sure they will know something very soon."

When he looked up, it was without hope or fear, just uncertainty. "I heard on the news that the FBI is looking for her, too."

"That's true, and I also happen to know the woman in charge of the FBI in our area. She's amazing. There's an outstanding team looking for Jada. I know they'll find her."

"And you're looking too." Just the hint of a smile touched his worried expression. "You're good at talking about claims and finding evidence and stuff like that."

She chuckled. "Yes, I am, and so are you."

Shelly came back to the room carrying her phone. "I'm sorry, that's my husband. We are meeting him for lunch up at the clubhouse."

MJ stood up. "I will let you get on with your day. I appreciate you taking a few minutes to talk with me."

"Of course. We want nothing more than for Jada to come home safe and sound," Shelly said as she and Cade walked with MJ to the door.

As MJ started her car, the thought of a second home, one that perhaps no one else knew about, intrigued her. She wondered if real estate paperwork might be somewhere in the Lausches' home.

Would the police still be there? Should she call Detective Hughes?

She shrugged off any concerns. As Cade had said, she was good at claims and finding evidence and stuff.

With no definite plan, she drove over to Jada's house, certain she could figure something out.

***

Yellow crime scene tape ran across the front door, but no one seemed to be in or around Jada's house.

MJ tapped her steering wheel, trying to work out a plan. What would happen if the police left a door unlocked, and she just tripped and the door opened? Is that like trespassing, contaminating a crime scene, breaking and entering? But if no crime had actually been committed...

Before she could finish the thought, a woman came bursting through the front door of Jada's house, screaming.

"Help, someone, help! There's a man in my house! Help!"

MJ scrambled from her car and met her in the driveway.

The frantic woman grabbed her shoulders, staring at her with wild eyes. "A man, he's in there! Call the police!"

"Is he chasing you?"

"I don't know!" She ran her hand over her slack brown hair. "I think he might have run out the back."

By this point, a couple of neighbors were tentatively venturing onto their porches, curious about the commotion. A woman who looked to be in her seventies was walking toward them on the thinnest two legs MJ had ever seen. She had a phone to her ear.

"Heather, dear," she called out in a concerned voice. "I've called 911, don't you worry. And Russ is getting his gun."

Sure enough, a tall bald man emerged onto the neighbor's porch, a conspicuous handgun swaying at his side.

The spry old woman reached them quickly, talking with the 911 dispatcher and putting one skinny arm around the shaken woman. "It's good to see you, dear," she whispered.

Heather. This was Jada's mom.

MJ had so many questions, but first, she would take this chance to get into the house. If someone had been in there, Heather's screaming exit from the house likely sent him bailing out the back, just as the woman had said.

"Heather." She looked directly into the woman's eyes to ensure she had her attention. "Do you mind if I go check it out, see if anyone is still in there? I'm MJ Brooks, by the way. I have Jada in my language arts class at school. I stopped by to see if there was any news."

Heather's brows furrowed in confusion as she stared at MJ, attempting to unravel all the words coming at her.

"Oh, I know you," said the older neighbor. "You helped the police after that horrible bombing at city hall." She turned to Heather. "You can trust her, dear. She works with the police." Turning back to MJ, she added, "Russ can go too, in case someone is still in there."

MJ glanced at Russ, his face filled with a mix of curiosity and suspicion, now standing on his neatly trimmed lawn. Despite his pleasant appearance in a green plaid shirt, MJ's greater concern was the potential for a gun accident rather than a run-in with the intruder, who she was more confident than ever had already fled following Heather's noisy departure.

"Thanks for the offer, but I'll just peek in, and if it looks clear, I'll check out the rest of the house."

Heather sniffled. "Thanks."

Yes! Permission to enter.

***

The door stood wide open as MJ approached. She listened before stepping over the threshold. Hearing nothing, she pressed on.

Unlike Cade's lavish modern house, the Lausch residence had a more understated charm. The traditional craftsman design featured an abundance of dark wood, which framed the windows and formed the square posts and railings leading to the second floor.

MJ stopped again in the entry, listening for any movement on the floor above. Still nothing, so she moved through a small hallway to the back of the house where the kitchen combined with a family room into one enormous space. French doors to the back patio were wide open. Beyond the doors, the fairway stretched out before her, a vibrant green carpet framed by majestic pines and a serene pond.

The course was empty. If the intruder left this way, he was long gone.

Her gaze shifted back to the hall, revealing two doors waiting to be explored. One was closed, and the other was slightly ajar, but not enough to see inside without further inspection. She hoped it was an office.

Bingo.

A large oak desk stood in the middle of the room. Built-in bookcases covered every wall, but the books that should fill them were mostly covering the floor as if having been flung there without a care. Whatever the intruder was after, he thought it was in this room.

The desk drawers were open, too, making it easy for MJ to find a bunch of hanging files. Flipping through the tabs, she saw cars, dental, insurance, medical, and others before she landed on real estate.

With a swift motion, she pulled it out and placed it gently on the desk. She nervously fumbled through the papers, her fingers seeming to have a mind of their own and making a mess of the documents. A deep breath helped to calm her down. If Lausch owned another house, the information should be in this file, but she needed a clear head to make sense of it.

As she quickly scanned through the file, she realized it contained documents specifically related to the Lausch residence, the very house she was currently in, as well as the Fairview rental she suspected housed her former student, Trevon.

A further perusal of the documents confirmed that thought. Stapled to the back of the home's sale documents was a lease agreement with Trevon. It surprised MJ to see that Lausch wasn't charging the young man any rent. Instead, the agreement read "lessee will pay in employment service to Fairview Golf Club."

Those guys really love their golf club, she thought. And it was a sweet deal for Trevon. The kid not only got free housing with his job, but he got housing most people could never afford.

While interesting, this information did not lead her any closer to Jada. The police already spoke to Trevon. The young man was as worried as everyone else about the missing teen.

Then she noticed a green tab marked "vacations."

As she opened it, slick brochures fell to the floor. She kneeled to pick them up, the bright cover of one catching her eye. It had pictures of laughing children riding on a gigantic yellow tube pulled by a boat. "Get your piece of Lake Cushman today," it read. "Cabins starting at $400,000."

Before she could read any further, the sound of creaking steps on the wood floor reached her ears, making her heart skip a beat.

MJ stuffed the brochures in the waistband of her skort and pulled her shirt over them as she hid behind the desk.

Maybe the intruder had been upstairs the whole time. She had to admit that once she got into the office, she'd forgotten about checking for the mysterious man.

The steps stopped at the office door, and someone pushed it open, hitting the book and paper debris in its path.

MJ held her breath, her heart pounding in her ears. This was probably one of her all-time, most reckless ideas.

"MJ, I know you're in here."

She didn't move but mouthed a silent "Darn it."

Jefferson Hughes.

Chapter Fourteen

On a city bus—route twenty-nine from downtown to the West Sound Mall—a woman died somewhere between boarding the bus and the last stop. At the end of the route, when the woman failed to disembark, the driver tried to rouse her without success. Paramedics pronounced her dead at the scene.

Larson received a call just after Amber Wells finished sharing the FBI file on Nico.

It was Officer Fogarty. He and Officer Evie Hanson were on the scene, and they were communicating with a city transit official. The man wanted to know if the transit authority could put the bus back in service once the medical examiner arrived and removed the body.

Larson rolled his eyes. A woman just died in one of their seats. There might have to be an interruption in service.

"Tell the official we'll be holding the bus as long as it takes to view the security footage," he said to his phone, which was on speaker and lying on the desk for Amber and Mendez to hear. "The sooner we get the footage, the sooner he can have his bus. We need to assume it's another drug overdose, and if she bought something while on that bus, there could be fingerprints or other evidence."

"Yes, sir," Fogarty replied. "Should he send the footage to your email?"

"That works. Tell him I want it from the time that woman got on the bus until the termi—" he stopped, shaking his head at Mendez and Wells as he realized the unfortunate pun he almost uttered. "Until the end of the route," he finished instead. "If there's no drug purchase made or other suspicious interaction, we'll release the bus."

"Got it," answered the young officer.

"Oh, and Fogarty, I know the guy is just trying to do his job, but so are we, so don't let him give you any crap about that, got it?"

"Got it. No crap."

"I'll be watching my email."

He ended the call and stuffed the phone in his pocket.

"The drug deal on a bus would only be too perfect," Mendez said as he flipped a pen around his fingers.

Larson snorted. "Yeah, right. Those guys know there are cameras on the bus, cameras with good lighting, not like the dark corners and alleys dealers like to scurry around. But who knows, this one could be more stupid than the usual scumbag. Let's hope they find something more than we've got so far."

Other than his parents positively identifying the body, they'd struck out with Christian Greene. All the so-called friends they'd talked to had lost contact with the guy. Christian hadn't held a job in a year. They figured he'd spent all that time living on the streets.

Amber Wells stared at her phone during this interaction, lost in something on her screen. A stiffness in her posture suggested that whatever she viewed there captured every aspect of her attention.

Guys," she said. "I think we have a location on our 'N' tattoo character."

She looked up. "How do you feel about a stakeout?"

***

Mendez and Larson parked three houses down from the target property, a tiny mustard-colored thing with white trim. Crooked, mangled blinds covered the front window, and the door had no windows, only a peephole. The overgrown yard, encased by a chain-link fence festooned with a Beware of Dog sign, seemed designed to keep the casual visitor away. No mistaken pizza deliveries or Jehovah's Witnesses were likely to risk opening the gate.

All the houses on the street were packed together as if put on display to show the consequences of not properly caring for your home. Their target house, however, had a further sad and menacing aspect to it, like a dog that had been beaten enough to be mean.

Amber and Special Agents Julia Liufau and Ron Benton were in a van a block away. They didn't have a view of the house, but they had a view of the detectives' location. If the neck tattoo guy showed himself, Larson and Mendez would approach him from the west side, forcing him, if he ran, toward the FBI van to the east.

Amber Wells had a "friend" inside the DEA. That friend had a confidential informant who spotted their man of interest at this house. Amber wouldn't share any more than that. She might not even know more than that since her DEA source feared compromising the CI. The fewer people in the loop on his or her identity, the better.

"What snacks did you get?" Larson asked, looking in the backseat at a grocery bag. They didn't do stakeouts often. Mostly, they were boring as all get out. They were also usually fruitless. Like babies who won't smile for the camera, you couldn't count on the target of your stakeout to oblige you by being present or doing anything noteworthy.

"Eating already, Larson? We just got here." It was Ron on the radio.

"You're just mad cause you don't have a caring partner who brings you licorice and soda."

Mendez put a finger up. "Correction. I brought salsa verde and tortilla chips, mango con chamoy, and Coke."

Larson reached for the bag. "Sounds good to me."

"Oh my gosh!" Julia said on the radio. "Save some of that mango stuff for me, please. That stuff's delicious."

"Maybe," said Larson.

Mendez motioned toward the house as he picked up a set of binoculars. "We got a female leaving the residence. White, short black hair, pink beanie, and a long gray coat. Looks to be in her twenties, ring piercing on her nose and I can barely make out a few tattoos on her neck. Don't see any 'N' tattoos from this side. Headed east on foot."

Larson groaned. "Man, I hope they are not selling that stuff in there. Amber, did your guy say what they are doing in this house? Cooking? Selling? Both?"

Silence on the radio. Either Amber didn't know, or she was mulling over how much to share.

"I think we can assume nothing good is happening here."

Larson pursed his lips. Mendez shook his head, warning him not to say anything else. Without Amber's information, they wouldn't even have this place to check out. Working between agencies could be like walking a tightrope. Not because they were territorial or trying to beat you to the punch, but because everyone wanted to protect their assets, especially those working in dangerous situations. Larson understood that, but he'd always struggled with red tape and people wasting his time. This better get them something.

Chapter Fifteen

"Come on, MJ. I can see you're behind the desk."

She inhaled deeply to steady her still-pounding heart before standing up slowly. "How could you see me?"

His crooked smile appeared. "I couldn't. I guessed."

She rolled her eyes as she stepped over a pile of books to get out from behind the desk. "Is that how you do most of your detective work?"

With a chuckle, he leisurely scanned her from head to toe, a smirk playing on his lips. "When did you pick up golf?"

She ignored his question, though she felt a flash of heat in her cheeks at his inspection of her. While brushing some non-existent lint from her white skort, she regained her composure. Her curiosity forced its way to the forefront and pushed away any lingering self-consciousness.

She was on to something, and she wouldn't let Jefferson Hughes dissuade her from finding out what happened to Jada. With determination, she met his gaze head-on, refusing to look away.

"What are you doing here?" they said simultaneously.

Their eyes locked. As the seconds passed, the intensity of Jefferson's gaze deepened. The silence between them grew, but it was filled with a palpable energy that charged the air. When Jefferson still didn't look away, her insides began a pleasant fluttering dance that made her cheeks blush. Her heart raced, pounding against her chest. He was so close that she could see the tiny specks of color in his changeable blue eyes.

What was she thinking? Stop it, she screamed inside. She tore her eyes away, breaking the spell.

"I asked first," she insisted, staring past him.

Jefferson sighed. She could feel his eyes still on her. "I think it was a tie. Besides, I am investigating this case and have cause to be here. You do not."

She flicked her eyes back to his. "Mrs. Lausch asked me to come inside."

Jefferson narrowed his eyes. "Mm, did she? I'm not sure even Mrs. Lausch should be in this house."

"She was in the house when I got here."

"And ran into an intruder." He said flatly, one eyebrow arched like the top of a question mark.

Planting her hands on her hips, MJ glowered at him. He seemed to be dismissing the other woman's claim. But MJ saw the distress when Heather came flying out of the house. The fear on that woman's face was all too real.

"She was scared out of her mind. But you look like you don't believe her."

He sighed. "To be honest. I'm not sure what to believe with her. Did you see anyone in the house?"

"No, but the patio doors were wide open. It looks like the guy ran out that way, onto the golf course."

Without another word, he turned and walked toward the family room and kitchen. MJ followed on his heels, noticing for the first time how his suit accentuated his tall, athletic frame. She almost stopped and slapped her own face. If she didn't know any better, she'd say he was trying to charm her off of this case with those annoyingly attractive blue eyes of his.

"And what about the mess in the office," she said as he surveyed the open doors. "Someone was looking for something in there."

He took out his phone and snapped some pictures of the door and the doorjamb. "You mean like you were?"

"I did not make that mess. I would never throw books on the floor."

He glanced up at her with a grin before shaking his head. Then he went back to taking pictures and moving without acknowledging her claim of innocence. "So, what were you looking for?"

Watching him scan the outside patio, MJ debated whether to tell him her theory, if she could even call it that. When Cade's mom talked about the Lausches selling their Las Vegas property, it hooked MJ's brain like a wild blackberry branch. Her idea was less theory and more intuition. Still, while Jefferson Hughes could be frustratingly rule-bound and skeptical, she'd seen the goodness in him last year, and while she didn't want to, she knew she should trust him with the truth.

"MJ," he said before she could explain anything. "Did you go outside at all?"

"Nope, I stopped there, at the door."

The detective stepped outside and walked to the edge of the patio where a row of recently pruned azaleas created a border with the lawn. Jefferson bent down and studied one shrub in particular. He took a picture of the plant and the dirt below it.

When he stood up, MJ could see the azalea had a damaged branch on one side.

"Why did you take a picture of the dirt?"

He was dialing his phone as he walked back inside. "Footprint," he said. "Don't touch anything else. I need to get forensics out here. And you and Heather are coming to the station."

***

The detectives waited for the arrival of patrol officers, who would guard the Lausches' house until forensics could get there. Afterward, they departed for the station, with Heather accompanying the detectives and MJ following in her car.

When they arrived, Detective Jackson took Heather to an interview room. MJ attempted to make the case that she should join them, but Hughes shot her down.

"I'll make you a deal," Jefferson said as he escorted her to the waiting area next to the interview rooms. "When we are done with Mrs. Lausch, I'll tell you some of what we know about Jada's family if you tell me what you were looking for in their house."

Since she planned to tell him anyway, MJ saw this as an excellent deal.

"Fine, but if you decide you need me," she smiled sweetly. "You know where to find me."

"Not gonna happen." He looked around the room. "You know where everything is?"

She glanced at the area behind her. The last time she was here, her mom was with her. She had flown up from Las Vegas after the explosion at city hall, worried out of her mind about MJ. She could almost feel her mom's arm around her shoulder as they sat exhausted on that waiting room sofa. The memory hit her with a sudden desire to see her parents.

"I remember." The words came out with a solemn softness she hadn't intended.

When she turned back, he was watching her as if wanting words to say, his blue eyes in search of the meaning behind the shift in her tone.

Unable to find it, he nodded once and then left her alone.

***

With Jefferson gone, MJ pulled the brochures from the Lausches' house out of her backpack. She'd stuffed them there on the drive to the station.

Lake Cushman. The place brought back a buried memory of the one time she'd been there.

Justin's army buddy, Grant, owned a cabin in that area and had generously invited them to join him for a weekend of waterskiing. Since the cabin was tiny, Justin suggested they set up camp close by, a decision that brought joy to Edgar. The dog loved the feeling of the packed sand beneath his paws as he ran along Stanton Inlet, but he despised retrieving sticks or toys from the salty water. On the other hand, the lake's freshwater transformed into a vast aquatic playground for him.

Grant's wife, Jessica, was a trail runner. She suggested one night, as they all sat around a campfire, that MJ join her on a run the next day. While running wasn't her favorite way to stay in shape, MJ did a fair amount of it and felt like she could keep up. Justin had laughed out loud and declined the invitation before MJ could say anything for herself. She'd stared at him, silently seething, but saying nothing. In the end, she just swallowed her anger, the red embers of it falling on a growing pile of hurt already collecting in her heart.

She closed her eyes and banished the memory. Because that's what it was. Just a memory.

Focusing on the brochures, she read the first one, which pitched Lake Cushman, sourced from the Skokomish River in Mason County, as the perfect family destination. It raved about exciting activities like water sports, camping, hiking, and the best fishing anywhere. There was even a golf course nearby.

She remembered it being a beautiful place. Commercialism hadn't yet spoiled the area, so it felt rural and untouched, though it was one of the most popular day trips for people in southwestern Washington. Thick forests and the proximity of the Olympic Mountains, their iron backs often dusted with snow into late spring, created a picture perfect scene at every turn.

The other two brochures were for Mason County real estate agents. Both boasted the ability to find the best Lake Cushman properties at the best price. Max Allen looked to be about fifty, with his salt and pepper hair and bleached white teeth. Poppy Alaya was much younger, a smiling, dark-haired woman who wore fiery red lipstick with confidence. If Lausch purchased a property, or was hoping to purchase one, she bet these two would know.

Even if he bought property there, none of this meant for sure that Jada would be there. Lake Cushman wasn't just down the street. If MJ remembered right, it took more than an hour to get there. If Mr. Lausch owned a cabin somewhere in the area, MJ couldn't see how Jada would get there without an adult's help, or the help of someone who was at least driving age.

The map app on her phone said it would take one hour and thirty minutes to get there.

Realizing she still had the visor on her head, MJ pulled it off and dropped it into the seat next to her, wishing she'd been able to change her clothes.

Working the phone screen with her fingers, she examined the travel route from West Sound to Lake Cushman.

Would a taxi or other ride-share service take someone all the way out to rural Mason County? Could a kid even book such a ride?

The map app could switch between directions for driving, walking, taking a train, or a bus. She doubted any of those other options were viable, but she clicked on the icon for bus, just to see what would happen.

According to the app, it would take almost five hours to reach Lake Cushman by bus. The process required a lot of bus changing and waiting at various stops, but to MJ's surprise, it proved to be doable.

Something like excitement bubbled up, making her jump from her seat. She paced the little waiting area, chewing on a thumbnail. She stepped out into the hall and looked toward the interview rooms.

Still quiet.

Just then, her phone buzzed in her pocket.

Chapter Sixteen

"**W**hy did you run?"

Jefferson stared at Heather, waiting for an answer.

The woman seemed to shrink into the chair, appearing even more frail than in their earlier interview.

When she didn't answer, Rory chimed in. "Imagine my surprise when I came to get you from your smoke break, so we can work on finding your daughter," said Rory, his disgust riding just under the surface, "and you've gone and taken off. As a dad, I can't even understand what could be more important to you than finding Jada."

"It's not more important," she shot back, anger flashing in her sunken eyes. "But if you find her, I can't help her. I have nothing. Dan had everything. If the police take it, we'll be penniless."

This wasn't the first time she'd complained about the police seizing her husband's money.

She knew something.

"Why would the police take it?" Jefferson asked as if he and Rory weren't a part of the police she feared.

It didn't work. She folded her arms and gave him a side-eye full of suspicion. "I'm not saying anything else."

Dealing with her was like playing a never-ending game of patience. He was determined to find Jada, not only because of the Nico case, but also because he feared for her safety and the uncertainty of her fate if they continued to waste time.

Despite the underlying tension, Jefferson maintained a soothing demeanor as he stated, "Without knowing the full story, it's impossible for us to help you."

She didn't budge.

Rory leaned across the table. "If you won't tell us that, then at least explain why you lied about getting a hotel and rental car."

Her eyes widened. "How…?"

"We traced the plate. Not that hard really." Rory shrugged. "I just don't get why you'd lie about that."

Releasing her arms, she ran a hand through her hair, her resistance deflating for the moment. "I suppose it was stupid to lie, but I didn't want my friend getting dragged into anything. He's had his trouble with the law, and he wouldn't appreciate me sharing his information."

"So, who is he?" Rory grinned.

With a half-hearted glare, she sighed. "His name is Wes, which I'm sure you already know, and he's a friend. He picked me up from the airport, let me sleep on his couch, and lent me his car. He doesn't drive much, living in Seattle." She glanced at the two detectives. "That's it, I swear. He's been good to me, so I was just trying to keep him out of it."

The story seemed feasible enough. "You met him in rehab," Jefferson guessed.

She nodded. "When Dan first told me I had to leave, Wes let me crash at his place for a couple of weeks. Then I got a place in California."

Rory cocked his head. "Why California? My partner here is from California. It's pretty expensive there, isn't Detective Hughes?"

"It is, Detective Jackson."

The glare was back. "I know what you're doing," Heather said.

"What are we doing?" Jefferson asked flatly, his eyes not leaving hers.

Sitting forward, she folded her hands on the table, her thumbs restlessly rolling over each other. "You want me to talk about money. Well fine. Dan paid for my place and all my living expenses. I went to California because he wanted me far away from Jada. He wouldn't let me near her unless I was completely clean, which I am now."

That's what they all say, thought Jefferson. Then he said, "So that's why you're worried about money. But I still don't understand why you went to the house in Fairview."

Turning her head to stare at the wall, she clammed up again.

"Ma'am." said Rory. "You don't have to be here, you understand?"

She nodded without looking at him.

"So, if you aren't going to tell us everything and anything that could help us find your daughter, then you might as well leave so we can get on with the search."

A tear dropped out of one eye as Heather stared at the wall beyond the two detectives. She wiped it with the back of her sweatshirt sleeve.

When she finally spoke, it was quiet and measured, the most sincere she'd been all day. "I went back to find the cash. In the past couple of years, Dan's business took off. I'm not sure why. He always said he finally hit the high-dollar real estate market." Her eyes drifted back to the two detectives. "I always thought it might be a little shady, but I didn't ask. For some reason, he always kept a lot of cash on hand, in his office safe. And I mean a lot, like a couple hundred thousand dollars."

The detectives exchanged wide-eyed glances.

"I must not be the only person who knows about it," she said. "That guy in the house, he must have been looking for it too. And if the cops look into it, they'll take it all and probably the house and everything else. Jada and I will have nothing."

A silence settled over the room as the detectives took in this information.

Heather jumped as a rapid knock sounded at the door.

Jefferson opened it to see MJ Brooks standing there, holding out her phone. Her eyes were glowing with excitement, like the blue center of a flame.

"MJ—"

"Just look," she said, thrusting the phone at him.

There he saw an email with one simple word. "Help!"

***

In the chief's office, MJ sat on the edge of a chair, explaining the message on her phone to Chief Carlson. Jefferson stood against the wall with his arms folded.

Using the school email system, MJ had sent a message to Jada when she first disappeared. The one-word email came from Jada's account.

Amber's words echoed in his mind. "If you want to find this girl, call MJ." It shouldn't surprise him that calling MJ wasn't necessary. Once she had an idea in her head, she refused to let go, like a pit bull. Scratch that. She was more like a hound dog that couldn't leave a scent alone, never looking up to see that she was headed straight for a cliff.

And here she was with the first genuine lead in Jada's disappearance. He had to hand it to her. MJ had a way with the kids, and they trusted her. Grudgingly, he admitted to himself that the trust MJ had with her students and parents could prove invaluable in getting to Jada, wherever she was.

As he listened to her explain, his mind wandered briefly to their encounter at the Lausch home earlier. The charged air between them wasn't his imagination. She'd felt it, too. He was sure of it. Letting out a breath, the memory alone was enough to make his pulse race. He hadn't felt that way in a long time. But the idea of him and MJ together was crazy. She was too unpredictable, careless, and rash, he told himself. It could never work.

"And I have an idea where she could be," MJ was saying. She glanced up at Jefferson and then quickly back to the chief as she pulled some papers out of her backpack.

Jefferson stepped forward, curious.

"These are brochures for Lake Cushman." She shifted uncomfortably in her seat.

Picking one up, Jefferson realized why she'd been so sheepish. "This is what you took from the house."

MJ cleared her throat but didn't admit or deny his statement. "I met with Cade McCann and his mom," she said. "The McCanns are good friends of the Lausches. They own property in Las Vegas, and Mr. Lausch used to own a place in the same neighborhood, but he sold it when he decided to file for divorce." Her eyes narrowed as she sat forward even further. "But that got me thinking. Maybe he bought a place that nobody knows about. There's even a bus route to get there, which explains how Jada could get there by herself."

That must be the reason for the golfing get-up, thought Jefferson, amused. While the outfit complimented her curvy, athletic figure, he still couldn't believe she used a golf lesson or something to weasel her way back into the Fairview gates. MJ was something else.

The chief looked at the brochures thoughtfully. "It's possible, but tracing the email is probably our best bet for finding Jada's location."

Smiling gently, the chief added, "You've done some good work here, Ms. Brooks. I think your insight and your relationship with the missing girl could be extremely valuable."

Jefferson, lost in his thoughts, had focused his eyes on MJ. He looked up to see the chief watching him.

"Detective Hughes, if Ms. Brooks is on board, I would like you to work with her on bringing Jada home."

Surprising himself, and probably the chief and MJ, Jefferson said, "Yes, sir," without objection.

The teacher glanced up at him. He couldn't be sure, but he thought he saw gratitude in her expression.

"I'm on board," she said.

"Alright, now that we have that settled," said the chief, "you need to get a trace on that email. I suggest you call Jared at the FBI office. Amber has already agreed to provide any resources we need, and young Jared has the skills to do this thing faster than anyone I know."

"Yes, sir."

The chief's steely eyes regarded MJ before addressing the detective again. "I suspect the school district is going to want a warrant. Even if Jada could be in danger, releasing student information is a tricky situation. Better safe than sorry. I'll put a call into the courthouse. What's the deal with her mother?"

Looking at MJ, Jefferson decided she might as well hear what they knew. "She hasn't provided help in finding her daughter, but she shared that Dan Lausch may have some questionable and even criminal business transactions. According to her, he kept a lot of cash on hand at the house. Rory is digging into that now."

"Good, keep him on that while you get the girl's location."

"Will do. Any news on Nico, sir?" Jefferson asked.

The chief sighed. "No sightings of the man himself yet, but Larson and Mendez are currently monitoring a house where the 'N' tattoo man has been spotted. I have received no updates yet, so as far as I know, nothing has come of it."

Jefferson felt a momentary pang of missing out. He hated stakeouts, but this was one he wouldn't mind being on. He brushed the thought aside.

Find the girl, then find Nico.

Chapter Seventeen

The snacks were gone.

A few people had come and gone from the little yellow house, but none of them were the man with the 'N' tattoo.

Larson was on the phone with Fogarty as Mendez watched the house.

"Hmm, that's interesting. I assume forensics took that stuff to the lab since there was no arrest?" He paused for a response. "Good. Let me know if anything else comes up."

As he put the phone away, Mendez put the binoculars down. "So, what's the stuff?"

"Gina Tillman, our latest victim, had a couple of pills on her. Blue, stamped with an F130. That's unusual. They usually try to mimic the stamps of the popular opioid prescriptions. It could be this new stuff making its way around, a new cook doing his own thing. That's a risky business. Makes it easier for us to mark him."

Mendez wrinkled his brow. "That is insanely stupid."

"Hey, Amber and crew," Larson said into the radio. "You ever hear of little blue pills being stamped with F130?"

"We haven't," replied Amber, "but I can put in a word with my DEA source. See what they know."

"Alright, well," said Larson, "how much longer before you think we head back to the station?"

"I'd give it a few more minutes," Amber said. "Patience. Patience is a virtue, Detective Larson."

"Yeah, whatever," he grumbled.

"Hey, you guys got any of those mango things left?" asked Julia.

Mendez snickered. "Are you kidding?

"Larson." she said. "You're such a hog."

"Yep, proud of it," Larson said. "I tell you what. We catch this guy today. I will buy you an entire bag of those things."

"You got a deal," Julia agreed.

"Hey. Hey, guys," said Mendez, putting the binoculars up to his eyes. "Think we got something."

Larson sat forward, looking through the driver's side window. "We sure do. We got a guy of medium height, a shaved head. I can see some tattoos on his neck, but I can't quite make them out. What do you see, Mendez?"

"No 'N' on his right side, but Joey said left side, anyway."

The man stopped in the middle of the scrubby yard and took out a cigarette. He started smoking and blowing smoke rings into the air. He casually watched his surroundings, but didn't seem to be on high alert. If he had been, the detectives and their car might have caught his attention. He wore faded baggy jeans and a black zipper hoodie.

"I think he's barefoot," said Mendez.

"That's got to be good for us, right?" said Ron from the radio. "Maybe even Larson can keep up if this guy decides to run."

Larson regularly took this kind of jab because he regularly handed them out to others. It didn't bother him in the slightest. Having spent twenty-five years on the job, he had grown tired of chasing scum through the streets of West Sound. He didn't hesitate to acknowledge that his young partner had a speed advantage over him. Still, he couldn't allow insults from the feds to go unanswered, even if they were meant in jest.

"Ha-ha. Says the desk jockey. When was the last time you had to chase anyone, Benton?"

"Let's stay focused, gentlemen," Amber broke in. "Mendez, what else do you see?"

Their target turned back to the house when someone opened the door and let a dog out into the yard.

He'd turned just enough.

"Yep, there it is. A big fat 'N' on his neck," Mendez said.

"That's it. That's our guy," said Larson. "Everybody ready?"

"We're ready here," came Ron's voice over the radio.

"Alright, we're going to make our move."

Larson and Mendez left the car without closing their doors all the way to avoid spooking him. As they approached the target house, they could see the man still standing on the lawn smoking, looking away from them.

They were almost at the front of the gate when someone shouted from the house. "Correr, hermano! Correr!"

The man jerked around and saw the two detectives.

He dropped the cigarette and ran, leaping over the chain-link fence and then hauling it down the road, bare feet and all.

"Dang it," Larson grumbled as Mendez took off after him. Larson examined the house to see where the shout had come from.

A short, heavyset man stood in the shadows of the doorway so that Larson couldn't make out any other identifying traits.

The 'N' tattoo guy was fast, but Mendez was faster, staying close on the man's heels.

Just as they reached the van, Ron and Julia stepped out from behind it, both holding up their pistols.

"Stop! FBI!" shouted Ron.

In a sudden motion, the man came to a halt, his arms instinctively shooting up for a split second. Then he turned and bolted back toward the detectives.

Mendez also had his weapon drawn. "You're not going anywhere, hermano. Just stop. Now."

Finally realizing he had nowhere to go, the man put his hands up.

Mendez ordered him down to the ground, where he cuffed him before searching his pockets for a weapon.

Larson walked up beside him. "Man, we just wanted to talk to you, and then you had to go run. What's your name?"

Mendez stood the guy up, having found nothing in his pockets. The detainee stared at Larson with hard eyes.

"Okay," Larson said. "You want to be that way. Who's your friend?" He motioned back toward the house with his head.

Still, the man stared.

"Quien es tu amigo?" Mendez tried.

The man turned an even colder stare on Mendez before spitting on the ground at the detective's feet.

"I think he likes you guys," Ron said.

Amber stepped forward, keeping a wary eye on the house as she spoke. "I think we need to get out of this area as fast as possible. We'll meet back at the station."

There seemed to be a growing crowd in the shadowy doorway. The hairs on the back of Larson's neck stood out as he recognized their unprotected position in the street. Taking their detainee back to the unmarked unit would mean crossing in front of the house.

"Mendez, take him to the van. I'll drive the unit back."

The younger detective eyed his partner. "Don't be stopping for lunch without me."

"But you can stop and buy some of those mango con somethings," threw in Julia.

Chapter Eighteen

The chief expected the warrant to come through within the hour. He'd also spoken to Brian Williamson, the superintendent of the West Sound Public Schools. While Williamson expressed his desire to help in any way he could, the district appreciated the chief had already requested a warrant.

Rory and a few patrol officers went to search the Lausches' home again, this time looking for financial records, computers or phones, and hidden cash. Forensics had a few fingerprints from the patio door, and they were in the process of eliminating family matches. Rory also called the office manager of Sound Home Title, Lausch's company, who agreed to meet him at the office. If Lausch had sketchy business dealings, his title company likely provided the cover.

Since nothing could be done to trace the email without the warrant, Jared, the FBI tech guru, came to the station with his laptop so he could get to work as soon as the judge approved the search. As he was setting up, Jefferson talked on the phone with Poppy Alaya, one of the real estate agents from the brochures MJ took from the Lausches' house. MJ sat at an empty desk, on the phone with Max Allen, the other real estate agent.

They'd already checked the property records for Mason County. Nothing for Lausch came up, but sometimes people used trusts or corporations to buy the property, keeping their name off the record. Knowing what to look for became the problem.

MJ's call with Max Allen didn't last long. She hung up and put her elbow on the desk with her chin resting on her hand, watching Jefferson have more luck.

"Yes, I understand you don't want to share that information, but I'm sure you've seen the news reports," he was saying. "Mr. Lausch is deceased, and his daughter is missing. The information you share could help us find her."

He glanced up at MJ. Her intense blue eyes bored into his as if trying to hear both ends of the conversation by drilling her way into his brain. He held her gaze just a beat too long, and feeling awkward, looked away abruptly.

"Okay, thank you," he said into the phone as he began scribbling on a pad of paper. "We are doing our best, thank you. Finding Jada is our top priority. Thank you, again Ms. Alaya."

He hung up.

MJ came over to see what he'd written. "Two addresses?"

"Yeah. Lausch didn't end up buying a house with her, but she showed him a couple of properties he was interested in. These are the addresses. We can compare them with the county records and see what comes up, at least until the warrant comes..." His voice trailed off as he became distracted by Stacey Underhill walking in the door from the lobby.

Seeing Stacey in street clothes always shocked Jefferson. He was so used to seeing her in her full-coverage protective suit or the scrubs she wore when doing an autopsy that seeing her outside of work was like seeing a different woman. With her blonde hair free from hairnets and hoods, she strode gracefully into the room like a runway model in her sleek, perfectly tailored tan slacks and navy floral blouse. She carried a manila envelope.

Stacey was a beautiful woman, but talking to her broke the spell for Jefferson. She always came on strong, whether or not she meant to. After only a couple of dates, Jefferson knew she was way too much for him.

MJ turned to see what he found so interesting.

"Uh-huh," she said turning back to him.

He did not meet her eye. "She's the medical examiner."

"Examiner," repeated MJ. "Interesting."

He cleared his throat, suddenly feeling hot knowing that these two women in the same room, talking to him, talking to each other, was going to be murder.

"Detective Hughes," said Stacey as she reached his desk. "I'm so glad you are here. I have some news for you." She pulled a chair over from an empty desk and sat across from Jefferson, setting her envelope on the desktop.

"Hello, Dr. Underhill." He knew his voice sounded miserable, but he found Stacey Underhill so unpredictable. He never knew what might come out of her mouth.

Her eyes widened, and as if noticing MJ for the first time. Stacey gave her a very obvious once-over.

"And who is this? Oh wait, don't tell me. I recognize you from the news last year. You are the teacher. TJ isn't it?" Stacey positioned her head so that her hair fell in a perfectly smooth wave across her shoulder.

MJ snorted. She actually snorted, as if holding back the eruption of a Mount-Saint-Helens-sized laugh. The worst part was that Jefferson felt the urge to join her.

"I'm sorry," she said. "Nobody's ever called me that. It's MJ." She swallowed hard, as if the urge to giggle hadn't subsided. "It's nice to meet you, Dr. Underhill."

"Oh please, call me Stacey. Jefferson usually does." She shot Jefferson a look from under her lashes.

The detective cringed at her overt flirting. He knew she did it just to get under his skin. After their brief dating history, he felt sure she wasn't any more interested in him than he was in her. The woman just enjoyed making him squirm.

"Well, MJ," Stacey said with added emphasis on her name, "you are so much prettier in person."

"Thank you," MJ said, flicking her eyes up to Jefferson's when Stacey turned back to face him. The mirth he saw there told him how much MJ was enjoying his discomfort.

Jefferson tapped the envelope. "So what have you got?" He'd had enough of the...whatever it was.

Stacey cast a wary eye back at MJ.

"She's okay," Jefferson assured her. "The chief gave permission for MJ to help on the Lausch case, which I assume is the case you want to talk about."

She nodded. "You assume correctly." She opened the envelope and pulled out a stapled report. "I will give you this whole thing, but I came to share the most important parts because most of this report is boring gobbledygook."

"I'm all ears."

She flipped forward in the report to the third page. "Here is what I found in Mr. Lausch's lungs. If you look through this list, you will not find pond water or the things associated with pond water."

"So, he didn't drown," stated Jefferson.

"No, and even more importantly, based on his face-down position in the pond, he had to be dead before submerging in the water."

Jefferson sat back and considered what this news meant. If Lausch was already dead, he didn't put himself in the pond.

"He was murdered," MJ said in a whisper.

Glancing back at her, Stacey said, "That's not for me to say. There were signs of pulmonary edema, consistent with a drug overdose, which can occur even with small amounts of fentanyl if that's what he injected. Toxicology is so freaking backed up. Who knows when we'll have that test back?"

Running a hand through his hair, Jefferson racked his brain for how Lausch could end up in the pond without someone else's help.

He rubbed his chin. "Could he have passed out next to the pond and then rolled in?"

Stacey raised a brow at him. "The dead man rolling in the pond theory. Interesting."

Jefferson shrugged. "I'm trying here."

MJ had said nothing, which Jefferson knew from experience was highly unusual. Chewing her thumbnail, she was watching Stacey and him, but she wasn't really seeing them, as if something else played out in her mind.

Suddenly, she jumped from her chair. Looking at Stacey, her eyes wide and alert, she said, "You said injected, right?"

"Yes, I found a slight wound consistent with injection on his arm."

"Which arm?"

Stacey smiled and nodded. "Yeah, I know where you're going, and it was his left arm. Since he wasn't a habitual user, he would use his dominant hand for the injection, which is what he did."

MJ was shaking her head. "No. No, he didn't."

With a furrowed brow, Stacey gazed at her. "Let me guess..."

MJ did not let her guess. "Mr. Lausch," she said with breathless excitement, "like his daughter, was left-handed."

***

Stacey and Jefferson stared at MJ.

The detective spoke first. "How do you even know that Lausch is left-handed?"

"Well, I know Jada is, but when I went on my tour of Fairview this morning—" She stopped, seeing the crooked smile creeping up Jefferson's face. "Don't say anything," she warned.

"I wasn't," said Jefferson.

Stacey looked between them. "This sounds like one heck of a story."

"It's not. I just needed to get into Fairview, so I took a tour of a club I could never afford in a million years."

Stacey laughed. "You are something else, girl."

"Yes, she is," agreed Jefferson, his eyes locked on MJ.

His comment caught Stacey's attention, and she studied Jefferson with narrowed eyes. He didn't see her, but MJ did, and a blush rose to her cheeks.

"Anyway," she said, attempting to get the three of them back on track. "The kid who conducted the tour, one of my former students—"

"Of course," said Jefferson.

"He said something about Jada needing to get left-handed clubs, like her dad."

The air in the room felt electric, at least to MJ. Something about Mr. Lausch killing himself never felt right, but this recent evidence suggesting that Mr. Lausch may have been murdered likely also meant that Jada was in real danger.

The detective directed his eyes to Stacey. "What do you think?"

"I think it makes more sense than a dead man rolling into a pond."

Jefferson stood. "I can see I'm never going to live that one down."

The doctor stood as well, "Nope, but you can keep that report. If anything else comes up, I'll let you know."

"Thanks for coming down."

"Of course. It was nice to meet you, MJ." She said this to MJ, but her eyes were on Jefferson, her brows raised.

The detective narrowed his eyes as if confused by her gesture. If he understood her meaning, he showed nothing. MJ knew what that look meant, and she didn't like it. Stacey Underhill seemed to think MJ was only involved in this case because she was some kind of romantic interest to Jefferson Hughes.

When Underhill finally left, MJ felt a whole heap of tension leave the room. Jefferson, if possible, looked slightly less stiff, more like his usual self.

"I should update the chief," he said.

"Yes, you should." Her tone was perhaps a bit icier than she meant.

Sensing the change, he paused like he was trying to decide where to step next. "You should come. This is your discovery."

She wanted to go talk to the chief, but the insult of Underhill's insinuation still rankled her. "Okay, but I just want it to be clear that I am here for Jada, because I can help find her, and for no other reason."

Standing straight and perhaps a little more rigidly, he replied, "Oh, believe me, that is completely understood."

"Fine."

"Fine. Shall we go?"

He walked away. After a second of watching him go, she followed.

***

They were just about to enter the chief's office when Mendez came in, leading a man in handcuffs—a man with a slew of tattoos.

Jefferson veered away from the office door and toward Mendez and his detainee, MJ close behind. Amber, Ron, and Julia were also making their way inside.

As Jefferson got close, the man with the 'N' tattoo pulled up and stopped, staring at the detective with smoldering, hate-filled eyes.

"Hey, keep moving," Mendez said, attempting to pull the man's arm.

"Detective Hughes," the man shouted.

Jefferson stopped in his tracks. MJ pulled up next to him.

The detective's blue eyes glared with laser focus, his posture stiff and deliberate, as if trying to determine if the man in front of him was a threat.

"Ah, it is you," said the tattooed man, a vicious smile curling his lips upward. "My boss knows you, knows where you live. He hasn't forgotten and he wants to make sure you don't either."

"Get him outta here," said Larson, who had just walked into the room. "That's enough flapping your worthless gums."

The man snickered as Mendez pulled him down to the interview rooms.

When he was gone, Jefferson let out a breath. MJ could see the tension in his jaw but couldn't tell if it was alarm or anger.

"Who was that guy?" she asked, watching Mendez drag him down the hall.

"A guy I need to be in that room interviewing." The hardness in his voice surprised her.

"No, you don't," said Amber, walking to meet him. "Hi MJ," she said with a gentle smile. "It's really good to see you." She said this with a sincerity that MJ appreciated.

"What was that all about, Hughes?"

MJ and Jefferson turned at the same time to see the chief standing outside his office. He'd witnessed the whole interaction.

Jefferson and Amber exchanged a look that MJ couldn't quite read.

"So, you haven't told him," said Amber.

"I was getting around to it," said Jefferson.

The FBI boss tilted her head in the chief's direction. "No time like the present."

The detective nodded with an air of surrender. "MJ," he said. "I need to talk with the chief on my own for a few minutes."

"Of course," she said, not in the least understanding what was going on but sensing it was important.

"Hey, Hughes," said Amber. "Not alone. I'm going with."

At first, MJ thought the detective would protest, but Amber Wells' face held no room for argument. This must be serious.

"By the way, Hughes," the chief said as Jefferson and Amber walked toward him, "I just got word that the warrant came through."

"That's good news, sir. MJ can get started with Jared. We need a moment if you have the time."

The chief said he did, and the three of them disappeared behind the closed door of his office.

***

Jared asked MJ to forward the email from Jada to him.

She did as he asked and sat nearby while he worked, trying to contain her desire to ask questions.

The two of them worked together last year to build a composite sketch of a suspect after the bombing of city hall. Jared didn't say much, he took his work very seriously. MJ doubted he said much when he wasn't working, whenever that was. As she watched him watch the computer screen in total concentration, his face framed by mop-like brown curls, she wondered if the young man might have an autism spectrum disorder.

Jared's focused and intense brilliance on the computer, coupled with his discomfort in making conversation, reminded her of students with autism she'd either had in class or known from other activities at school. People on the autism spectrum were as varied in their skills and abilities as anyone else, but there were some characteristics she recognized in this young man.

Whether he was on the autism spectrum wasn't her business, so she just watched and waited for when he needed something from her.

Ron and Julia came over to say hello and see what MJ and Jared were working on. Ron was one of the tallest men MJ knew. She guessed him to be close to seven feet tall, and he had a face that could put the fear of God into anyone—dark hair, dark bushy eyebrows, and a severe face that always looked serious. In truth, he was the least serious of all the FBI agents in the group. He was just a laid-back guy who liked to crack jokes at the wrong times.

Julia had probing black eyes that always made MJ feel like she could read into her soul. She had a mass of black hair that she almost always wore under a ball cap with the logo of one of Seattle's sports teams. Julia's softness came out when she talked about her little boy.

Together, Julia and Ron could find information no one else could find, and they did it with lightning speed.

After MJ explained the situation, Ron and Julia said they were going to investigate a different avenue related to the Lausches.

"Detective Jackson is over at the title company, and he has questions about some of Mr. Lausch's financial transactions," Ron said. "Funny how no matter what we investigate, it always ends up coming back to the money."

"Always," agreed Julia. "So, we better get moving, Ronny."

The big man looked up at the ceiling. "Work, work, work. That's all you think about. I need lunch before I can focus on anything."

Julia rolled her eyes. "Fine, we'll order in."

"My favorite four words." Ron smiled like an excited kid.

After checking if MJ or Jared wanted anything, which they declined, the two wandered off to order their food and get down to work.

"I have an address," Jared said suddenly.

"Already?"

"Would you prefer it to take longer?" He said without looking at her and without humor.

"No, sorry."

He glanced at her and then back to the computer. "It's okay. That was a joke. I will send the addresses to your email and the email for Detective Hughes."

She smiled. He was also funny.

"Do you want to see it on the map?" he asked.

"Ooh, yes." She peered at the screen as he zoomed in. "Is that Lake Cushman?"

He nodded as he continued zooming to get a good look at the property.

"I knew it!"

"There it is," Jared said when the map stopped moving.

The house itself was on the lake, as in beach-front property. There was one residence within walking distance, but the roof view from the satellite showed the house otherwise surrounded by the spikey tops of the pine forest.

"What's the address?" MJ asked as she grabbed the pad of paper where Jefferson had scribbled the information from the real estate agent.

"It is 5891 Lakeview Loop."

Scrunching up her nose, MJ stared at the addresses on the paper. "Well, that's weird. That's not one of the addresses from the real estate agent, but it's super close. I've got 5889 Lakeview Loop."

Jared pointed at the screen. "That's the one next to it."

MJ puzzled over this for a minute. The discrepancy likely meant nothing. Poppy Alaya said Mr. Lausch didn't end up buying a house from her, so maybe both houses were for sale, and he bought the other one. Whatever the reason for the slight mismatch, they had a location, and it was time to go get Jada.

Chapter Nineteen

"Alright, friend. If we can count on your cooperation, I'm going to take the cuffs off," Mendez said to the tattoo man.

"I'm not your friend," he replied with a sneer.

"Leave 'em on," Larson said as he pulled out a chair from the other side of the metal table. "Victor here is going to cooperate with the cuffs on. Or do you prefer Vic?"

The man glared at him.

Larson sat back in his chair and smiled. "That's right, friend," he said, emphasizing the word. "We ran your face through the system and bam, there you were, Victor Cano. The, uh, neck tattoo there," he said, pointing to the left side of his own neck, "that must be new. It's not in your last photo shoot. Is that for a girlfriend or something?"

The guy looked like he wanted to eat Larson alive.

"Maybe you touched a nerve, Detective Larson," Mendez observed from the chair next to his partner. He looked at their detainee thoughtfully. "That makes me wonder if our friend maybe wishes he didn't have that tattoo. Maybe it holds some terrible memories for him."

Victor Cano looked away from them, turning to face the wall, somewhat obscuring his 'N' tattoo.

Larson sat forward, his hands on the table. "You see, Vic, we're not interested in your love life, but we would like to know why you ran off and left Christian Greene to die in the street."

With lightning speed, the man's head snapped back to the front. He jumped from his chair with a primordial growl, lunging at Larson across the table. Although the man's hands were secured behind his back, he barely missed head-butting the detective. Larson jumped up and out of the way just in time. Cano abruptly swung around the table and dashed towards Mendez, who had quickly risen from his seat.

The young detective moved deftly to the side while throwing his elbow over the top of Cano's upper back, jabbing with a quick and exact movement that sent the detainee to his knees.

Hearing the noise, two patrol officers rushed in and wrestled the man back to his seat. They secured his ankles to the chair and his hands behind him around the back of the chair.

Larson and Mendez returned to their chairs, Mendez taking a little extra time to smooth his shirt and tie. The two officers, on assurances from Larson that they were fine, stepped back outside the room.

"That was fun," smirked Larson. "So, what's Christian Greene to you?"

Cano pulled at his restraints, his neck muscles bulging with the effort.

Clearly, Larson thought, hitting him hard with Christian Greene only made the man more angry. It seemed Christian Greene's death was a bigger deal to Victor Cano than just some random kid's overdose. He decided to try another direction.

"Look, we have a witness who saw you taking care of Christian. I don't think you wanted the kid to die. And I can tell you firsthand that breaking this news to his mother... Well, let's just say I won't forget the heart-wrenching sobs of that woman for a long time."

Cano squeezed his eyes shut and lowered his head. All the fight deserted his muscles, his shoulders drooping as far as his cuffed hands allowed.

Mendez sighed. "Yeah, his parents showed us how he used to be a star three-sport athlete—football, baseball, basketball. Then he started using. Man, that stuff just destroyed his body."

"The sores on his skin, and he was so emaciated," continued Larson. "When I saw his driver's license—"

"Just stop it," came the mangled, tortured plea from Victor Cano. "Please."

Larson and Mendez looked at each other. Was Victor Cano crying?

Sitting forward, Larson appealed to the remorse Cano seemed to express. "Victor, talk to us. Whatever killed Christian, this tranq mix, is killing a lot of other people right now. We just want to find the stuff, so no other parents have to lose a kid."

Victor sniffled but didn't look up. "I don't know what you want from me. I don't know where that stuff is coming from. Chris got it when I wasn't with him." He moved his head to the side, trying to wipe his eyes on his shirt without using his hands.

"Come on, Victor," Larson urged. "We know that 'N' is for Nico, and you work for him. Nico has quite a drug trafficking reputation. Word is, he's back in the area. Nico comes around. People die. What are we supposed to think?"

Cano raised his head. His eyes were red, and a layer of moisture glistened under his nose. "You don't know nothing."

Mendez got up and opened the door. He asked the patrol officer to bring him a box of tissues. Then he closed the door and dropped them on the table.

The younger detective sat forward. "I'd like to give you another chance. I'll take the cuffs off your wrists and let you clean up your face.

Then you tell us the parts we don't know. We are not trying to string you up, Victor. We need to find those drugs."

Cano didn't verbally agree one way or the other, but he relaxed his arms when Mendez took off the handcuffs. He rubbed his wrists as Mendez pushed the tissue box closer to him.

"So, what is it we don't know?" Larson asked.

Without looking at them, Cano shrugged. Then he gruffly pulled a tissue from the box, holding it in his hand as if he didn't want anyone to see him using it.

"Chris was my friend. I would never let him use anything like that stuff. I don't know who he got it from, but..." He looked off to the side, his face contorted by an inner battle. "You guys don't get it, man."

"You afraid of Nico?" Mendez asked.

The man's gaze bored into him, his intense stare implying that he found the answer to be blatantly clear

Larson nodded. "Okay, we get that. But I'm sure, after what happened to your friend, that you understand why we need to find Nico, or at least where they're cooking the pills."

Cano sat back in the chair and swiped his nose. He stared at Larson like he was trying to discern the very nature of his soul. What he found there would determine how much he said.

None of the men spoke, and the silence seemed to stretch on. Larson glanced at Mendez and stood up, about to end the interview, when Cano finally spoke.

"Nico didn't tell any of his crew to make them pills."

Larson sat back down, keeping his facial expression neutral, afraid that if he interrupted or looked skeptical, Cano would clam up. Both he and Mendez stayed quiet as the man continued.

"The only reason Nico came up here is to find out who's been cheating him."

With a hand on his chin, Larson narrowed his eyes. "How are they cheating him?"

"By cutting his supply with cheap stuff like that animal tranq drug, then making their own pills and selling twice as much, cutting Nico out of the extra cash."

This was an interesting twist. Larson glanced at Mendez, whose eyes were wide like he'd just seen the Easter Bunny. A drug dealer trying to get dangerous drugs off the street was about as real as the Easter Bunny.

"Does he know who it is?" Mendez asked.

Victor snorted. "If he knew, you two would be cleaning their guts up off the sidewalk."

Larson shook his head. "Actually, we don't do that part."

"Whatever, man," Cano said with a sneer.

Lifting a foot onto his knee, Larson sat back in the chair. "See, what I don't get is how Nico doesn't know who's doing it." He raised his finger in the air. "So let me see if I got this straight. Nico supplies drugs ready to be made into pills or whatever, and someone in his network is making and selling what Nico expects, but they're also using some of his supply combined with fillers to create extra, and that is the dangerous stuff that killed Christian Greene. These mystery people line their own pockets, and Nico is none the wiser. Except that he is. How am I doing?"

Cano stared. "I'd say you're not as stupid as most cops."

With a chuckle, Mendez said, "I think that's the nicest thing anyone in this room has ever said about my partner."

"I won't let it go to my head," Larson smirked. He studied Cano. "So, I'm betting that having the cops all over town searching for this stuff also has Nico riled up."

Cano folded his arms. "Yeah, you all should stop that. You're going to get somebody killed."

That was almost funny, thought Larson, except that it was all too true. They could end up leading Nico to the people he was looking to punish. Larson found it hard to believe anyone in Nico's network could be so brazen.

"I've been thinking," said Mendez with a look of concentration. "If we know who all the cooks are for Nico's network in West Sound, where they're making the stuff, we could help find them. Of course, we wouldn't hand them over to Nico, but they wouldn't be selling the drugs anymore."

Cano looked at him with disappointment. "Maybe you're not as smart as your partner." He paused to run a hand over his shaved head. "Even Nico doesn't know that. It keeps his network secure. No one can snitch too much information because it ain't in their brain." He shook his head slowly. "And that's not how Nico works. He's out for blood."

Larson watched him with a steady stare. "Nico staying at the yellow house?"

Screwing up his face in disgust, Cano said, "No way, man. Nico only stays in style."

"So where is he?" Larson pushed.

The man shrugged. "He don't tell me that."

Larson nodded. "I just have one more question." He tilted his head. "How do you know Detective Hughes?"

A wicked smile spread up his face like a kid stealing the last cookie. "I don't know him. But Nico does, and he got a bad grudge against that dude. All Nico's guys know that cop's face. He should run and hide."

Chapter Twenty

When Jefferson and Amber finished explaining the detective's ties to Nico, including his brother's role in the network and the case in Medford a decade ago, the man's eyes seemed more flinty than usual.

He put his elbows on the desk and folded his hands. "I wish you'd told me this earlier, but you're here now." His lips formed a thin line. "Given this history, I think it best that you stay off the search for Nico. If Amber is right, he could be gunning for you, and that is not something I can risk."

It took all the self-control Jefferson could muster to keep from launching into a passionate appeal. Instead, he responded with his emotions carefully controlled. "Of course, I'll respect your orders, sir, but please hear me out."

He nodded once. "Go ahead."

"If Nico is here to exact some kind of revenge on me, then not being involved in the case won't keep me out of danger. It will only keep me less aware of what is going on. I know more about Nico than anyone else in the station. I can help get him off the street."

The chief sighed, his eyes softening somewhat as he regarded Jefferson. The detective knew that look did not bode well. It said the chief felt for him but wouldn't relent.

"Hughes," he said. "I don't doubt your desire to protect the citizens of West Sound from this monster. Your safety is important, and so that plays heavily into my decision, however, that's not all. This is too personal for you. Your brother's addiction, that he could be involved somehow... I'm concerned it could compromise your judgment, and I just can't risk it."

Jefferson hung his head. This was unbelievable. As much as he respected Chief Carlson, he was wrong about this.

"Have I ever given you a reason to question my judgment, sir?"

"Jeff," warned Amber. She had mostly listened quietly, only helping to fill in some details regarding what happened in Medford.

"It's fine," said the chief, waving her off. "That's a reasonable question, and no, son, you haven't, and it will not happen now. Besides, is Jada Lausch back home?"

"We're working on it, sir."

He stood, a signal that his words would be the last of the meeting. "That is your job right now. I appreciate you bringing this business with Nico to my attention, and you have my decision."

***

MJ waited impatiently for Jefferson and Amber to come out of the chief's office. Once she had a direction, like the address for Jada, sitting still felt like physical torture.

Finally, the door opened, and the three of them stepped out. MJ rushed to meet them with the address clutched in her hand.

Before she could say anything, Detectives Larson and Mendez came from the opposite direction and beat her to it.

Larson spoke first. "Chief, Cano gave up some interesting info the team should hear."

"Not just interesting," threw in Mendez. "It's shocking information."

"There's new information related to Mr. Lausch as well," added Jefferson.

The chief nodded at the detectives. "Sounds like we need a quick briefing. Let's meet in ten minutes."

They all agreed. MJ's heart sank. How long could a briefing take? Jada's life could depend on how fast they got to her. They still didn't know if she was being held by someone or was on her own.

"What's the matter?" Jefferson asked as they headed toward his desk.

She stopped to face him. "Jared confirmed that the email came from Lake Cushman. We have an address. Why can't we just go? I'm really worried, Jefferson."

The way his name came out, even to her own ears, sounded unusually intimate, which seemed to surprise both of them.

He searched her face with troubled eyes, like oncoming storm clouds overtaking the blue of the sky. She wondered how much of that look had to do with her or Jada, and how much had to do with the meeting in the chief's office. Whatever it was, there was a deep part of himself that Jefferson never showed, a part that she knew was suffering. She'd seen glimpses of it last year, too.

Maybe it was just the fact that he was finally taking her seriously, but she felt a pang in her heart for him.

He closed his eyes and turned away as if shielding himself from her. "Look," he said with a sigh, "I know it's hard to wait, especially for someone as reckless as you." He said the last part with his annoyingly attractive crooked smile. "But it is safer for us and Jada if the rest of the team knows what we are doing. We don't know what to expect when we get there, and you are an unarmed private citizen. We'll need backup."

"I am not reckless," she insisted. "I'm just..." She couldn't think of a good replacement word.

This time, his smile was broad, and the clouds cleared from his eyes, if only briefly. "Get a snack or whatever you need before the briefing. We'll leave immediately after it's finished."

***

Everyone gathered in the briefing room, including MJ, whom the chief allowed as an observer only and instructed not to share anything with anyone outside the meeting.

If only she wasn't still wearing that stupid skort. She felt like a high school cheerleader. Thank goodness she'd already taken off the Las Vegas visor.

She walked awkwardly into the room and was immediately relieved when she saw Amber waving her over to sit next to her.

As MJ took her seat, Amber said, "It's been a whirlwind, so I haven't had a chance to say how important it is that you're helping Detective Hughes on the Jada Lausch case. Whatever she is going through, when we finally find her, the familiar face of someone she trusts will be very important."

"Thank you. I couldn't agree more. I'm just grateful that Jefferson seems more open to the idea."

"Yes, that is good." A slight, almost indiscernible crinkle at the corners of Amber's eyes made MJ wonder if the agent had something to do with the detective's change of heart.

Once everyone was settled, the chief invited Larson and Mendez to get started.

Larson explained that Cano, the man with an 'N' tattoo, indeed worked for the drug trafficker named Nico. They released him because they had nothing to charge him with except resisting arrest.

According to Cano, Nico had a rogue crew. Larson explained what Cano had told them about one of Nico's crew using cheap ingredients to cut his drugs.

"So, if we don't figure out who it is before Nico does, we could have a bloodbath on our hands," surmised the chief.

"Exactly," Larson agreed. "Cano said we'd be 'scraping guts off the sidewalk.'"

MJ listened in horrified silence. She knew about drugs; she had plenty of students who lived a life surrounded by family members using drugs, born to addicted mothers, and even experimented on their own, especially with cannabis. However, she had no experience in this world of peddling and killing. How could people have so little concern for their fellow humans?

"Our ace in the hole," Larson continued, "is the DEA's CI. If that guy or gal can keep us updated on what Nico knows, we may be able to head off the carnage." He looked at Amber. "What do you think, SSA Wells?"

She acknowledged his question with the tip of her head. "I can pose the question."

"What's the probability they'll agree?" Larson pushed.

Amber's expression remained neutral. "I can't promise anything, you know that. It depends on whether using the CI in that way could compromise the goals of the DEA investigation. All I can do is inform them of the situation and ask for their help."

Larson looked like he wanted to say more, but the chief put his hand up. "We are not debating this here. The fact of the matter is, we can only control our investigation. Where we get help from other agencies is a bonus." He held Larson with his steady, gray eyes. "What do you think are your next steps, if, let's say, you don't have an inside informant?"

"We keep tracking down the movements of our OD victims. Where did they go? Who did they buy from? Find some low-level dealers and follow it up the chain."

The chief nodded. "Take as many officers as you need to interview people on the streets who may have seen something."

Amber added that the FBI could assist with getting access to security cameras, databases, and phone records, usually with speed.

"You have anything else, Sergeant?" the chief asked.

Larson's eyes fell on Jefferson. "Nico is pretty set on taking out our man Hughes. What's that all about?"

MJ wasn't sure she heard right. "Take out" as in kill? This crazy drug dealer wanted to murder Detective Hughes? She looked at Jefferson, unable to keep the alarm and confusion from showing.

He met her eyes briefly before directing his gaze to the head of the table, as if he expected the chief to answer the question.

The chief exchanged a look with Amber before speaking.

"There is a history there that we don't have time to go into. So yes, Hughes will be extra vigilant, as will the rest of us, ensuring he stays informed of anything we know about Nico's movements."

So, it was true, MJ thought. Jefferson Hughes' life was in danger.

Larson nodded his understanding. "That's all I have for now."

"Hughes," said the chief.

"Thank you, sir. We have an address at Lake Cushman where we believe Jada Lausch is located. We will head out there as soon as we finish the briefing. As we are not sure what to expect, we will need some backup. Jada could be alone, or someone could be holding her hostage. She emailed MJ with just the word 'help.' Jared traced the IP address to the Lake Cushman address."

The chief's gray eyes narrowed. "By 'we,' you mean you and Detective Jackson?"

Jefferson cleared his throat, but he didn't hesitate. "No sir. I mean Ms. Brooks and myself, along with the officers you allow to accompany us."

All eyes in the room were on Jefferson. The tension weighed on MJ like she lay buried under a mountain of sand.

"Chief," said Amber, breaking the awkward moment. "If they find Jada, I highly recommend that MJ be present. The girl could be hurt, confused, and wary of men she doesn't know. MJ may be the only person in this room she will trust. I know you are worried about Ms. Brooks's safety, but she knows the risks and will follow Jefferson's lead. I'm sure of it." Her eyes fell on MJ as if to warning her not to make a liar out of her.

The chief's unwavering gaze held firm, refusing to soften. Regardless, he nodded once to signal his approval. "Take a couple of patrol officers with you. I'll make a call to the Mason County Sheriff, let them know what's going on. They'll need to send out a car or two to be onsite with you. It's their jurisdiction. And make sure Ms. Brooks here wears a vest." The chief said with a stiff but not unfriendly smile at MJ.

"I will," Jefferson assured him. "I have something else related to Lausch. I received a preliminary autopsy report from Underhill. Some details lead us to believe that someone else injected Mr. Lausch, intending to kill him."

"Whoa," said Larson. "That changes things. Maybe we should check for forced overdose with all our cases. We could have some mad addict murderer on the loose."

Jefferson shook his head. "Not likely, Larson. I'm not sure Lausch is connected to the rest. He may have had some shady financial deals in his business. Maybe one of them turned deadly. That's what Rory is checking on now."

Ron cleared his throat. "I can throw a little gas on that fire."

"Please share," said the chief.

"Detective Jackson sent us some records, first relating to Lausch's house and then to other properties he's helped settle, all with corporate owners." The big man sat up and started outlining his talking points with his finger on the table.

"Dan Lausch paid cash for his home in Fairview." He moved his eyes around to see the reactions of the others. "I see you are all sufficiently shocked. It's unusual to have that kind of cash lying around, and it is especially unusual for a man who owns a small title company in West Sound, Washington."

"But that's not even the weirdest part," he continued. "Julia and I have been tracking down the other deals he's assisted with closing, and all of those were cash deals as well."

Amber sat up, her posture alert. "Money laundering."

"Sure sounds like it," Ron agreed. "The government's been cracking down on this kind of thing, but only in the big cities. It can go unnoticed for a long time in little corners of the world, like West Sound." He grinned like a jack-o'-lantern. "We are about to open a whole can of worms with this one."

MJ's mind was reeling. Jada's dad was laundering money? She wondered if Jada discovered her dad's illegal business dealings, and that's what made the girl so sensitive to Cade's jokes about too many clothes—some kind of misplaced guilt.

Could that same knowledge have put her in danger? MJ felt more anxious than ever to get moving. They needed to find Jada now.

Chapter Twenty-One

T he day had moved into late afternoon by the time MJ and Jefferson got on the road, followed by a patrol car carrying Officers Fogarty and Hanson.

"Are you cold?" Jefferson asked as they started down the highway.

"No, not really," she lied.

"Are you sure? Because you look cold." He held the wheel with one hand and reached into the back seat.

"Here's my coat," he said, putting a long navy overcoat on her lap.

She spread the heavy coat over her legs. The ghost of Jefferson's scent clung to its fabric. "Thanks."

"Sure," he said.

"This vest is uncomfortable," she said. "Can't I take it off until we get there?"

He gave her a side-eye. "Nope. Chief's orders."

They both fell silent.

It amazed MJ how quickly they left the city behind. Within only a few miles, the noise and traffic were already fading in the distance. The dark forest drew close to them, blotting out the world beyond the moment, with the road as the only reminder of where they'd come from.

The dull sky felt heavy. The air felt heavy. The colors outside the car window were bold and demanding, greens so vivid and varied that they dared you to look away.

MJ leaned back in her seat and watched the earth fly by. So much weighed on her heart. What if they were too late? This young girl had lost so much—no contact with her mother and now her father, murdered.

Closing her eyes, she willed herself to think more positively. They would make it in time. Jada would be alive.

The detective sat silently beside her, but she could feel his preoccupation. What must he be thinking, knowing that a violent drug trafficker wanted him dead?

Without opening her eyes, she asked, "Why is this man Nico after you?"

Though she couldn't see it, she could feel him turn to look at her. "Well, you just jump in deep, don't you?"

Opening her eyes, she kept her head resting on the seat back, but rolled it to look at him. "Did you put him in jail or something?"

He sighed. "Sort of."

"How does someone sort of go to jail?"

"He didn't go to jail, but about ten years ago, I helped in an operation that put a lot of his network in jail. Nico fled to Mexico to avoid prosecution, but he lost his entire business."

She lifted her head off the seat and shifted to face him, waiting to hear more.

He glanced at her and then back to the road. She thought he would say more, but he didn't for a long minute.

Finally, he said, "I used my little brother to do it."

It sounded like a confession, and he kept his eyes on the road as if expecting her to judge him for it.

"How?" she asked gently.

Once again, he took a long pause before responding, and when he did, his voice reflected a deep wound, the words coming with an effort. "He's an addict. He worked for Nico. He may still work for Nico."

There it is, she thought, that strand of sorrow woven into the fabric of Jefferson, not always visible, but always there.

"What's your brother's name?"

He told her, and as the drive continued, Jefferson shared his brother's story, the one that had become his story in so many ways. He never cried, but the deep love he had for his brother only made the addiction and loss of their relationship more devastating.

She said little, just listened. Given his intensely private nature, she doubted Jefferson had revealed this much about himself to many people. Maybe not anyone.

With the trust he placed in her that day and the man he showed himself to be, MJ realized she might like Jefferson Hughes much more than she wanted to.

***

They were almost to the Lake Cushman turnoff when Jefferson finished talking about Alex. He hadn't meant to tell MJ as much as he did, but she made it so easy. She never tried to explain it away or offer condolences, she just wanted to know about Alex.

And Jefferson wanted to talk about Alex. Before he got into drugs, his brother was smart, funny, and athletic. She let him say it all.

The burden he constantly carried felt some measure lighter having shared it.

"I'm sorry for rambling on," he said, putting a hand through his hair.

"You weren't rambling," she said. "I appreciate getting to know your brother...and you."

The way she hesitated before adding those last two words shot a wave of unexpected gratitude through him. He turned to look at her, but she was gazing out the window, some of her dark curls having fallen from her ponytail to frame her face.

A smile played on his lips as he recalled her crazy charade to gain entry into Fairview.

"Here!" she said suddenly, bringing him back to the moment. "This is the turn."

He tapped on the brakes and checked his rearview mirror to ensure Fogarty didn't hit them. All was clear, and he took the left-hand turn.

To get to the house, they had to drive around the lake. This meant a two-lane road with multiple tight curves as they drove in and around the surrounding forested area.

When in full view, the lake reflected the deepest coal-colored shades of the sky, and though beautiful, it didn't appear inviting for any activity other than viewing from a cozy spot inside. Steep, evergreen foothills jutted straight from the lake to the sky, like natural prongs holding a prized onyx.

On a hot summer Saturday, people would pack this road bumper to bumper, looking to picnic, camp, fish, or cool off with water sports. It was still moderately busy with campers and hikers. Trails abounded around the lake, and an entrance to the Olympic National Forest wasn't far.

"Left at the next turn," MJ said. She'd printed a map before leaving the station. According to her last experience near Lake Cushman, the cell service was spotty and non-existent in some places.

The turn took them onto a narrow gravel road. The occasional pothole jostled them as they navigated the windy track. Trees and other vegetation choked the roadway so much that Jefferson wondered what he would do if a car came from the other direction. He knew people lived down this way, though they had passed no cars or seen signs of any homes yet.

Soon, however, they passed the first gated dirt lane of a private residence.

"That one said 5887, so it's coming up," MJ pointed out.

When they came to the next house, they noticed an SUV parked just outside the gate.

"This is the house Poppy Ayala showed to Dan Lausch, but it's not the one Jared traced the IP address to. That one is still further down."

"Looks like someone is at that house, anyway," said Jefferson, eyeing the car as they passed. "Nice G-Wagon."

MJ glanced at it briefly before turning her attention back to the road. "There," she said. "That's got to be it."

Jefferson pulled up to the gate and off the road. Fogarty pulled in behind them.

MJ jumped out of the car as soon as it stopped. Before anyone else was even out of their vehicles, she was checking the gate.

"Whoa, MJ," said Jefferson as he climbed out of the car. "Hold up. You can't go busting in there by yourself."

She turned around. "There's a padlock on it, so we'll have to climb it."

The two officers joined them at the gate. "I got some bolt cutters in my patrol car," offered Fogarty.

"No," said Jefferson. "This may not even be the right house. We are not going to destroy property. We're on shaky ground even entering the property because we should wait for the county sheriff."

Balling her hands into fists at her sides, MJ growled. "You can wait. I'm just your average citizen checking on a friend. So I'm going."

As much as it bothered him to admit it, she was right. They were wasting precious minutes, and Jada's life could be at stake. There were just too many unknowns.

"I didn't say we would wait. I said we *should* wait," Jefferson explained as he surveyed the gate. "But we will have to climb over."

"It's not much of a gate anyway," Evie Hanson said.

She was right. It was the type of metal three-bar gate farmers and ranchers used to separate animals from each other or parts of the pasture. Jefferson only knew that because he'd spent time out at Rory's place riding horses and helping fix fence posts. It had horizontal bars and with no barbed wire or other sharp protective features.

"And MJ, no matter what happens, you need to stay behind me and the officers here," Jefferson warned. "Agreed?"

"Fine, agreed. Can we go now?"

"Of course." With one lithe move and very little effort, he was over the gate, looking back at her and trying to suppress his triumphant smile.

MJ rolled her eyes and grabbed the top bar.

Jefferson watched in barely concealed amusement as she swung her right leg over, stepping on the bar closest to the top, and then carefully brought the left leg over. While the gate didn't have any purposefully pointed hardware, she was wearing a skirt. The rough metal could still scratch her bare skin.

He walked over to assist her.

"I got it," she growled.

"Fine," he said, raising his hands and backing away.

She jumped down on the other side. Fogarty and Hanson were right behind her.

Jefferson led the way, the two officers behind him, and MJ in the rear. They approached quietly and cautiously, but without weapons drawn.

The house didn't come into view until they were a few yards down the dirt lane. It was a spring green a-frame cabin with a wrap-around wooden deck furnished with chairs and a table on one side, with a cluster of vibrant red Adirondack chairs on the other.

Other than a few trees in the way, they could see that property backed up to a stunning view of the lake.

The red front door was solid with no way to see inside, but the windows were without blinds or curtains. The place looked dark inside.

"Fogarty and Hanson, you two head around the back. Don't get too close to the house yet. Just check for lights and any movement. I'm going to check the front. MJ stay here."

Thank goodness MJ didn't protest, thought Jefferson as he crept up the steps to the door. He wanted her out of the way in case something went sideways.

Looking behind him, he glanced down at the part of the deck he'd already crossed. His footprints were clearly visible in a fine layer of dust and fallen pine needles. If someone was here, they hadn't come through this door.

Before knocking, he glanced briefly in the front window. Though dark, he could make out the furniture of a small living room.

He knocked and waited. When no one came, he knocked again, louder this time. Still nothing.

Walking back down the porch, he said, "I don't think anyone is here."

Fogarty and Hanson returned to the front. "We checked around the back. It's all dark," reported Fogarty. "No sounds. It's completely quiet."

MJ knit her brow. "She has to be here."

"It looks as if no one has been here in a while," Jefferson said, looking out toward the lake. "But now we'll give it a more thorough check."

She nodded, but he could see the distraction working on her face as she tried to figure out what to do next.

"Fogarty, Hanson. You two check around the property, any sheds or outbuildings. Don't break any locks or anything, but look in windows, listen for movement. Check for anyone on the dock. I'm going to check all doors and windows of the house."

The three of them dispersed. As Jefferson walked along the side of the house, he looked in the windows he could reach. He saw a kitchen through the side windows and a sunroom along the back. A door from the sunroom opened onto the deck. As he got closer, he could see a slight misalignment between the door and door frame.

He pulled, and the door opened easily. Splintered wood around the latch suggested someone had pried it open. He looked down to see a mass of small shoe prints, just barely visible in the fine layer of dirt.

Warily, he stepped inside. "Hello. Police."

He took a few steps. "Hello. Police. Is anyone home?"

The house was completely quiet and grew darker inside as the daylight began its descent outside. He explored the main floor without having to take a single step because it all seamlessly blended into one joint area. He took the stairs and checked each of the bedrooms and a small recreation room with a TV. Nothing.

As he turned the corner to go back down the stairs, his heart skipped a beat as he ran into MJ.

Stepping back and taking a breath, he said, "MJ, what are you doing? I told you to stay put."

"I know, but listen. That SUV we passed..."

"The G-Wagon?"

"Yes!" Her eyes were wide with alarm. "Yes! Brent Miller has a white G-Wagon, just like that one. Those are rare. It's just too much of a coincidence that he would be at the house that Poppy showed Lausch. Jada has to be at that one."

"But why would Brent Miller be there? He claimed to not know where she was." Jefferson's unease grew as he realized where this was headed. Despite the deepening shadows, the fear on MJ's face was impossible to miss.

He pointed down the stairs. "Let's go."

Chapter Twenty-Two

When they got to the other house, Jefferson looked in the passenger window of the G-wagon while MJ looked through the driver's side.

"In the cupholder," MJ whispered.

An insulated cup with the words Fairview Golf occupied one spot.

Jefferson nodded and motioned with his head toward the gate, where Fogarty and Hanson waited.

"Since we don't know the situation here, it's important that we enter quietly and prepared," Jefferson cautioned. "Officer Hanson, I'd like you to stay here at the gate. Stay under cover and watch in case Miller tries to run. Fogarty, weapon out. MJ, stay behind me and Officer Fogarty. When we get close to the house, I want to check what I can see from the windows before we make any moves."

MJ's stomach fluttered with fear. Without knowing why, she couldn't fight the feeling that Brent Miller intended to harm Jada. She had no basis for this other than intuition and the vicious pounding of her heart.

They scaled the gate noiselessly and stuck to the darkening shadows as they made their way down the drive. Like the other property, the house didn't come into view until a few yards in. Unlike the other house, lights blazed from the bottom level of the yellow a-frame cabin.

MJ and Fogarty waited just on the edge of the wooded area, watching as Jefferson made his way silently up the porch. Pressing himself against the side of the house, his gun pointed down at the deck, he turned just enough to see inside the window while staying hidden.

He snapped his head back and quickly made his way off of the porch. "Jada is there."

"Oh, thank goodness," breathed MJ, her hand on her chest where her heart slowed a beat with relief.

Jefferson's jaw tightened. "Yes, she is alive." He said evenly. "But Miller has her tied up in a chair. He has a gun."

"No," she whispered, covering her eyes with her palms. She felt frozen. The image of Jada at the mercy of Miller, with a gun, sent an icy chill down her spine. They were so close, only to have her so close to danger at the hands of a man who pretended to care about her and her family. Just beneath this despair, anger flared.

Suddenly, she threw her hands down and thrust her chin out. "We have to go in. That man will not get the chance to hurt her."

"We," Jefferson said, pointing to himself and Fogarty, "are going in. You are not."

She protested, but he took her shoulders in his hands. "MJ, I cannot risk you getting hurt. Fogarty and I know what to do. We trained for this. Taking you with us only puts you *and* Jada at risk. Please trust us and stay here."

There was just enough light left in the sky for her to see the pleading in his eyes. She did trust him, especially after everything she learned about him today. She knew Jefferson would risk his own life to save that girl.

She swallowed hard and nodded.

"Thank you." The changeable blue of his eyes had grown dark with the oncoming night and the intensity of the moment. Still, their softness lingered on her for just a few seconds longer than necessary. Regardless of the imminent danger, she flushed, grateful for the shadows.

When he released her shoulders, he turned to confer with Fogarty. The two of them slipped quietly onto the porch. Jefferson took the front, his back against the side of the house and his shoulder near the front door. Fogarty took up the same position behind him.

***

Jada pulled her hands apart, trying to loosen the duct tape that bound her arms behind the chair. He'd wrapped them too tightly. Her hands were going numb.

Mr. Miller paced the floor in front of her, a handgun swinging at his side with each step. "It's not so hard, Jada. Just tell me where the money is, and this will all be over."

Sweat glistened on his forehead. He looked insane, and she knew he'd probably kill her the minute she told him anything. "I don't know what you are talking about," she insisted. "My dad just told me to come here. He didn't say why, and he only gave me a few hundred bucks. I already told you. It's in my backpack."

Miller sat on the couch and faced her. With a bitter chuckle, he waved the gun in her direction. "I can't believe your dad thought he could hide you away with all that money. Like I'm not the one who taught him how to buy property with a shell company." He shook his head. "It hardly took any effort at all to find you. Almost as little effort as putting that needle in your dad's arm." His white-toothed smile was menacing in his dark expression.

Her heart froze. "What do you mean? What needle?"

"Oh, you haven't heard?" He slowly shook his head with a solemn expression. "I guess I get to break the news."

His face darkened as he stood in front of her. "I'm sorry to inform you that," he said in mock sincerity, "your father passed away after a drug overdose."

Jada stared. Tears prickled her eyes, but she fought them. He wanted her to cry. "You're lying."

"Nope. I'm afraid it's true. And everyone thinks you ran away, which you did," he said, swinging the gun and using it to point at her.

Jada could feel herself trembling. Her stomach hurt, and she tasted vomit at the back of her throat. She never liked Mr. Miller, and she didn't want to believe he could be horrible enough to actually kill her dad. But looking at him now, she felt sure he wouldn't hesitate to kill her. He'd already searched the entire house for the bag of money. She couldn't understand why her dad had so much cash, but she was confident that Miller would never find it.

There was a sudden, explosive noise as the door burst open, shattering off its frame.

Startled by a man's urgent shout of "Police!" Miller quickly leaped up from his seat, his gun already pointed toward the door.

Jada squeezed her eyes shut as a shot rang out.

***

For a split second, MJ stood frozen to the ground, part of her afraid of what that shot meant, and part of her trying to do as Jefferson asked and stay put.

Forget that. With a shot of adrenaline, MJ bolted toward the house. There was no grand plan in her mind. She just had to go. She had to know what happened and try to help.

She turned at the sound of footsteps behind her. Officer Hanson and two other police officers were running to the house, their weapons drawn.

MJ had just run up the porch when Hanson came up beside her. "Stay back," the woman ordered. Hanson inched toward the door with the two men, who MJ realized were sheriff's deputies.

"All clear," they heard Fogarty yell.

Hanson lowered her weapon, as did the deputies, before cautiously peering in the doorway. MJ pushed forward to see inside.

Jefferson had his knee in the back of Brent Miller with the man's hands behind his back, snapping on handcuffs. Fogarty was carefully using a pocketknife to cut the duct tape and rope that bound Jada to a kitchen chair.

The young girl seemed to be in a daze, not crying or speaking, but staring at Brent Miller as Jefferson stood him up and forced him to sit on the couch.

Slipping between the officers in the doorway, MJ stepped into the room. When Jada saw her, the girl's eyes flew open as if seeing the most amazing sight of her life.

"Ms. Brooks," she cried out. Immediately, her eyes welled up and tears cascaded down her cheeks. When the girl tried to say more, no words could make it through the sobs that were coming in rapid succession.

MJ knelt beside her just as Fogarty cut the last binding. The girl reached around and squeezed MJ around the shoulders with her shaking arms.

"My dad...is...dead," Jada waled.

"I know, sweetheart." She hugged the girl tightly and stroked her hair as the girl's tears rushed out of her.

"But you're safe now," MJ assured her as she held her. "We've got you. You're safe. Miller won't hurt you anymore."

MJ glanced up with misty eyes to see Jefferson watching her. He looked away, but what she saw there was not the neutral gaze of a detective, but the empathetic look of a man acquainted with pain.

Chapter Twenty-Three

The evidence that Brent Miller attempted to shoot Jefferson Hughes was buried in the wall under a painting of an empty blue canoe floating on a serene lake.

When Miller saw the detective's firearm pointed at him as well as Fogarty's, he'd dropped his gun in the face of such diminishing odds of escape.

Jefferson pulled a kitchen chair over and set it in front of the couch Brent Miller occupied. "Mr. Miller. I'm interested to hear your explanation for holding a teenager hostage."

Miller looked away without speaking. He wore a polo shirt and shorts as if he'd be hitting the course later.

Jada blew her nose on some toilet paper Fogarty found for her. "He..." she sucked in a big gulp of air. "He wanted the money."

Turning to look at her, Jefferson narrowed his eyes. "What money?"

"The money in the bag my dad gave me," she said, wiping her nose. "I hid it at the house next door."

Ah, this must be the same money Heather was after, thought Jefferson. He wondered if the mysterious man who broke into the Lausches' house was Brent Miller, also on the hunt for a bag of cash.

Brent Miller scowled at Jada. "I knew you had it, you little liar."

With a look of disdain, Jefferson turned on the man. "If you want to answer my questions, then you can talk. Otherwise, keep quiet."

The detective turned back to Jada. "Why did your dad give you a bag of money?"

Tears fell from her eyes again, and she dabbed at them with fresh toilet paper. "I think he knew something bad was going to happen to him." She glared at Miller. "He killed him. He just told me so, said he stuck a needle in his arm."

"She's lying," Miller shouted. "The spoiled little brat is making it all up."

"I am not," Jada said. She turned to MJ. "I swear I'm not making any of it up. I heard them fighting in my dad's office, too. Mr. Miller said Trevon would keep making the stuff, and my dad would keep doing his part of the deal, or else he'd do something to him. I couldn't hear that part very well."

A jolt of recognition hit MJ. "Do you mean Trevon from the pro shop?"

Jada nodded.

"You better shut up if you know what's good for you," Miller warned.

Jefferson grabbed Miller by the arm and pulled him up from the couch. "Fogarty. Hanson. Take this guy out to the sheriff's vehicle. I'm sure they'll want to book him, and he can wait in the Mason County jail until we get to him. Then you two can head back to the station. I appreciate your help here today."

"Yes, sir," said Fogarty.

"There are a couple of our guys out there who can take him off your hands," said one of the sheriff's deputies to Fogarty, who had Miller by the arm. Then, addressing Jefferson, he said, "I'm Deputy Williams, and I assume you are the West Sound detective."

"Hughes. It's Jefferson Hughes." The two men shook hands.

"Glad to meet you, Hughes." He had a good-natured smile. "My guys will set up a perimeter outside. The county forensics will need to collect evidence of the shooting and the hostage situation. We'll need initial statements from each of you."

Jefferson expected as much. "Sure," he said. "However, Miller will be up for a murder charge in West Sound, so I'm sure we'll be extraditing him immediately."

The deputy shrugged. "I'm sure the lawyers will figure out all the details."

After Fogarty and Hanson left with the suspect, Deputy Williams sat with MJ, Jefferson, and Jada, taking notes as they each recalled the events of the night. When finished, he thanked them and said their detectives would be in touch if they needed further information.

With the deputy off doing other tasks, Jefferson turned to Jada.

"I know it's been a long night, and you are tired of talking to people. But I'm going to ask you to tell me everything you know, from the beginning, before everything that happened here. What you've seen or heard could help us ensure people like Mr. Miller go away for a long time."

Jada's red eyes checked with MJ.

"It's okay. You can trust him. He's here to help. Do you need some water or something?"

Jada nodded, her face puffy and pale. "There's some bottled water in the fridge."

After she got the water, MJ handed it to Jada and sat on the couch. "Before you go into too much of the story, I just have to know one thing. When we traced the email from your school account, we were led to believe it came from the house next door. Which house did your dad buy?"

"This one," she said. "The people next door aren't ever there. I thought they might have internet, so I..." She glanced at Jefferson and then at the floor. "I broke in the back door." Raising her head back up, she tucked her long hair behind her ears. "You know, sometimes the router has the password on it. My dad told me not to bring my phone, but he didn't say anything about my school computer." She let out a ragged breath. "I was going to write more, but I heard a noise and got scared. So I left. I think it was just the wind."

The smile creeping across MJ's face said she approved wholeheartedly of the girl's cleverness. "I'm glad you figured that out. That's how we found you."

Jefferson leaned forward with his forearms on his knees. "So, let's start at the very beginning. Tell me the first thing that didn't seem quite right to you?"

The girl rubbed her palms on her jeans and sniffled. "It was that fight with Mr. Miller. I was supposed to be asleep, but I'd been on my phone just scrolling through stuff. I heard yelling. With just my dad and me, our house was quiet. No one ever yelled. I thought maybe my dad was watching something too loud on the TV. He did that sometimes." A tear escaped, and she wiped it away.

"I went downstairs to tell him to turn it down, but then I realized it was coming from his office. The man yelled to my dad that he made a lot of money and he shouldn't complain, that drug addicts died all the time."

MJ handed her some more toilet paper as the tears picked up again.

"I thought maybe they were talking about my mom," she said with a sudden gulp of air. She shook her head. "But I don't think they were. I heard my dad say something like, 'It's not worth the risk' or something like that. He wasn't yelling like Mr. Miller."

She took a drink of water.

"Take your time, Jada," Jefferson said. "I know this is all hard. You're being very brave."

With a long breath through her nose that she let out slowly through her mouth, the girl continued.

"My dad said something about Trevon getting in too deep, and that's when Mr. Miller got really mad and said something about just doing his part or he'd ..." She couldn't continue as a sob took over the words.

MJ went to her and put an arm around her shoulders. "Maybe we should take a break."

Jefferson agreed. "I'm going to get some water. Can you show me where it is, MJ?"

Cocking her head to the side, she gave him a confused look. After a second, her eyes widened as she grasped his meaning.

"Sure. I'll be right back, Jada."

In the kitchen, Jefferson opened the fridge and pulled out two bottles of water. He handed one to MJ. "Who is Trevon?"

"He is the student I told you about who gave me a tour of Fairview."

"Based on what you know, is it possible Trevon is cooking drugs?"

Shocked, she wrinkled her brow as she tried to imagine Trevon doing such a thing. "I don't know. He was a nice kid in middle school, but it's been a long time since then. He didn't give me that vibe, but I didn't figure Brent Miller for a murderer, either."

Jefferson opened his water. "She said something earlier—'Trevon will keep making the stuff.' And then something about him getting in too deep."

"You think these country-club types could be mixed up with that drug trafficker that hates you?"

"I know. It's weird."

With her arms folded, MJ squinted as she considered this prospect. It was just crazy enough to be true. Brent Miller wasn't the saint he played for the public, that was for sure. Who else was living a double life?

She saw Trevon in her mind, and the full meaning of Jefferson's conclusion sank in. She touched a hand to her heart. "That drug dealer will murder Trevon. We have to do something."

He already had his phone out, swiping the screen. "No service. We should get going. I'll get reception as soon as we get back on the main highway."

Just as he said this, the front door opened, and another Mason County deputy came in, followed by an officer with a camera.

The young girl sat alone on the living room chair, her arms folded and hunched over her knees. This next bit would be tough for her to navigate with her dad gone and her mom less than reliable. And MJ couldn't promise that the worst was over. If only she could make it all go away.

***

Outside the house, the red and blue lights of the sheriff's vehicles cut through the newly fallen night. The vehicles stretched down the narrow dirt road, including around the house next door. Jada had explained to the deputy where she'd hidden the bag of money. The deputies were now securing the outside of the house and waiting on the owners to give permission to enter or a warrant, whichever came first.

After thirty minutes of driving, Jefferson pulled off at a convenience store so he could call into the station. The store stood out in the surrounding darkness like a singular buoy in a black sea.

"Do you want something to eat?" MJ asked Jada.

The girl nodded. "Yeah, I'm kinda hungry. But I don't think I can eat much."

"Let's go in and get some snacks and use the bathroom."

Jefferson had just got Larson on the phone and was relaying the events of the night.

MJ grabbed her backpack and then gently touched his arm, motioning toward the store.

He nodded that he understood.

As they walked inside, MJ explained people might look at Jada with some confusion because of the news reports. She didn't want the girl to be weirded out if someone stared at her.

Sure enough, as they paid for their snacks, the cashier, a woman with brown hair that was just beginning to gray, kept a wary eye on them as she bagged their chips and cheese sticks.

Finally, her eyes stopped on Jada. "Everything okay with you, honey?" Her suspicious eyes flicked to MJ.

With a relaxed smile, Jada said she was. "You've probably seen me on the news. This is my teacher, Ms. Brooks, and she and the police found me. So, I'm good."

The woman clapped her hands. "Well, hallelujah!"

Jada's face reddened. "Thanks."

"I'm sorry hun, but we don't get enough good news these days. I'm so glad you are safe." She shook her head sadly. "I'm so sorry about your daddy."

Moisture filled Jada's eyes, and she put her head down.

"I'm sorry," said the woman. "I'll just shut up now and let you two get going."

With a gentle smile, MJ thanked the woman, who only meant well. She wrapped an arm around Jada's shoulder and led her back to the car.

Earlier in the day, on the drive to Lake Cushman, MJ discovered that the detective liked to drink sparkling water. She'd picked up one with lemon in it, but when she opened the car door, nothing but a shadow filled his seat. Jefferson was gone.

Turning back to the store in confusion, she couldn't believe he had slipped into the store without passing them. He's tricky, she thought as she and Jada climbed into the car, Jada in the back and MJ in the front passenger seat.

They said little while they waited, both crunching on potato chips.

"You should know," said MJ, turning to sit sideways and face Jada, "that it was Cade who first came to talk to me about you. He was worried because you hadn't been on your phone or anything for a long time."

Jada cringed. "I was so mean to him that day I threw the marker. That was the day after I heard my dad and Mr. Miller fighting. What they said made me feel guilty, sort of like my dad was doing dangerous things to make money just so I could have lots of clothes and stuff."

The girl took a chip out of the bag and stared at it before dropping it back in.

"That night, after the marker thing, Dad told me I had to go. He had a backpack ready for me and everything." She stared straight ahead, watching the scenes unfold in her mind. "The backpack was heavy, and he told me it was full of money. If he didn't come to meet me at the cabin, he said I should wait a month and then use the money to buy a bus ticket to my aunt's house in Texas. I've never even been there." She wiped a silent tear away.

"He took me to a bus station and told me how to change the buses to get to Lake Cushman. It only took me to the entrance, so I had to walk to the cabin with my hair up in a hat. He said it was important that no one knew where I was for a while. I couldn't take my phone because he knew I'd be too tempted to use it, and bad people could trace it."

She went quiet again.

"Your dad loved you more than anything," MJ said. "I don't know everything about what happened to him, but from what you've said, it sounds like he was trying to do the right thing."

She nodded and slowly chewed a chip. It felt like a signal that she was done talking for now. MJ turned back around in her seat. Where was Jefferson? It'd been at least fifteen minutes.

Watching the door to the convenience store, she saw a tallish man exiting. She was disappointed to see he was wearing an orange construction vest.

"Jada," she said. "I want to go check on the detective. Maybe he got hung up on a phone call or he thinks we're still in there and is waiting for us. I don't want to leave you alone, so I need you to come with me."

The girl agreed with no argument. She most likely didn't want to be alone in this dark, lonely place.

The two retraced their steps into the store. After a minute of going down the aisles and checking the bathrooms, MJ stopped to ask the cashier.

"Did you see a tall man in a nice suit come in? Blond and," she hesitated, "and good-looking, blue eyes."

"Maybe in my dreams," the woman laughed.

MJ had a terrible feeling. This was not like Jefferson at all. He should be standing by the car tapping his foot, eager to get to the station. There was no "mill or mess around" in Jefferson Hughes. Something was wrong.

"Do you have cameras outside?"

"Yeah, hun, but I can't just show them to anybody."

"Right," MJ said absently. "Okay, thank you."

She had to get in touch with the station, with Detective Jackson or Amber Wells. The fastest way would be the police radio in the car.

"Let's go back to the car," she said to Jada, trying to keep the panic out of her voice.

"What's the matter?"

Deciding to be as honest with the girl as possible, MJ said, "I'm not sure, but Detective Hughes wouldn't just leave us here. Get back in the car. I'm going to check a couple of things."

Moving around to the driver's side, MJ opened the door and popped the trunk. She searched inside, hoping to find a flashlight. She moved aside a heavy winter coat to find a plastic box the size of a cooler. Flipping the lid open, she was relieved to find a box of supplies—rubber gloves, what looked like evidence bags, crime-scene tape, and a flashlight.

Before grabbing the flashlight, she grasped the edge of the trunk, squeezing her eyes shut. She willed Jefferson to walk around the corner of the convenience store. He'd apologize and say he had to check something in the back or find a spot with better cell service. But she knew he wouldn't. A sense of dread settled deep in her bones; something terrible had happened to Jefferson.

MJ didn't know exactly what to do, but she knew that letting him down wasn't an option. Her next move could mean life or death for him.

With a deep breath, she steeled her spine, shaking the despondency from her attitude. A new sense of resolve flowed through her as she reached in and grabbed the flashlight, ready to do whatever it took to get Jefferson Hughes back, safe and sound.

First, she'd see if anything was left behind, any clue about what had happened in this parking lot. Jefferson would have found some way to communicate the situation; she was sure of it.

Lighting up the ground on the driver's side of the car, she thought there were a few torn weeds that grew through the concrete, but she couldn't be sure. Even if that were the case, it could be from anyone's shoe or boot as they got out of their vehicle.

"Come on, Jefferson, give me something," she pleaded in a whisper as she continued searching for signs from the missing detective.

A glint of metal just under the tire caught her eye. It was a key fob. No, it was *the* key fob for the unmarked car they'd been riding in.

Whatever else had happened, she felt sure Jefferson dropped the key for her to find. Energized, she continued sweeping the flashlight around the car.

Just as she was about to open the driver-side door, the flashlight illuminated a marking in the dust coating the rear door. She shined the light directly on it.

With their finger, someone had hastily scrawled the letter "N."

Her heart sank. Jefferson had left this mark to let her know Nico had taken him.

She jumped in the front seat, pulled out the police radio, and pushed the button. "Hello, is anyone there?"

Static.

"Hello," she repeated. "Are you there? West Sound PD, are you there?"

The static continued, but this time she could hear the faint outline of a voice.

"Listen," she said. "I can't understand you, but I hope you can understand me. This is MJ Brooks. Detective Jefferson Hughes is missing. I believe he may have been taken by Nico. Please get this message to the chief and Amber Wells. I am going to try calling the front desk with my cell phone."

She let go of the button to listen. Again, static and a faint voice.

Reaching to the floor of the passenger side, MJ found her backpack and dug out her phone. First, she called Jefferson's number. A buzzing from under the driver's seat revealed its location. She reached under the seat and grabbed it. Of course, it was password-protected.

Jada sat forward and grabbed the headrest of the passenger seat. "What are we going to do?"

"I'm going to get that store video." She found the number for the station in her contacts and was just about to call when her phone buzzed in her hand.

"Hello?"

"MJ, this is Amber. The dispatcher relayed your message. Tell me what happened."

As quickly as possible, MJ relayed what she knew.

"Here's what we'll do. The Mason County Sheriff can handle getting the video and sending it to us. It would be best if you got Jada to the station. Can you drive the car?"

"Yes. I have the keys. Am I allowed to drive it? I feel weird. It's a police car."

"Technically, no, but I don't like the two of you waiting there, since Nico's men know your location. Just be careful and, as tempted as you might be, don't touch any buttons and don't use the blue lights."

MJ tried to smile at the image of her racing along the highway, blue lights flashing, but the growing pit inside of her prevented it. "We're going to find him, right?"

"Yes, we will find him. I promise you that."

Chapter
Twenty-Four

The only light in the room came from a crack under the door. Someone on the other side of that door was smoking weed. The smell choked Jefferson as if they were blowing the smoke in his face.

His arms ached. They'd taped his wrists together behind his back and around a pole in a surprisingly immaculate garage. When they first dragged him to the chair and removed his blindfold, the lights were still on. Jefferson had observed as much of his surroundings as possible in the short time before they turned out the lights.

The walls were white and unmarked. No tools hung anywhere. The floor had a gray epoxy coating that appeared flawless, and there was an empty workbench with a couple of stools in front of it. Otherwise, a black SUV appeared to be the only thing in the room with Jefferson. The faint smell of oil and rubber mingled unpleasantly with the weed.

Just before the garage went dark, he'd noticed just the tip of a man's shoe, as if someone were lying on his stomach on the farther side of the SUV.

Jefferson's stomach turned. Nico had likely already started his killing today.

The lights went out and duct tape covered his mouth and held his ankles to the chair they'd forced him into. He hadn't seen Nico yet, but Jefferson knew he was there.

The three men who had ambushed him at the convenience store worked for Nico. One of them had the same tattoo as Victor Cano.

Jefferson tried to shift his body to relieve the pressure on his shoulders. It didn't help.

He thought of MJ and Jada and hoped that they would get away. The idea of Nico's men going back for them stabbed at his gut.

Earlier, while MJ and Jada were in the store, Jefferson had finished his call and stepped out of the car to stretch his legs. That's when he felt the gun in his back.

"Do exactly what I tell you or those pretty ladies riding with you will pay the price. Play nice, we leave them alone."

The man smelled of body odor and cigarettes.

"Alright, I understand. You'll get no problems from me."

"Wise man." The guy took Jefferson's gun from his shoulder holster. "Pop the trunk."

He knew then that they were after the money. How Nico knew where they were, and that Lausch's money was in Mason County, was a mystery. They were about to be very disappointed.

Jefferson opened the door and pulled the latch to release the trunk. At the same time, he dropped the key fob next to the tire, hoping MJ would find it. She and Jada needed to get out of there before any of Nico's men got the bright idea of coming back for them.

The man pushed Jefferson toward two other men, also Nico's goons. "Watch him." One of them turned Jefferson around and thrust his gun into his back, attempting to conceal the nature of this little meeting from any passing prying eyes.

"Where's the money?" the first gun-toting man asked, staring into the trunk. A sliver of light from the store fell across one glaring eye as he faced Jefferson. The look was intimidating, but the detective also heard a note of fear in the question..

Jefferson couldn't hide a smirk, revealing how much of an idiot he considered the guy in front of him. "Oh, you thought I would have the money?" he asked, playing up the incredulity of the idea. "Man, this isn't my jurisdiction, so that evidence will stay with the Mason County Sheriff."

The malignant stare he received held equal measures of fury and dread. This man had failed in at least one of two tasks Nico assigned him. People who failed Nico regretted it.

"Check the inside the car," the man ordered the other henchmen.

As they did, Jefferson reached out with his pinky and, with little movement, carved an 'N' in the dust covering the rear door of his unmarked police car.

The men reported finding nothing inside.

"Get him in the truck," the man sneered.

Once in the SUV, they kept him blindfolded, so Jefferson could only guess that they'd driven back to West Sound.

He hadn't expected Nico to have his men following Miller, and now, trapped in this garage, he hadn't a clue how to get himself out of this situation. At least he'd been able to tell Larson about Miller and the possible connection to Trevon. He hoped they had units on their way to Fairview to get the kid.

He leaned forward in the chair, trying to break the duct tape around his wrists. While taping his hand behind the pole had the effect of creating more discomfort and pain for him, it also created a small space between his skin and the tape, enough to move the tape back and forth against the pole. It had already loosened a fraction.

Suddenly, the light in the garage flipped on.

Squinting against the sudden brightness, Jefferson could see a man coming toward him. As his eyes adjusted and the figure came closer, there was no mistaking that the man was Nico.

He pulled a stool over from the workbench and sat in front of Jefferson.

"We meet at last, Detective Hughes." He slouched on the stool like a man without a care. In his mind, he'd just bagged his prize in a years-long vendetta.

Nico sat with one foot on the ground and the other resting on a rung in the middle of the stool. Though still a young man, he looked worn beyond his years. His hair had receded, so he'd shaved it, which is probably why his guys also shaved their heads. No need to incur the boss's wrath by reminding him he was balding.

He wore tan chinos and a light blue button-down shirt with muted off-white stripes—more country club than drug boss.

"This place is nice, eh?" said Nico. "You should see the inside. Es hermosa. I always stay in such style here. I have friends, you know. They run part of my business where we buy beautiful houses." His teeth glistened as he proffered a cheesy grin. "They are a good investment—an excellent way to use the cash we take in around here."

"But," he said, suddenly turning serious, "they have gone off my rails." Nico cocked his head. "Off the rails?" He waved his hand. "Whatever. They have been cheating me out of money, and I can't have that."

"Ty!" He yelled toward the door.

The door opened and a burly man, also with a shaved head, dragged a boy, who looked no older than sixteen, down the steps into the garage. Another henchman followed with a chair.

The kid's face matched the color of the floor. He was going to pass out or throw up. Duct tape on your mouth and throwing up could be a deadly combination.

"So, this here is Trevon," Nico explained as the two men forced the kid into the chair and taped him to it. "I have to take this Trevon—this little a boy because Brent Miller made him cut my drugs with that cheap poison. Well, to be fair, drugs are dangerous. I never touch them. But you," he said, pointing at Trevon, "you cooked that poison. You killed people."

Jefferson's heart sank. Nico had been a step ahead of them this whole time. His message to Larson had been too late.

The kid whimpered and turned his wild eyes on Jefferson. The detective tried to project calm, but it didn't help.

"I mean, you even marked your stupid stuff with an F, like I couldn't figure out that was Fairview. Miller loves that name so much. He wears it on all his clothes." The chuckle that rolled out of him had no mirth in it. Instead, Nico was like a simmering pot of violence that could boil over at any minute. He could whip out a gun and shoot them both before finishing the next sentence.

"After we put a tracker on Miller's car, figuring he was trying to find the money his stupid partner hid, he led us right to it. We planned to get it, then put a bullet in his head, and all would be fine." He gestured toward Jefferson. "Then you showed up, and now Brent Miller, who I really want to get my hands on, and my money, are locked up."

Nico sighed. "You have been a pain in my side for too long, my friend. First, you lied your way into your brother's good graces, and then you used him to destroy my entire business. Man," he chuckled, "that little bro hates you. He probably hates you more than I do."

Despite facing a probable death, this statement pierced Jefferson with more pain than any bullet could. He wished Nico was lying, but he realized he didn't know his brother anymore. He'd been naive, just like Amber said. The truth stung.

"So," continued Nico, "that's why I have a special surprise for you. A reunion you could say." The enjoyment with which Nico said these words came from the darkest of places. He could only mean one thing, and Jefferson felt his heart turn cold.

"Alex!" Nico yelled with his eyes fixed on Jefferson, waiting to see the horrible realization the moment it manifested in the detective's expression.

The door to the house opened. It was Alex, but it wasn't Alex, because the man walking into the garage bore almost no resemblance to the little brother he'd seen just a year ago at his father's funeral.

When Alex stood in front of Jefferson, hatred filled every feature of his face with menace.

Nico put an arm around his shoulder. "Alex here has requested to have the honor of killing you."

Chapter Twenty-Five

Officer Fogarty and Detective Jackson met MJ and Jada outside the station. When she handed Fogarty the key, a flush of anxiety rested on his boyish face, but he couldn't seem to get any words out. She smiled weakly, knowing there wasn't much reassurance in it.

Detective Jackson walked them into the station, asking if they were okay and if they needed anything. The sparkle of humor he normally carried about him was absent. Instead, rings of worry hung under his eyes.

Inside the station, people moved with frenetic energy. It looked as though every officer in the city, county, and state, as well as FBI agents, were in this one room.

Some turned to look at them. The strained concern on their faces made Jefferson's disappearance all too real. A lump formed in her throat, and she had to stop and take a deep breath.

"MJ, you need to sit down," Rory insisted, trying to lead her to a chair.

"I'm fine," she said, putting an arm around Jada. "Where should we go?"

"There's a room for children down the hall from the regular interview rooms. It has a couch, TV, drinks, and food, anything you might need."

A woman MJ had never seen at the station came forward. She was in regular street clothes, and she didn't seem like a police officer or detective.

"Hi, MJ and Jada," the woman said, sticking her hand out. "I'm Deanna Michaels. I'm a youth advocate with Rainier County here to help Jada with whatever she needs and to make sure she is in a safe place."

"Hi," Jada said in a sound barely above a whisper.

"Let's head down to the children's room, and you can sit down, rest, and get what you need. We can talk more when you're ready," Deanna said with a friendly smile.

Rory led them all down toward the room. On the way, they passed the waiting area for the regular interview rooms. MJ was shocked to see Shannon sitting there with an older woman. Shannon had her arm draped around the woman's shoulders, seeming to console her.

"Shannon?"

Her friend looked up with tired, lackluster eyes. "MJ! I'm so glad to see you. And Jada! Thank goodness, sweetie. We were so worried about you."

"Thank you, Ms. Davis."

MJ told Jada to follow Deanna Michaels and Detective Jackson to the other room. "I'll catch up in just a minute."

She nodded. The girl was exhausted.

"What are you doing here?" MJ asked as she hugged Shannon.

"Well, you remember my Aunt Susan," she said, putting a hand on the woman's shoulder.

MJ realized the older woman was the bride's mother from the wedding reception.

"Of course," she said. "It's good to see you again, though this doesn't look like a happy occasion."

Shannon's aunt could only shake her head and take in a ragged breath.

"No," said Shannon. "It's my Uncle Glen. He's missing, and we are really worried about him. We are waiting to see if they can track his phone."

This was not good news, and MJ struggled to keep the dread out of her expression. Glen was most likely embroiled in whatever got Mr. Lausch killed and Brent Miller arrested.

"I'm sorry," was all she could say.

Shannon squeezed her aunt's shoulder. "Everyone seems very busy. Do you know what's going on?"

MJ rubbed her face, trying to force the sting away from her eyes. "Jefferson—Detective Hughes. He's missing."

Her mouth fell open in shock. "No! How?"

Blowing out a breath, MJ looked down at her feet. She was tired, and it'd been a stressful night. Her emotions were too close to the surface.

When she met Shannon's gaze again, she'd tamped down the tears. "It's complicated, but I don't think it's good. I'm going to see what I can find out. Give me your uncle's number. Maybe, if he has a minute, I can get Jared on it. He's this really smart FBI tech guy."

"That would be great, MJ," said Shannon.

Her aunt pulled a pen and a small scrap of paper from her purse. "Here it is," she whispered, barely able to get the words out.

"I can't promise, but I'll try." She squeezed Shannon's hand. "If I hear anything about your uncle, I'll come to tell you right away."

They hugged again, and MJ headed to the hub where everyone was working.

***

"It's not like the DEA can just call up this source," Amber was saying. "It has to be very orchestrated, or they risk getting him killed. I've briefed my DEA friend on the situation. They're working on it. Trust me, Larson, I want to find Jefferson as much as you do."

Larson had his hands on his hips and turned away, running a hand over his bald head. "Come on! We have to do something," he said. "He doesn't have much time."

"What do you mean he doesn't have much time?" asked MJ as she joined them.

Amber cast a fleeting glance back at Larson.

The detective sighed, bending his head and rubbing his forehead.

Leaning against a desk with her arms folded, Amber seemed to debate what to say. Finally, a grim determination settled over her expression. "We think Nico wants to clean up this mess and get out of town as fast as possible. He won't drag this out."

MJ closed her eyes and bowed her head. This couldn't be happening. They'd been through so much already today. She heard again in her mind Jefferson apologizing for rambling on about his brother, saw his hand through his hair and that stupid crooked smile.

In what universe did an evil, violent man like Nico get to decide the fate of a man like Jefferson Hughes? She could feel the anger rising. Not the type of anger she needed to control, but a motivating rush of injustice. This good man could not die this way. No, this would not happen. Nico would not win.

She opened her eyes, realizing she'd balled her hands into fists. She unfurled them and flexed her hands.

"Then let's find him," MJ said with defiance blazing in her eyes, her muscles taut with the need to act. "Nico does not get to do this. We will find him."

Amber nodded, but MJ had the distinct feeling there was something they hadn't told her.

"We think they also have Trevon, the boy Jefferson called about." Amber tilted her head toward Larson.

His jaw tightened. "We sent a couple of units out to pick him up at the Pro Shop. It was closed, but a clerk was still there and said Trevon left for lunch and never came back. We got an address for an apartment in town, but no one was home there."

This news added to the urgency. MJ felt another surge of energy pulse through her. "That's what Miller would want you to think. But we know more than they think we do, and we have a resource they didn't count on."

Larson narrowed his eyes. "What do you mean?"

She pointed to her legs. "A skort."

"What's a—"

"What do you know?" Amber asked, pushing away from the desk, a light in her eyes that hadn't been there a few seconds ago.

She explained that when she took the tour at Fairview, Trevon had told her he lived in a house in the neighborhood, a house Lausch owned and had supposedly wanted to rent. Now she knew he was living in that house for free, likely in return for his services with the drugs.

"That's where he was cooking the drugs," Amber said, her hands moving up to her head. "MJ, I could kiss you right now!"

Suddenly and shockingly, Amber climbed on the desk and gazed around the room. "Everyone," she called out. After a few seconds, the room went eerily silent, the fear that there was bad news hanging on the faces of the men and women working so hard to prevent it.

"Listen up. Ron and Julia, I need you two over here now. Everyone else, get in the briefing room now." She glanced down at MJ. "We are going to find him."

Chapter Twenty-Six

"Hello, bro," Alex sneered.

Jefferson could only stare. He knew his eyes shone with naked hurt, but there was no hiding it.

Alex laughed. "You still thought I could be saved, didn't you?" He leaned into Jefferson's face. "Well, I don't need to be saved," he hissed.

Bending his head, Jefferson tried to escape the hatred that confirmed his deepest fears, the reality he didn't want to believe. Any fight he needed to survive this moment had vanished. He felt vulnerable, an unfamiliar feeling of weakness invading him physically and mentally.

"Look at me," Alex yelled, his spittle hitting his older brother.

Trevon wept next to him. Jefferson turned to see his shoulders shaking as the sobs and fear wracked his body.

Alex grabbed his chin and forced his face back to his. "You can't save him any more than you could save me, big brother. You've just wasted your whole life trying to fight what everyone wants." He straightened up and gestured toward Jefferson. "Man, drugs are what everyone wants, and we just make sure they get it. You," he snickered. "You think you're some kind of hero."

A spark of anger flickered in Jefferson's eyes.

"What? You think I'm lying?" Alex turned to look back at Nico. "I need to hear him crying."

Nico nodded. "You can take the tape off his mouth, bro, but if he yells, shoot him."

With one move, Alex ripped the tape from Jefferson's face. It felt like he took a layer of skin with it.

Jefferson licked his lips. Then he set them in a thin line with the small amount of defiance left in him. He wasn't going to give Nico the satisfaction of witnessing his complete and utter horror at Alex's act of brotherly betrayal. He thought briefly of their mother, but pushed the thought away. Imagining how his death would crush her, how she would lose two sons to the dehumanizing and cruel drug trade wouldn't serve him now. He had to focus his anger on Nico, on the system, the continued influx of drugs that killed and ruined so many lives, and the money changing hands between the lowest of humankind.

"Ah, there it is," said Alex. "That look of disgust. The look that always said you were better than me."

"I was never better than you," Jefferson croaked, his throat dry and raw from the duct tape. "I missed you."

Nothing. No small sign of affection, regret, love, or even hurt showed in his brother's narrowed brown eyes, once so large and innocent.

"You're pathetic."

"While I am enjoying this walk down memory lane, you need to do the deed, little bro," warned Nico.

Alex turned around to face him. "Man, you promised I could torture him first."

"Did you just mean mind torture or am I gonna see some blood, bro?"

"Oh, there will be blood. But..." he whispered the last part. "I need a hit first, you know, to be more effective."

Nico snorted. "Shoot, you see what I deal with?" he said to Jefferson. "This guy using up all our supply." He stood up. "Put the tape back on his face. Then, as soon as you got your mojo on, you do the deed, both of them, then we split."

Alex pulled off a piece of fresh duct tape and slapped it over Jefferson's mouth. "I'm going to give you a little time to think about all the painful things I am going to do to you."

Jefferson cast his eyes down, not wanting to see the bloodthirsty aggression in his brother's once innocent eyes.

Alex kicked Jefferson's ankles as he left.

Then the two were gone, having turned the lights out again.

Chapter Twenty-Seven

While MJ had glimpsed the sale agreement for Trevon's house in Dan Lausch's home office, she couldn't recall the address. Ron tracked down two properties belonging to Lausch in Fairview, one being his residence, meaning the other had to be where Trevon lived and possibly cooked drugs.

The team focused on that house first, surmising that Lausch likely let Trevon live there in return for using his drug-cooking skills.

MJ was not invited to come along, which was fine with her. Although she wanted to be there to see that Jefferson was safe, she knew that breaking down doors and facing a possible shootout was not within her skill set or on her bucket list of desired experiences.

Instead, when the team was gone, she wanted to go check on Shannon and Jada.

First, she found Jared.

The young man gazed intensely at his screen, which wasn't very unusual for him, but this time, he was not typing or working on anything. He looked at a map with a series of red dots moving along it.

"Is that them?" she asked quietly.

"Yes. It's the GPS trackers on the vehicles."

They didn't spare any personnel for this operation. The show of force would be extreme with several law enforcement agencies, including the West Sound police, county sheriff, state troopers, and federal agents. MJ didn't know who all of them were or which agencies they served, but they were a threatening force, with most of them in tactical gear and serious weapons.

"Another man is missing who may be involved."

Jared flicked his eyes to her before returning to the screen. "Who?"

"My friend's uncle. He hasn't checked in with his family, and they are anxious."

"Has it been twenty-four hours?"

MJ shook her head with a long sigh. "No, in fact, I saw him this morning."

"I am going to guess that they want to track his phone."

"Yes. I have his number."

Jared continued to watch the screen. "Do you think Nico has him?"

"My gut tells me he does."

The mop-headed young man turned to her. "Do we have anything that ties him to the current operation?"

MJ considered his question. The only thing she knew for sure was that they had some business dealings together, they were friends, and they shared a weekly golf game.

"They were business partners, probably on this whole drug scheme."

"That's not enough for the cellular network to give us the information." His voice betrayed no feeling on the matter. Some might see him as cold, but MJ knew that was just his way.

She smoothed the scrap of paper with the phone number between her fingers, trying to come up with some clever way to get around this issue of rules and compliance. What would an eighth grader do?

Somehow, she didn't think hiding her phone under a desktop while texting or spending long minutes in the bathroom would help.

"Leave me the number and his name. I'll see what I can do," Jared said, moving his eyes back to the map on his screen. "They're almost there."

The red dot moved along the winding road to the Fairview Gates. MJ's stomach did an uncomfortable flip, and she found that watching the screen was not comforting.

She picked up a pen and wrote Glen's name on the scrap with the phone number. "Thanks, Jared. I'm going to go check on Jada."

***

MJ updated Shannon and her aunt on the way to check on Jada. She told them it could take some time to trace the cell phone because they had to clear some legal hurdles. But she let them know Jared was working on it. MJ would have told the two women to go home, but she did not want Shannon trying to take her aunt back to Fairview right now. The potential for a gun battle or dangerous men fleeing into the neighborhood was all too real.

When she walked into the children's room, the lights were dim and Jada was fast asleep on the couch, covered in a smiling emoji-themed blanket.

Deanna Michaels sat in a chair nearby with a blanket on her lap. Her eyes were closed, but flew open the moment MJ entered.

"Sorry," MJ whispered.

Deanna shook her head and whispered back. "No problem. I was awake. Just listening to a podcast in one ear." She pulled out a small earbud and smiled.

MJ moved closer, careful not to make too much noise, and sat in an armchair across from Deanna. "How is she?"

The other woman tilted her head to the side. "Remarkably well for all she's been through. I think your being with her today has something to do with it. She couldn't stop talking about you and how you and the detective saved her." She smiled, her eyes soft and kind. "The fact that she is even talking about it...That's a good sign. But there's a lot she'll still need to process."

"What will happen to her?"

Deanna looked at the sleeping girl, her eyes soft but with tiny creases in the corners. "I'm not sure yet. Her mom doesn't seem to want legal custody, and I think, given her history, that's a good thing. Maybe her mom can get herself in a better place someday, but she's not there right now. Jada has an aunt in Texas, but given the time difference and all that's happened, we won't contact her until Monday. Jada says she has friends she can stay with for now. The McCanns?"

MJ nodded. "Yes, they are a wonderful family, and I believe they've been like a second home for her. That would be a good place."

"Well, hearing that from you helps."

Watching Jada sleep, MJ felt her own exhaustion, but it was quickly overpowered by the restless dread burrowing itself through her bones. She was afraid of the moment the news about Jefferson came.

Sure, he had annoyed her and tried to keep her out of his investigations, but MJ knew that had more to do with his rigid determination to do things the right way. It also had a lot to do with him trying to keep her out of danger. She tended to walk into it, she knew that. Jefferson fiercely needed to protect people, especially people he cared about, like his brother. Not that he cared about her…She wouldn't go that far, but he was a good person; the kind the world needs more of. He didn't deserve whatever he was going through right now.

She couldn't sit any longer. "I'll check on her again later," MJ said, trying to hide her agitation. She had to find some place she could be alone.

Deanna nodded, but watched her with careful eyes. "Be sure you are taking care of yourself, too."

"I will. Thanks."

MJ hurried out of the room, not sure where she was going. She ran into Julia as she entered the hub.

"MJ," Julia said gently, holding her shoulders. "Are you okay?"

"Yes, I just need to step outside to get some air."

The agent's face softened as she studied her. "I'll let you know when we hear something."

"Thanks."

When MJ made it through the lobby and out the front doors, she walked a few feet away, out of the glare of the streetlight, to a spot covered in shadows. The cool air brushed her face with the salty mist rolling in from the sound. She breathed it in, holding her arms out as it covered her. She loved this feeling. Closing her eyes, she could almost imagine being at home on the beach with Edgar.

The damp air had grown colder as the sun escaped to warm another part of the world. Despite this, she barely registered that her legs, still in a skort, were chilled and covered in goosebumps.

The streets were quiet as the entire city seemed to hold its breath, wanting to know but not wanting to know.

MJ folded her arms around her waist and waited.

Chapter Twenty-Eight

The lights struck Jefferson's eyes with a momentary blindness as Nico and Alex came back into the garage.

Trevon raised his head with a whimper. Jefferson wished he could have at least talked to the kid while their captors were out of the room, but the tape made it impossible. Even with all of his effort, he hadn't made more than a centimeter change in loosening the tape around his wrists.

Alex grabbed one stool and dragged it noisily to a spot in front of Jefferson.

To the detective's horror, he saw that his brother now had a fat-bladed hunting knife in his hand.

"You like that?" Alex asked, holding it gripped in one hand with the pointer finger of the other hand on the sharp tip. "I took this off some wasted guy when I was tent living in Portland." He rotated the knife around. "If you don't know how to drop out properly, people will scavenge your stuff." He said it with an air of pride, as if his ability to survive and thrive in lawless homeless camps was a skill he could put on a resume.

"It's too bad George can't be here," Alex said, referring to their older brother. "This would be quite the reunion of the Hughes brothers."

At the mention of their brother, Jefferson closed his eyes and lowered his head. At least their mom would have George who still lived in Redding, the one brother who'd married and brought the joy of grandkids to their mom's life. But even that joy would be overshadowed by what happened today in this garage. Alex killing Jefferson would devastate both their brother and their mother. That realization cut through him worse than whatever Alex planned to do with his knife.

"Let's go, bro," called Nico behind him. "We don't got all day."

Alex moved his stool closer to Jefferson, his eyes appraising his brother's appearance. "You always loved your clothes." He took the knife and stabbed Jefferson's left pant leg and slit the fabric up to his knee.

"You still like to play basketball, bro?" Alex licked his lips as a wicked smile slowly widened to show his teeth. "Let's start with a little thigh muscle. I always hated that you beat me at every game. But today, this is one you won't win."

He set the tip of the knife on Jefferson's thigh. Then, with a gleam in his eye, he twisted. Jefferson didn't look down, but the immediate pain of his flesh being opened by the knife made him lightheaded, and he thought he might vomit.

He stared at Alex, whose eyes were focused on his with fierce, dark enjoyment. He didn't look down, but Jefferson could feel the blood trickling down his leg as Alex continued to twist, slowly but continuously moving the tip of the knife deeper into Jefferson's thigh.

"Not even a sound. The stoic older brother, always a man of strength and determination. Top of his class in high school, law school, and then he does what? Becomes a dirty cop."

Jefferson's eyes watered from the pain.

"Let's try the other leg, shall we?" Alex once again sliced his pants up to the knee.

Alex chuckled. "You remember how I used to say I wanted to be a doctor? Well, look at me now! I got meds and here I am doing surgery."

Nico chuckled behind him. "Bro, that's the lamest torture speech I ever heard. You need to work on your evil side. And I'm getting bored. You need to just kill the dude."

"I'm getting to it," Alex promised.

"Well, I need some more entertainment, so I'm gonna take out the kid." He stood up and pulled a pistol from his waistband, pointing it at Trevon's head.

Bang!

But the noise came from inside the house. Booming voices and thundering feet reached their ears like a herd of wild horses had broken in.

Nico dropped the gun to his side. "What the—"

Gunfire erupted inside the house and Alex stood and turned wide eyes to Nico.

They heard a chopper overhead. Lights flashed outside, and it sounded like an army had surrounded them.

Suddenly, the garage door to the house burst open.

Alex whipped back to Jefferson and bent down to look into the detective's face, the knife still in his hand.

Jefferson wished he could speak. Tell him not to do this. If he puts the knife on Jefferson now, one of the officers will take him out.

To his surprise, this time Alex's eyes were wide and clear, more like the old Alex. His face was so close to Jefferson's that there was only a slice of air between them. His little brother smiled gently and whispered, "They made it. You're going to be okay. I love you, big brother."

"Drop the knife!" A group of officers in tactical gear was spilling into the garage, their rifles ready, and one pointed at Alex.

He dropped the knife and raised his arms.

Chapter
Twenty-Nine

A paramedic cleaned the wound in Jefferson's leg.

"It's not too deep," she said while taping a bandage on his thigh. "But you'll likely need a stitch or two. We can take you in."

He sat on a gurney in the back of the rig. There was no way he would tell this paramedic about the lightheadedness washing over him. He knew the cause. The extreme emotional duress of thinking you are going to die—and that you are going to die because someone you love is going to kill you—is bound to cause a physical response. Doctors couldn't fix that. He would just deal with it. The feeling would go away soon.

"Thanks, but if you just put a couple of butterfly bandages on, I'll get it taken care of in the morning."

She gave him a stern look. "Don't blow it off, detective. You don't know what else could've been on that knife. You need a deep tissue cleaning and stitches."

"And some new pants," added the boisterous Rory, approaching the back of the rig in his black tactical gear and vest. "You'll do anything to buy a new suit, won't you Jeffy?" He grinned through his ginger beard.

They clasped hands. "Seriously, man. I'm glad you made it out of there," Rory said, his voice heavy with genuine relief. The steadiness of his gaze betrayed the weight of the night's events.

Jefferson nodded, not trusting himself to speak about it yet. He'd scaled the range of emotions tonight, and he wasn't sure yet where he'd landed.

"We done here?" he asked the paramedic.

"If you say so," she said, putting her hands up.

"Thank you, I mean it. I will take care of it," Jefferson promised. Then he gingerly climbed out of the rig, using Rory's shoulder for assistance.

His leg stung, but once on the ground, it handled his weight just fine.

The lights of the different law enforcement vehicles flashed on the surrounding stately Fairview homes like garish holiday strobe lights. A few residents watched the show of force from their doorways.

A smiling Amber approached, still wearing her FBI vest. "Am I glad to see you, detective." She reached on her tiptoes and wrapped him in an enormous hug.

"Not half as glad as I am to see you all." When she released him, he asked in a low voice, "Where's my brother?"

Without changing her smile, she said simply and quietly, "We'll talk about that later."

The finality in her tone meant he wouldn't get any more than that out of her right now. He sensed that any conversations about Alex would happen outside of anyone else's earshot.

"How's the kid?" he asked, wincing at the stinging in his wound.

Her smile faded as she sighed. "He's physically unharmed, but given the amount of drugs he's manufactured, the deaths that occurred, he's likely to spend time in prison, unless he can implicate people farther up the chain."

At least he is alive, thought Jefferson. They were just seconds away from Nico putting a bullet in his head. He was glad he didn't have to give MJ that news.

MJ. Had she got away? Did she find the car keys? He was almost certain she had. MJ was too sharp to miss the clues he'd left, but he was almost afraid to ask.

He cleared his throat. "What about MJ and Jada? Did they make it back to West Sound?" Keeping his voice professional was difficult. There was a softness in the words that he hoped only he noticed.

The flashing lights played across Amber's face so that he couldn't be sure, but he thought he saw a poorly suppressed grin there.

"They made it. And it is because of MJ that we are here. Or I should say, because of MJ's skort."

"Still don't know what a skort is," said Larson, walking up to join them, with Mendez and the chief close behind.

Jefferson looked askance. "Her skort?"

Amber laughed. "In a way. Something Trevon said while escorting her on the 'fake' tour led us here." She tilted her head toward the house where Nico held him captive, a monstrously large French Chateau-style home that was now crawling with law enforcement.

He couldn't believe it. After mocking her for going to such extremes, MJ's ruse to get into Fairview came back to save his life. She'd never let him forget it.

"Detective Hughes," said the chief in his low, rumbling voice. "You should be heading to the hospital."

Jefferson shook the hand the chief offered. "The paramedic patched me up. If it's okay with you, sir, I'd like to go to first thing tomorrow."

"I don't blame you, son. You've had a long day. Did your paramedic make a record of the injury?"

"Yes, sir, she did."

"Fine, but get there soon." He looked down at Jefferson's legs with one bushy eyebrow raised, creating a thick row of wrinkles above his eye. "I'm assuming one reason for your hesitation is the state of your pants."

Mendez slapped him good-naturedly on the shoulder. "I think I might have finally out dressed you today."

"Whatever, Mendez," said Larson. "I bet Jeffy here has sweats in his locker nicer than your pants."

Jefferson laughed along with the rest. Just a few minutes ago, he wasn't sure he would see any of their faces again. He'd been certain of his impending murder at the hands of his own brother. But in the end, his crew found him.

Larson guzzled a bottle of water. Even in the cool darkness of the night, his face was glistening with sweat. "On a more awful note, the other guy didn't make it. The one on the ground beside the car. He was already dead when we got to him."

"Who is it?" asked Jefferson.

Rory cringed. "It's the uncle of MJ's friend, that pretty blonde school counselor we met at the Lausches' house. She and her aunt have been waiting at the station, hoping to get his phone tracked. We were all a little tied up, and he's an adult man who has been missing less than twenty-four hours." They all knew what he meant. They could track cell phones, but without a warrant or knowledge of immediate danger, the legal requirements meant to protect the public's privacy also bound their hands.

"I got a look at him," said Larson. "He'd been dead for a while. No warrant to ping his cell phone was going to save him."

Jefferson could feel the exhaustion kicking in. He rubbed his forehead. "Her uncle must have been in on the scheme."

Amber patted his shoulder. "Let's head over to the van. Larson and Mendez here can take an initial statement from you and then I will take you home. Ron and Julia have been working on all the financial stuff. We'll go over everything right after you visit the doctor tomorrow."

He grinned. They would not let him get out of seeing the doctor.

As much as he wanted to know everything this minute, Jefferson had to admit that home sounded pretty good.

Chapter Thirty

The wind picked up just enough that MJ felt the night's chill as she stood in the shadows outside the station.

Yellow rays from the streetlight washed the sidewalk before the light faded into black around the edges, and then the next streetlight picked up the task of dispersing the darkness. No matter how many street-lights dotted this city, they would never eliminate the deep, churning pools of night where the dark did its business.

She hated that it existed, that good people with a powerful light had to go in and sweep out those corners. Danger hid there, waiting for opportunities to take those good people from their friends and family. Misery loves company, or at least loves to hurt the company.

She had to get out of this darkness. It was invading her mood, filling her with dread and fear. She needed to think with light and optimism.

She walked back under the streetlight. Jefferson had to win. The people out there risking their lives to save him had to win. Nico needed to lose. He was part of the underbelly that stunk up this world. Maybe he was innocent once, but he'd made his choices, and his choices were hurting people she cared about.

She turned at the sound of light footsteps behind her.

Julia came to stand next to her, staring ahead into the street. She stood silently for a few heartbeats. Then she said, "They got him."

She spoke so quietly that MJ felt a hitch in her heart. What did "got him" mean? Taking in another breath of the sea-soaked air, she dared to turn her face toward Julia.

With a guarded smile, Julia met her gaze. "Jefferson is safe. He refused to go to the hospital, so Amber is taking him home."

"Hospital?" MJ asked, her eyes wide with alarm.

"He's fine," Julia assured her. "Otherwise, they'd never in a million years let him go home, no matter how much he fought it. No, he's fine. So is that Trevon kid."

"Oh, thank goodness." MJ bent over and rested her arms on her knees as she processed the relief that broke over her at the news. They'd made it in time. They'd won.

Before long, she realized how quietly Julia stood beside her. MJ stood up and watched her warily. Julia had more to say, and whatever it was, she didn't want to say it.

MJ wondered if someone had been hurt in the raid, maybe Rory or Amber, or one of the other detectives.

"What is it, Julia?"

The woman, with her intense eyes, seemed to calculate whether MJ could handle what she needed to tell her. Finally, she folded her arms, either against the cold or the words she had to deliver. "They found a man at the scene, already deceased. It's the uncle of your friend, Glen Donovan."

MJ's hand flew to her mouth and tears sprang to her eyes. She didn't know Glen well, but this would devastate her friend.

"I'm sorry," Julia said. "An officer is with them now."

"I should go. I should be there," MJ said, starting toward the station.

Julia touched her arm. "Wait a few minutes. The police have their way of doing things. They are trained and ready to handle whatever the family needs. Give your friend some time to absorb the information."

All MJ could think about was Shannon sitting by her bedside all night long after the explosion at city hall; Shannon giving her the news of their principal's death and staying to comfort her; Shannon always taking care of others in their time of need.

"But either way," said Julia, "It's freezing out here. Let's go inside."

MJ agreed. She would give it five minutes, and then she would go see her friend. Shannon needed her, and she intended to be there.

***

MJ stayed at the station as long as Shannon would let her. She held her friend's hand as she made a soul-crushing phone call, one her inconsolable aunt could not make. The call was to her cousin, Aubrey, who was on her honeymoon on Victoria Island.

The new bride, devastated, pledged to take the next ferry from the island, which wouldn't depart until the early morning.

Then Shannon insisted MJ go home while she took her aunt back to Fairview, where several other cousins, aunts, and uncles were gathering.

The McCanns came by to pick up Jada. MJ promised she would check on the girl the next day after they'd all had a good night's rest.

And that's what MJ did. When she finally crawled into her bed, the loneliness of no dog and no neighbor was quickly swallowed up in a dreamless sleep.

Chapter Thirty-One

T he next morning, a doctor at the urgent care center examined and cleaned Jefferson's leg wound. He couldn't stitch it after so many hours, but he said the butterfly bandages seemed to have done the job. It wasn't too deep, the doctor said, adding that if Jefferson had a little more fat on his legs, it might not have hit muscle at all.

Jefferson wasn't sure if he should consider it a compliment or if the doctor thought he was too skinny.

Whatever. It was done.

The detective had called as soon as the clinic opened and pleaded his case as a public servant to be seen first thing. It worked, and they made room for him. He didn't sleep well, anyway. Between his aching leg and bizarre dreams, he could only doze off and on.

The times he drifted off, he kept seeing his brother as a little kid, his round and innocent brown eyes laughing as they played on the trampoline. Then the boy Alex would disappear, and he would instead have Nico's face, laughing like a demon, spit dribbling from his mouth onto Jefferson.

It only took a few rounds of dreams like that to get Jefferson out of bed.

His phone buzzed as he walked to the car. It was Wells.

"You all patched up?" she asked.

"Yep. I even got a sticker for good behavior."

"Wait, is this Jefferson or Rory? It's pretty early for jokes from you."

Jefferson chucked. "I think he's wearing off on me. So, when are you going to tell me where Alex is?"

"This morning if you're up to it."

"You know I am."

"Then meet at the address I am going to tell you. I will not text it, so you'll have to remember. Don't write it down."

Now, he was sure. Alex was in some kind of protective custody. There wasn't any other reason for such secrecy around his location.

"Go ahead."

"3343 Rogers Road. Drive to the Scenic Shoreline neighborhood. Cross street, Beacon. Got it?"

"On my way."

***

The house on Rogers Road was a tiny pink bungalow with a camper trailer and a massive black pickup truck in the driveway.

The Scenic Shoreline neighborhood's first iteration was as a beach-front campground in the 1970s. Then the owners started selling off a few lots here and there, allowing people to build small homes. Before long, houses, cabins, and bungalows replaced all the campsites. The result was a hodgepodge of older homes nestled between towering Douglas Fir trees, a source of frequent power outages when the gentlest of winds rolled through.

Jefferson pulled in front of the house, checking the address again. This didn't seem like the right place. He must have remembered the numbers wrong.

His phone buzzed in the passenger seat.

"Are you there?" asked Amber.

"Yeah, where are you?"

"Look around and make sure no one followed you.

He turned and looked out the driver's side window. "No one followed me. I am the only one on this street who looks suspicious."

"Okay, so drive to 1565 Meherrin Drive. Same neighborhood. Cross street, Boatfield."

Jefferson sighed into the phone. "I think you are having fun with this."

"Maybe a little," she said. "Hurry."

Soon, the detective pulled in front of a nondescript gray, one-story house. Moss covered the roof, and one of the front gutters hung low so that Jefferson could see a massive dam of pine needles. The shedding fir trees, clustered in the front yard, reached their oversized limbs across the roof and surrounding area, and their giant feathery tops pierced the silver sky above.

Amber's car sat in front of the dirty garage. She met him at the door when he knocked.

"Good morning, Jeff."

He greeted her while checking out the surroundings.

The inside did not match the outside. Fresh paint, carpet, and furniture filled the updated living room, complete with carefully curated art that provided a pop of color against the basic white walls. He could see through to the kitchen, which had modern appliances, marble countertops, and soft sage cabinets.

Someone had cooked breakfast, and the smell of bacon made his stomach rumble.

Two large men, both in jeans and black button-down shirts, watched TV from a rust-colored sofa. They glanced up when he walked in, nodded greetings, and then moved their attention back to their show.

And there, at the kitchen table with a plate of food, was Alex.

His shaved head wouldn't grow in for a while, but the rest of him looked different—clean and dressed in a normal pair of jeans and a Washington State cougars sweatshirt, the Nico tattoo visible above the collar.

Jefferson walked toward him, not knowing if he should hug his brother or punch him in the face. What Alex put him through last night was easily the worst experience of his life.

Alex's demeanor revealed the same uncertainty; he only dared to make eye contact with Jefferson for mere seconds before dropping his eyes under a furrowed brow.

"You probably hate me pretty good right now," his little brother finally said.

Jefferson stared. "Get up," he said with a guttural force full of emotion.

Alex stood, seeming to accept whatever he got from his older brother.

"Jeff," Amber said quietly, touching his arm. "Don't."

Ignoring her plea, Jefferson walked to Alex and grabbed him into a hug that would squeeze the life out of most people.

Alex froze at first. It was clear he'd expected something more violent. Soon Jefferson felt his little brother relax and wrap his arms around him, squeezing with all his might.

When they separated, both had misty eyes.

"I'm so sorry, brother. It had to look real or Nico would never believe it," Alex said.

"I get that now," Jefferson said, "but at the moment..." He couldn't continue as the memory of the sorrow made it all too real again.

Just then, another man emerged from the hallway and stopped next to Amber.

"So, this is the detective," the man said. He wore a navy-blue suit, minus the jacket. The sleeves of his crisp, white shirt were rolled past his elbows, something Jefferson knew was a habit of former Marines. He also had a close-cropped haircut and the erect posture of the service.

"I'm with the DEA. Dakota Soucy. Most people call me Kota. Nice to finally meet you." He held out his hand.

Jefferson glanced at Amber as he shook the DEA agent's hand.

Training her eyes on Jefferson, a slight quirk on her lips and raised brow silently told him that Kota Soucy was her DEA source.

With sudden certainty, Jefferson knew Alex was Kota's confidential informant.

He glanced back at his little brother with a lowered brow.

"I'm willing to bet you have quite a few questions, Detective Hughes," said Kota. "Why don't we all take a seat at the table? I can explain what's been going on and then answer any question you might still have."

As they moved to the table, Kota took Alex's mostly empty plate and carried it to the kitchen. He rinsed it in the sink and set it in the dishwasher.

Kota joined them at the table, pulling a chair out and flipping it around so that he could straddle it backward.

"First, before we get into the operation, I want you to understand that we fully intend to keep Alex safe until Nico goes to trial," Kota said. "This safe house will be compromised after a few days, so we'll be moving Alex out of state. Once we do that, you will not be able to contact him until the trial."

Jefferson stared at Kota. "But what about..." He turned to look at Alex. "Sorry, but this is an issue."

Alex looked down, not surprised by Jefferson's concern.

"What about his addiction?" Jefferson continued, getting animated. "The kid has been in and out of rehab with no change. Do you all plan on keeping him high? Because he's an addict."

Sitting a little straighter and with a soft glimmer in his eye, Kota looked at Alex. "I think I'll let your younger brother here answer that."

Alex had his hands on the table, fingers interlaced. At first, he just watched his thumbs as he rolled them over the top of each other. He seemed to be searching for the right words.

Finally, his round brown eyes met Jefferson's. "I've been dreaming about this moment—how I would tell you. Outside of Mom, you stuck by me the longest. I'll never forget the night you kicked me out of Mom and Dad's house, dragging my sorry self to the bus station. The look on your face that night, it cut me deep." He shook his head at the memory of it. "Until that night, you'd always had sadness mixed in with the anger or frustration I caused you, but that night, it was pure loathing."

"Alex—"

"No, Jefferson, let me finish." He wiped his nose with the back of his hand. "It's not like I didn't want to quit the drugs all the other times, but I hadn't reached my lowest low, or at least I hadn't seen myself at my lowest. I finally saw what I'd become reflected in your face. Our dad was dead, and I was still trying to..." A sob broke through him. "I was still trying to take, and take, and take." A slow stream of tears trickled down his face. "You were right to kick me out, and I wouldn't blame you if you didn't want anything to do with me." His words were so choked with emotion that he had to stop and take a breath.

Alex gazed at Jefferson with tears and hope gleaming in his eyes. "I got clean, brother. I finally got clean."

Chapter Thirty-Two

Jefferson pushed back his chair and stood. As much as he wanted to reach out and hug his brother in glorious happiness, he'd been burned too many times. There were too many questions.

He faced away from the table, his hand on the back of his neck.

"How long?" Jefferson asked without turning around. The answer, if it were true, would tell him all he needed to know.

"It's been almost a year," Alex said softly, but with confidence.

The detective turned around. "But you were with Nico." He couldn't say the name without a sneer coming into his voice. "You said you were getting a hit last night. I don't understand why you would be with Nico if you were free of the drugs. He's scum. He kills people like Anna with the crap he puts on the streets."

Alex flinched at the mention of Anna. She was his girlfriend when he lived in San Francisco a decade ago. She overdosed in Nico's hotel room and died.

"I deserve your mistrust," he said, wiping his face with a tissue Amber had given him. "So, all I can do is tell you the truth and hope it will be enough."

Kota cleared his throat. "I can see there is a lot for you two to unpack here, but maybe I can shed some light on Alex's involvement with Nico."

Jefferson reluctantly returned to the table. He wanted Alex's recovery to be true, but if he was honest, he was afraid. He was afraid to trust his brother. He was afraid of feeling the hurt and betrayal all over again. In the past year, he'd bottled it up and hid it away. If he opened those old wounds, he feared Alex would eventually cut them deeper, so deep they may never heal.

When Jefferson sat down again, Kota began. "About six months ago, Nico found your brother. We'd been tracking a lot of Nico's old network, anticipating him trying to bring them back in, build his business to its former glory." Still straddling the chair, he folded his arms on the seat back. "We also knew Alex had been in treatment with a local minister, who has worked some real freaking miracles," he said, shaking his head. "We weren't sure what would happen, but it was pretty obvious after a couple of visits that Alex wasn't interested in joining Nico." He looked steadily at the two brothers. "Nico still trusted Alex and wanted him on board. So, we saw an opening, and we took it."

Jefferson ran a hand through his hair before he turned a hard eye on Kota. "Were you trying to get him killed?"

"Jeff," said Amber, "Listen like a cop, not a brother. If you had the chance to get Nico, you'd take it, too."

"It's okay," said Kota, "I get it. He seems like a risky choice, but Alex could get in closer than any of Nico's other associates. And our goal in this operation was to get Nico this time, not just his network."

"But it's not just the physical danger," argued Jefferson. "If he was only a few months clean, you risked him getting on the drugs again, he could have—"

"But I didn't, Jefferson," said Alex. "It turns out I'm also a pretty talented actor." He offered a weak smile. "But hey," he said, grabbing Jefferson's arm. "We got him." His brown eyes implored his older brother to see reason. "And there is so much more to all of this than what went down here in West Sound. With what I know, Nico is never seeing the outside of a prison."

"So, you're planning to testify," Jefferson asked, matching his brother's intensity.

Alex sat back. "Of course I am."

The detective simply stared at the tabletop and nodded.

An uneasy quiet overtook the group. They all understood the danger Alex was in. Nico might be behind bars for now, but he had friends and enemies who would want Alex dead before he ever saw the inside of a courtroom.

Kota was the first to break the silence. "You can understand why we will move Alex. He'll need to remain isolated and on the move until the trial. Then," he tilted his head to the side, "he'll have the option of going into the witness protection program."

It was all too much. Jefferson needed time to think. "I need some air."

Without giving anyone time to stop him, Jefferson walked out the front door.

The crisp morning hit him like the first jump into a cold pool. He sucked the air deep into his lungs, trying to dispel his growing agitation.

He should be happy. Alex had finally kicked his habit, for now. The longer he stayed clean, the more likely his recovery would last. But evil people would be after him. And even if he lived to testify, he would be gone again, into a witness protection program that meant Jefferson could never contact him, because making contact would put them both at risk.

Standing with his hands on his hips, looking at the sheet of gray above him, he tried to reconcile himself with the situation. All he'd ever wanted was for his brother to have a shot at a good life. The opportunity was still there, and more possible than if Alex had continued down the road of addiction, which Jefferson knew would have ended in a premature death.

The door closed behind him, and Amber stepped onto the porch. She stood quietly for a moment, looking up as if she knew what he was looking for in the veil above them.

"Alex carries a lot of guilt," she said softly. "He probably should. The time he spent transporting and dealing drugs for Nico caused heartache and pain for other families."

She faced Jefferson, who still searched the sky. "This work he's done. He sees it as restitution. He can never completely undo the damage of his past, but he can help get this predatory, heartless man off the streets."

She turned away and gazed at the sky again. "It's cruel. You getting Alex back just to lose him again, but you are the reason he's here. You are the reason he's still alive and in recovery. Recognize the blessings when they come, Jeff."

Her words made perfect sense, and he knew Amber was right. But so much had come at him so fast, like waves hitting him with force one way and then the receding water pulling him in another direction. Should he stay skeptical and distant to protect his sanity? Or should he accept this new version of Alex and make peace with their past?

She looped an arm through his. "I don't know what's going to happen, but I know that if you don't take this chance to make things right between you, it might not come around again."

The sky had such little variation. One ominous shade of gray extended as far as Jefferson could see. The complete coverage of every inch of the atmosphere made it hard for him to imagine there could be any place in the world where the sun was shining, and the sky was any other shade.

He closed his eyes and surrendered to it.

Chapter Thirty-Three

An unusual solemnity hung about the briefing room when Jefferson and Amber arrived. It felt like walking into church.

Perhaps his mind associated Sunday with going to church, as he had almost every Sunday in his youth. Now he only went when he visited his mom, and she asked him to go. He didn't mind it. Seeing old friends and the adults who helped raise him reminded Jefferson of a more carefree time, when his faith was easy to come by.

His mom told him he struggled with his faith as an adult because he kept putting his faith in other people. Human beings will let you down, she said.

That was true, but he'd learned today that people could also restore your faith.

He'd finally let go of his fear and made peace with Alex. Kota gave them some time alone to talk, reminisce, and shed a few tears they didn't try to hide.

What he learned helped Jefferson see how incredibly brave his brother had been. Once the detective got past his anger at how the DEA risked Alex's life, he realized how much his brother needed this victory—not just over Nico, but also over the drugs.

He was proud of him, and he would miss him. Alex said he wasn't sure about the witness protection program; he would see how the trial turned out and then decide. If he entered the program, Jefferson and his family might get a few rushed minutes with him after the trial, but then he'd be gone and unreachable.

Alex asked Jefferson not to tell their mom and their brother the whole situation until after Alex left West Sound. The more people who knew where Alex was, the more opportunities there were for information to leak. Their mom wouldn't understand, and she would be angry at Jefferson, but it was for the best.

As Jefferson took a seat next to Rory, his partner gave him a side-eye. "So, how's the leg? Am I finally going to beat those long legs down the basketball court?"

"Keep dreaming, Jackson," Jefferson smirked, appreciating Rory's ability to lighten the mood.

Amber sat next to Ron and Julia. After a minute, the chief walked in and took his seat.

"Good morning, everyone. I'm sure most of you, like me, prefer to be home today, so let's get going."

He scanned the group with his steely eyes. "First, I am extremely proud of all of you, the rest of the WSPD, and our law enforcement partners. Today, because of the dedication and sacrifices of you and them, the people behind these drug cocktails, as well as many of those proffering it on our streets, are behind bars."

"And with a little civilian help..." He paused as a murmur went up around the room. Even the chief wore a hint of a smile as he looked directly at Jefferson. "With a little civilian help, a missing girl was brought safely home, and our own Detective Hughes is safe and sound."

"Here! Here!" Larson yelled as applause and whistles erupted around the room.

Jefferson cursed his father's Scandinavian genes as he felt color creep up his neck. Though it would only make his discomfort worse, he wished MJ could be there to hear the chief's praise. If she hadn't made the right connections, Jefferson and Alex could be dead.

His younger brother wouldn't have killed him. Jefferson knew that now. If the team hadn't found him when they did, Nico would have eventually realized Alex was stalling. Then he or his henchmen would have killed both of the brothers and Trevon.

This wasn't the first time Jefferson had underestimated MJ, and he would probably do it again. It was a good thing she was so darn obstinate.

"Alright, settle down," cautioned the chief, though he still wore a grin. "We need to get on to other matters. Larson, tell us who we have in custody."

Detective Larson consulted a piece of paper in front of him. "We have Nico in custody along with five of his associates. Brent Miller is in the custody of the Mason County Sheriff, but the DA has already begun the extradition paperwork. We also have Trevon Baldwin, the young drug chef out of Fairview. Victor Cano was not among those arrested last night, so we need to be on the lookout for him. He is just one of the guys we believe may try to keep Nico's West Sound network intact, if we don't find him."

Rory slouched in his seat and leaned his head against the back. "I'm still trying to wrap my head around the idea that those hoity-toity Fairview guys were running a drug lab out of their neighborhood."

"Wait till you hear what we took out of that house," said Larson. "We recovered an unspecified amount of heroin, cocaine, fentanyl, and a variety of chemicals used as fillers, including xylazine and crap like antifreeze."

"Antifreeze?" repeated Jefferson. Fogarty's question in their first briefing was right on the money. Those dirtbags were knowingly poisoning people.

"Pretty good for a night's work," said Amber. "It's also important to note the domino effect of your efforts here. The DEA is now closer to taking down Nico's entire West Coast network, and they have some even bigger names they will now be able to pursue." She gave Jefferson a meaningful look. No one else in the room knew about Alex's involvement and what he knew about Nico's network.

"So, let's talk finances," said Ron excitedly, clapping his enormous hands together.

Groans went up around the room.

"You simpletons might think this is the boring part, but what Julia and I have here," he glanced at Rory, "with a little help from Detective Jackson."

Bowing his head, Rory accepted this acknowledgment of his work as Ron continued.

"This is what keeps these guys in jail. When it comes to the drug networks, just follow the money, baby."

Julia rolled her eyes. "Great intro, Ronnie."

"Thanks. I've been working on it."

Julia paused, shuffling through her notes. "We have evidence that Nico and Brent Miller were working together on a real estate and money laundering scheme."

Rory leaned forward, frowning. "Talk about an odd couple."

"Greed makes strange bedfellows," Larson said with a sardonic chuckle.

Jefferson remembered Miller when they met next to the pond where Lausch's body had been found. The man had rolled up in his golf cart, all concerned for his neighbors. After Jefferson had asked him to identify Lausch's body, Miller showed an uncanny ability to fake surprise and emotion when he knew the truth all along.

"This is the strangest partnership," agreed Jefferson. "But I don't understand how they were getting away with it. Aren't there laws in place to prevent this sort of thing?"

"There are," Julia said, "But the feds focus on big players in big markets. Setting all of this up in a place like West Sound kept them from attracting attention. And therefore, they needed Donovan and Lausch."

Julia cleared her throat, "From what we've been able to piece together from records at the bank and the title company, we think it went something like this: Nico would deposit cash from drug sales into accounts set up by Miller, who then used those funds as trusts to purchase properties."

"And," added Ron, "Donovan at the bank and Lausch at the title company provided the cover."

"That's how they flew under the radar for so long. None of the players filed the required paperwork for cash transactions," Julia said. "An operation like this required all these people to look the other way. That's how you get a small bank manager and the owner of a small title company living in the priciest real estate in the county."

"Nothing like a little bribery to make people go blind," threw in Ron. "Both Donovan and Lausch lived in homes either owned by trusts or paid for in cash."

Sitting forward with his elbows on the table, Mendez tapped his chin. "It sounds like they had a good thing going. Why risk it with dangerous drugs and murdering Lausch? We may not have found this scheme, at least for a long time."

With a shrug, Julia said, "Greed. Miller and the others made the risky calculation to cheat Nico by cutting the drugs with fillers. They could dilute the base drugs—cocaine, heroin, fentanyl—whatever they got from Nico. Then they create maybe a quarter to a third more street drugs and Nico knew nothing about it. Sell them and pocket the cash. We think Lausch wanted out, and that's when Miller stabbed him with a syringe filled with a lethal dose of fentanyl."

Releasing a small puff of air, Jefferson said, "Miller as the murderer will be tricky to prove, even with Jada as a witness to their argument. We have very little evidence from that scene, and no one saw anything."

Amber, who had been listening with a look of concentration, spoke up. "That's probably the case, but his partnership with Nico makes him an accessory to any murder, kidnapping," she nodded once toward Jefferson, "drug trafficking, fraud, and other crimes committed by Nico or his men as part of this operation. Add that to what we know he is directly responsible for...Brent Miller won't walk away."

Julia sighed, closing her dark eyes and wiping a hand over her face. "Yeah, we have a lot of work to do to make all the connections and make sure we have uncovered all the potential evidence. There are still unanswered questions, but" she smiled, revealing her perfect white teeth, "we got 'em. Now it's just a matter of ensuring we give the prosecutors enough to bury them."

***

After the chief said a few last words, the group filed out of the briefing room. Most were heading home to take the rest of the day off.

Today, the large hub of desks was sparsely populated, with only a handful of people working. While a few patrol officers made phone calls, most of the room remained empty and quiet.

Amber walked alongside Jefferson, chatting about her plans for the day.

"We're going to visit Jerry's mom. She insists we come over for dinner on Sundays, and with my schedule, we don't always make it." Jerry was Amber's husband of thirty years. He was the reason Amber moved to West Sound.

With a slight wrinkle in her nose, she said, "I know the roast beef will be dry, but I love our visits there. She's an amazing woman."

She stopped as they were getting close to the exit. "So, are you going to go rest that leg?"

Looking ahead, Jefferson watched as his colleagues were making their way to their desks or out to their cars. Most had someone waiting for them, like Jerry waiting for Amber.

A hollow ache settled in his chest. With Alex gone—truly gone this time, not just another wayward disappearance—an unexpected loneliness weighed on him.

Maybe Amber's mention of her mother-in-law made him miss home. Jefferson hadn't been to Redding since his father's death. His mom deserved more from him. Perhaps it would be best to deliver the news about Alex in person.

With her curious light hazel eyes, Amber watched him. He realized he hadn't answered her question.

Drawing a deep breath, Jefferson surprised even himself. "I think I need to make a quick visit before I head home."

With a sparkle in her eye, Amber asked, "A visit up Stanton Inlet?"

Jefferson felt heat creep up the back of his neck. It shouldn't surprise him that Amber put it together.

Trying to sound nonchalant, he shrugged one shoulder. "Just need to follow up on a few things."

Amber's lips twitched in amusement. "With our civilian consultant?"

Rubbing the back of his neck, Jefferson gave an awkward chuckle. "Something like that."

Rather than let his discomfort linger, Amber simply nodded. "Well, don't work too hard, detective. You've more than earned a break." With a wink, she turned and headed for the exit, leaving Jefferson feeling both embarrassed and grateful for her discretion.

As he watched her go, Jefferson couldn't deny the truth to himself anymore. He needed to see MJ—if only to thank her for saving his life. This case wouldn't feel complete until she knew the important role she played in ending a deadly scheme.

At least, that was the reason he gave himself.

Chapter Thirty-Four

The water of the sound was as motionless as the flat gray sky above it. One kayak cut through its glassy surface, otherwise, all was quiet. It was the peaceful ride MJ needed. She paddled slowly back to the shore as a hawk glided over the water to roost in the tallest evergreen on the opposite side of the inlet.

After an intense weekend, this time alone centered MJ. It calmed her and got her ready to return to work tomorrow.

The range of emotions she had gone through had a draining effect on her, leaving her feeling depleted. She'd gone from the constant worry she had about Jada to the overwhelming despair she experienced upon learning about Shannon's uncle being killed. And of course, Nico had almost murdered Trevon. The kid needed to be accountable for his crimes, but he didn't deserve to be gunned down like an animal.

Then there was Jefferson. She didn't know how to categorize her feelings during the time he was in danger. Maybe she didn't want to. Feelings made her vulnerable, and vulnerability was not something MJ did well.

As the kayak scraped along the rocky bottom of the shallow water, MJ caught sight of a tall figure coming down the beach access stairs.

There was the devil himself.

A sudden flutter in her stomach made MJ curse herself. Stop it, she thought. He's just here to tell you to stay away from his next case. Get a grip.

The wet crunch of his footsteps on the packed sand emphasized how quickly his long legs devoured the space between them. She groaned inwardly, sure that his appearance was likely to cause a less-than-glamorous dismount from her kayak, in her dry suit no less.

Setting the paddles inside the craft, she began maneuvering her body to get over the edge. The kayak wobbled treacherously, and MJ closed her eyes, expecting an icy splash. But suddenly, the rocking stopped.

Opening her eyes, Jefferson's crooked smile greeted her as he held the nose of the kayak. "Good morning, MJ."

The gray morning softened the usual vibrancy of his eyes to a subdued, stormy blue. She tried not to stare, but a sudden sense of gratitude caught in her throat.

He was alive.

Of course, she'd known he survived, but some part of her had still harbored a niggling fear—one that could only be extinguished by seeing the proof with her own eyes. Relief washed over her, as the lingering dread, a dread she hadn't realized existed, finally unwound from her heart.

Moving with careful calculation, she gingerly stepped out onto the beach. When a sudden loss of balance threatened to send her backward into the kayak, Jefferson grasped her hand. His warmth soothed her cold skin.

"Careful there," he said.

"Thanks," she said, glancing down at their hands clasped together.

He cleared his throat and let go. With the warmth gone, she wished he hadn't.

"Sorry to barge in on you," he said, stepping back so she could get to her rain boots and jacket resting on top of a white log of driftwood. "We learned a lot in the briefing today that you might find interesting."

Sitting on the log, she brushed sand from her feet and pulled on her boots, her eyes on him.

"I appreciate that." She stood and pulled on her jacket. "And that you came all the way out here."

Inwardly, she smiled. Sunday and the detective still wore a suit, including his expensive shoes.

Following her eyes, he saw the sand already beginning to accumulate on his loafers.

MJ chuckled. "Jefferson, we are going to have to get you some boots."

Their eyes met, and she colored at her own choice of the word "we."

Looking away and down the beach, she asked, "Are you okay to walk and talk?"

His crooked smile returned. "I never really liked these shoes anyway."

They turned together and walked along the beach as the water lapped softly after them.

He told her everything Julia and Ron shared about the partnership between Nico and the men at Fairview. How they used the real estate market to launder money and traffic drugs in West Sound.

Once he'd told her all the important details, Jefferson stopped. She felt a gentle touch on her arm as he turned to face her.

Gazing toward the water, he breathed deeply. Then he cast his eyes to hers. "I need to say thank you. I know it was you who figured out where to find us." His eyes were soft and so liquid in their depths. She wanted to climb into them.

"You saved my life," he said. "And not just mine, but others, too."

Still holding her eyes, he reached out and took her hand again. She shivered at the rush of heat that coursed through her.

That shiver meant nothing, she told herself. Her hand was just cold; she'd been out kayaking all morning, after all. Still, she found it impossible to pull her eyes away from his. The pain he usually carried there was gone, and something else was in its place. Was it hope?

Just then, a loud bark rang out, and a ball of black and white fur came hurtling toward them in a spray of sand and water.

A shrill whistle followed. "Edgar! Come, boy!" It was Justin jogging down the stairs to the beach. The dog, too far gone in his euphoria, continued.

MJ quickly pulled her hand back and then immediately regretted it. Why did she care what Justin saw or his opinion about it?

Angry with herself, she didn't dare look at Jefferson.

"Edgar, buddy," she said as the dog ran into her legs. She kneeled to rub his back and head. She chanced a quick glimpse at Jefferson.

With slightly narrowed eyes, he watched Justin approach. His stance reminded her of the deer that sometimes wandered into the yard. If she were quiet enough, they would stand still, their long legs frozen and their huge eyes watching her, trying to determine if they should stay or run.

As Justin got closer, Jefferson chose to run.

"I should get going."

MJ stood, not knowing what to say. Begging him to stay felt weird, but letting him go also felt wrong.

He didn't give her a chance to do either.

"I'll see you around," he said, flashing her a very forced crooked smile.

"Jefferson," she whispered.

But he was already walking away.

* * *

Next in Series

Stolen Hearts on the Sound

Chapter 1

Detective Jefferson Hughes ducked out of the rain and through the door of Callie B's Cafe. The scent of cinnamon, freshly baked bread, and coffee immediately took some of the chill from his bones.

And he needed it. West Sound and the entire Puget Sound area had been in a constant state of drizzle or downpour since November. They were now well into December, a fact made all too clear by the constant strains of Michael Bublé Christmas music playing all over town.

"You're bright and early this morning, detective." The owner of the cafe, Callie Brown, stood at the counter, carefully adding muffins to the display case to the tune of Bublé's version of "White Christmas." Her shoulder-length brown hair was in a springy ponytail.

"I bet you're here for one of these." She motioned with her head to the freshly placed muffins, grinning so that her eyes smiled too. Callie's place had become extremely popular lately, and Jefferson guessed it was partly because the owner had a way of making every customer feel like her favorite.

"How'd you guess?" He gazed longingly at the muffins as he ran a hand through his blond hair, dispersing some raindrops gathered there.

"Oh, I think you can smell the muffins from the station, because you always seem to show up when they are fresh from the oven," she teased. "But this is a little earlier than usual."

"Station training today," he said flatly. "I need something to get me through it," he added with a sigh. "How about that coconut chocolate chip?"

"Ooh, excellent choice," said a bubbly voice next to him.

Surprised, he turned to see MJ's friend, the cute blond school counselor.

"I love that flavor," she said. "I think I snagged the first one." She held up a Callie B's bag as proof.

When he didn't say anything, she grinned at him with sparkling brown eyes. "You probably don't remember me. I'm Shannon Davis. I'm—"

"Sorry. Of course, I remember," he cut in. "You work at the middle school."

She was even more attractive than he remembered. They met earlier in the year when MJ and this counselor came to check on a missing student at the home of a man found dead in a golf course pond. MJ's presence there had surprised and somewhat agitated Jefferson. He didn't really notice Shannon that day, except to see how it irked MJ when her friend flirted with him.

"Yeah, I'm headed to school now, but I didn't want to miss my chance to say hello," she said brightly.

With a thud, Callie closed the display case and set his muffin on the counter. Jefferson flicked his eyes at her just in time to see her raise both her eyebrows and give him an encouraging wink. Then she turned to help another customer at the register.

Shannon had suddenly started digging in her enormous purse, either out of need or because she also saw Callie's facial signals.

Jefferson grabbed the muffin. "It is nice to see you," he said.

She glanced back up at him, holding a gaggle of keys and putting the purse back on her shoulder. "You too."

"I'm really sorry about your uncle," Jefferson added, lowering his voice.

She nodded. "I appreciate that. My aunt is doing much better." Her pretty features stilled as she momentarily remembered the grief of a few months ago. "I'm afraid that the holidays are going to be quite difficult, though."

The case involving the missing student also involved Shannon's uncle, who died at the hands of a ruthless drug trafficker.

"Hey," she said, shaking her head to recapture her sunny attitude, "I hope I'm not being too forward. I really have to get to work, but I'd love to see you again." She gave him a side-eye out of her long lashes. "I'm pretty sure MJ told me you're single. That's true, right? Because if not, I will feel really stupid."

Her brilliant smile lit up her face, and Jefferson found himself smiling back at her.

"I'd like that," he said, shocking himself. Why shouldn't he say yes? From what he'd seen so far, Shannon was both beautiful and intelligent.

Their eyes locked. She blushed slightly before saying. "Can I see your phone?"

He wasn't sure what to make of that, but he unlocked the screen and handed it to her with an amused version of his crooked smile.

With fingers flying at top speed, she typed something into it. "There. I sent me a message from you. Now you have my number, and you can call me."

"Well, okay," he said with a light laugh. Was she really afraid of being forward?

"Okay," she repeated, her eyes locked on his. "I hope to hear from you soon. Goodbye, Detective." She pulled the hood of her raincoat over her golden blond hair and headed out the door and into the downpour.

Jefferson looked at his phone to see what message she'd texted to herself.

"I'm free Saturday."

With a brief pause, he fixed his gaze on the screen of his phone before quickly stashing it in his pocket. A strange mixture of anticipation and dread washed over him. He knew the dread was MJ. There'd been a fleeting moment in the fall when he thought there might be something between them, but he quickly dismissed the thought as foolish. MJ's ex-husband Justin seemed to still be in the picture. The man definitely had feelings for MJ, but Jefferson had no idea how MJ felt about Justin, or him for that matter.

With nagging uncertainty, he wondered if he should have stayed more professional with Shannon.

He shook his head. Get over it, Hughes, and get on with life. While he'd always preferred being a romantically unattached detective, married to the job, the last big case made him realize he was ready to explore a relationship. The only trouble was that he hated the thought of dating women he didn't know. He knew some people used apps to find potential dates. He couldn't imagine anything more risky.

As he turned to go, he caught Callie's eye again.

She wore a knowing grin. "Enjoy your weekend, Detective."

A Letter from the Author

Thank you for reading *Deadly Deals on the Sound* — Book Two in the On the Sound Series. I appreciate you! I hope this series is one that you will recommend to your family and friends. My mission is to write twisty crime fiction that deals with real-life issues, but doesn't let the dark-side take over. (Trust me, writing criminals without criminal language is an art form.) In my books, you'll always know who the good guys are.

I love Jefferson and MJ even more after Book Two, and I can't wait to get Book Three in the hands of readers later in 2024. If you love romantic subplots, this series is right up your alley.

I'd love to hear your feedback. Please take a few minutes to check out my website and sign up for my newsletter. Stay up-to-date on new releases, special editions, and upcoming formats (like AUDIO!).

Visit Gemmacbooks.com to learn more.

All the best in life and reading adventures,

Gemma

Acknowledgements

Thank you to my family and friends for their support and encouragement in this writing adventure. Your opinion, advice, and belief in me are the underpinnings of my creative life. I love you.

Thank you to Becky Wallace for her amazing feedback and editing skills. I love how thoroughly you enjoy the process of story making. Your feedback makes me a better writer, and your celebration of a well-written passage brings me child-like joy.

Made in United States
Troutdale, OR
02/21/2025